The Voice of God

by

Larry Maness

Mainly Murder Press, LLC
PO Box 290586
Wethersfield, CT 06129-0586
www.mainlymurderpress.com

Mainly Murder Press

Copy Editor: Jack Ryan
Executive Editor: Judith K. Ivie
Cover Designer: Karen A. Phillips

Copyright © 2013 by Larry Maness
Paperback ISBN 978-0-9895804-3-4
Ebook ISBN 978-0-9895804-4-1

Published in the United States of America

Mainly Murder Press
PO Box 290586
Wethersfield, CT 06129-0586
www.MainlyMurderPress.com

Dedication

For Bill Maness and David Mayo

One

When the church caught fire, rumors spread like so many sparks in the night sky: Father Jerry set it himself. Hadn't faulty wiring popped up in one sermon after another over the past months? He could build a sermon around anything, but he chose old wires and imperfect circuits to prepare the congregation for what was coming. It's clear as a spring morning now. Father Jerry wasn't raising money to fix what ailed the hundred-year-old building. No, he was raising money for his own personal use once he caught the Provincetown bus to Boston, then on to Logan Airport, where two tickets to Rome waited for him. He burned the church to destroy evidence that would lead to his conviction.

But the tickets were never picked up, and Alitalia's Flight 725 left without Father Jerry and his companion. Where they got to, no one knows. Who Father Jerry was traveling with, no one is telling.

The silence only fueled the rumors: The airplane tickets were a hoax, a diversion designed to perplex. Father Jerry was as Irish as a Dublin pub; he wouldn't run to Italy. He'd go back home and disappear among all the Dublin Dunns. Or maybe South America. How long could you live in Argentina on three hundred thousand dollars, if indeed that was the correct amount stolen from the church? Father Jerry didn't keep all the money in the bank, and what records he did keep burned in the fire. Gossipers started out at eighty thousand stolen and, like bids shouted at an auction, stopped at half a million before people came to their senses. Where would Father Jeremiah Dunn, the parish priest of St. Peter the Apostle in Provincetown, Massachusetts, lay his hands on that kind of money? It couldn't have come only from the congregation. They gave small amounts weekly and willingly but nothing close to three hundred thousand in the six years that Father Jerry had urged their generosity.

Maybe it wasn't money that drove him to overload the wiring, feel the walls heat until flames shot through the roof, making sure the old wooden church could not be saved before he called the fire department. Maybe at fifty he'd fallen in love with someone other than God. Maybe a woman captured his innocent heart. Or maybe the suspicions about his sexual preference were true, and he gave in to a man. Or maybe, like the tickets to Rome, that second seat on the airplane was also meant to cloud clarity. There was no one else. There was only Father Jerry, who had vanished with the money like the smoke mixing with the sparks that rose into the night sky.

Ben Covey drove past the locked and unmanned ranger station at the edge of Herring Cove's nearly empty parking lot and backed his double slide Fleetwood into place. It was the last week in April, and a heavy northeast wind stacked choppy seas along the beach. Covey liked this time of year on Cape Cod. The campgrounds were officially closed, and large crowds were weeks away as were the sand flies, gnats and mosquitoes. Covey and his family had the entire beach to themselves.

Usually the Timlins joined them for the inaugural weekend of the camping season, but Joey Timlin said it was still too cold to hit the road. Joey, like the rest of New England's residents, had suffered through the longest stretch of bitter winter on record. Over one hundred inches of snow had fallen in Boston, making unbearable the subzero temperatures. In February the thermometer never rose above twenty degrees. Most nights were in the minus single digits. As bad as it was in the city, the Outer Cape, that thirty-mile stretch of sandy land between Chatham and Provincetown, received more snow than any other place in the state. Blizzards and nor'easters pounded the fragile shore, dumping feet of snow one storm at a time. The last storm in mid-March buried the dunes in more than three feet of white powder. For the first time in memory, the beaches were filled with more cross-country skiers than fishermen. Joey Timlin jokingly told his friend Ben Covey that when he got to Provincetown, a foot of snow would greet him at the Herring Cove parking lot. Joey would wait another week or two to keep peace in his family before driving down and freezing.

Ben found the cold wind refreshing. It cleared his head and gave him fleeting, anxious thoughts about exploration and traveling where no one had before. The RV salesman stressed adventure—pack up the family and set out on a trip of a lifetime. Ben believed in that adventure. He savored moments alone on the windy beach under low, gray clouds. You had to dress for the weather, but the Fleetwood had plenty of closets, enough even to please Janie, his fourteen-year-old daughter. Twelve-year-old Sam, Ben and Sarah's other child, got by on sweatshirts and shorts. No matter what the weather, Sam put on his red Patriots football sweatshirt and cutoff blue jeans. Freezing or not, he stayed true to his summer uniform.

Ben caught a glimpse of that uniform disappearing over the steep dune that bordered the tarmac parking lot. Janie led the way, hoping the dune's height would provide reception for her cell phone. When that failed, she pulled her fleece jacket tighter around her and picked her way around a thorny cluster of *rosa rugosa* full of tiny spring buds.

"Who you callin'?" Sam dashed past her, stomping across some beach grass flitting in the breeze. "I bet I know. Ryan."

"Shut up."

"Ryan, Ryan, he's my man. If he can't do it, no one can."

Janie spun and hurried off in the opposite direction. "I have other friends."

"Say what you want. It's Ryan."

Janie tried the number again, then glared at her awkward brother. "It's not anybody. The phone doesn't work out here in the middle of nowhere."

"It's not the middle of anything. It's the end, the end of the world. You can't go any farther unless you want to drive into the Atlantic and drown."

"I can swim."

"Not as good as me." Sam caught up to his petulant sister and reached for the phone. "Let me try."

Janie jerked it out of reach. "When you grow up."

"I'm almost as old as you." Sam lunged one of his famous, high-energy, fake-out lunges he used on the basketball court to steal the ball. Janie stepped aside and watched her brother fall in a heap.

"How's that beach plum taste?" Janie snickered. "You want to watch those stickers don't cut your baby face."

"Who you calling a baby?"

"You."

"You don't know what you're talking about." Sam squirmed to his seat.

"Do too. Mom taught us last year." Janie swept one arm over the mounds and hallows of sand chiseled and changed for thousands of years by the wind. The dune's immensity produced a loneliness in her that made her secretly glad her brother was with her. "Nature walks," Janie continued. "You should have paid more attention. If you had you would know you're sitting on a clump of dusty miller."

Startled at the thought, Sam put his hands down to push himself up only to jerk his right hand away.

"What's the matter?"

"I dunno. Something hard."

Janie bent down for a closer look as Sam clawed through the sand. In seconds he pulled out a tarnished silver cross upon which lay the delicate figure of the crucified Christ. The cross more than covered both of Sam's open hands.

"It's huge," he cried, not able to contain his excitement. "Maybe it's part of some buried treasure. I bet it is. Mom said explorers were here hundreds of years ago. They probably left stuff behind."

Janie took the cross and held it by the piece of short chain attached at the top. "It's not all here," she said, looking more carefully at Sam's find. "The chain's broken. See this link? It's opened the slightest bit."

"So?"

"So maybe it got caught on something and fell off somebody's neck or out of their hands. I don't know."

"I do," Sam blustered. "I say it got caught on an old nail in the wooden chest when the pirates went to bury it. Those old chests were heavy, especially loaded down with gold and jewels and iron muskets to fight off their enemies. I'm going to find it." Sam dug wildly, not waiting for Janie to join in. "I'm gonna be a billionaire." His hands sprayed sand like a digging dog. "I'm gonna buy a motorcycle and an airplane and a movie theatre so I can see all the films and eat all the popcorn I want free."

Sam's furious digging flung a clump of something that fell with a thud near Janie's feet. Could her boneheaded brother be right about the treasure? With the tip of her shoe, she nudged the offering, scraping off some of the caked-on sand.

"Sam?" A hint of revulsion and fear mixed with the words. "Samuel? Would you stop digging and tell me I'm seeing things? Sam, please."

Sam stopped his search, but he couldn't do more to ease his sister's mounting fears.

"Mother!" Janie's frightened voice quickly pierced the wind. "Mother, up here. Quickly!"

Ben Covey had never before been a news item, but now he stood beside his wife and children with their RV as a backdrop.

Adventure, indeed, he smiled to himself, knowing that the image of him and his family filled the airwaves all over New England.

"A family on vacation in a spot they'd visited for years has found what looks like human remains in the Provincetown dunes," stated the news anchor in the studio. "The local police will say only that they can reveal nothing at this time. It's too early in their investigation, but the State Police and their crime labs will be actively involved in identifying the tattered pieces of cloth, the two small bones, and the tarnished silver cross. Even when asked directly if the cross came from the church that burned to the ground last January in this small seaside community, the police would not speculate. And Father Jeremiah Dunn, the missing priest? Are the bones the children found his?"

Ben had his theory even if the police were saying nothing.

"Of course they are Father Jerry's," Ben said, looking solemn and straight into the camera. "We never miss a mass, even when we come to Provincetown. But wherever the church, the priest protects what belongs to God. That's his job. Father Jerry came out here to the dunes to get that cross back from whoever stole it."

"And who might that be?" the on-scene reporter asked.

"The guy who set the church on fire. That's obvious," Ben said. "That's the only thing that makes sense. Father Jerry was chasing the guy down and caught him. Only he found out too late that he couldn't defend himself. Priests fight for our souls, they don't do hand-to-hand combat. What happened to Father Jerry is proof that hand-to-hand combat is not a good idea. It cost the poor man his life, and I know one other thing."

"What is that?" the eager reporter asked.

"Especially for a priest, it was a terrible way to die."

Two

The two-story, red-shingled, three-bedroom house at 610 Commercial Street radiated the charm of an old farmhouse. Its small parlor offered spectacular views of Provincetown Harbor across the street. A spacious, low-ceilinged kitchen in the rear connected to an ell and small workshop. In back of the property, surrounded and hidden by trellised wisteria, sat a comfortable cottage Mrs. Katharine Cardosa used to rent out in the summers to help pay the upkeep on her house and the ever-rising property taxes. The cottage had housed her son since Lino moved back home. His older sister, Dr. Carol Cardosa-Stanley, lived in San Francisco with her own family, her own medical practice and her own set of problems. It was impossible for Carol to get away for more than a few weeks at a time, which added to her worries about her mother's failing health. Since Carol didn't need the money, she offered the family house as a bargaining chip. If Lino would accept responsibility for dealing with their mother's decline, Carol's share of the property would be his when the red house was finally put up for sale.

"Even in this market, that house alone is worth well over a million dollars," she reminded him. "That's not including the value of the cottage. What do you think? Another four to five hundred thousand?"

"It's not going to happen," Lino said when he'd first heard Carol's proposal.

"But there's plenty of room. You remember how big the house is. You could finish off the attic in your spare time," Carol said. "You and Linda won't even know Mom's there."

"Linda and I are splitting up."

Carol wasn't surprised. Only the strongest families survive the death of a child. "I'm sorry, Lino. Really, I am," she said, seeing in her mind a defeated Lino. He'd changed since Steven's death. Not in looks. He would always look like their father—five feet ten inches tall, jet-black hair, and the body of a trim middleweight boxer with wide shoulders that slanted down from his collarbone as if something were pressing on them. His dark eyes, surrounded by crow's feet, were direct and piercing to the point of unsettling those who didn't know him. What had changed was his attitude. He had buried all happiness with his son and now moved through life as if carrying the coffin on his back. "Not the best of times, is it?" Carol offered.

"Not the best."

"Do you want to talk about it?" She knew he wouldn't. Lino sailed with a level keel, keeping both sorrow and joy to himself until he ran aground and exploded. His emotional eruptions were his weakness and kept in check by withholding his feelings.

"There's nothing to say," he said. "It just didn't work."

"You need to bring closure to this, Lino. You and Linda both. You're never going to have a moment's peace until you find out what pushed Steven over the edge."

"Aren't there rules forbidding psychiatrists from counseling family members?"

"Friendly advice, that's all." Carol knew her brother well enough to change course. "What are you going to do with your house in Gloucester?"

"Linda's staying. I'm moving out."

"If you don't have a place …"

"I'm a grown man. I'm not moving in with Mother."

"There's the cottage." A memory jarred her. "And the bay. You used to do all right running dad's little skiff across the bay, taking clients fishing."

"That's ancient history, Carol. Nobody remembers."

"Not until you tell them you're back. You can't keep close-lipped about it. Guides get the word out. Besides, you love being on the water. What is it you used to say? All you need to be happy is a body of water, a trustworthy boat and a customer paying you to take him to the fish."

"I'm not listening, Carol. Tuned out."

"Think about it, all right? That's all I ask. We can't let Mom go it alone much longer. She needs help."

"She doesn't want any."

"I know what she says, but what she says isn't reality. You and I know that. She needs somebody with her."

"How about a rest home?"

"Don't be mean, Lino. Besides, Mom won't leave her house. She loves it there. Even if you were only nearby to check in, that would be a great help. We can hire someone else to actually take care of her."

"Someone like who?"

"Social workers, nurse's aides, caregivers." Lino could almost see his sister twirling her long black hair around two fingers as she worked toward a solution. "People trained to do that sort of thing. There's help out there, Lino, we just have to find it. I'm not asking you to do it all alone."

"It just sounds like it."

"What'd I say about being mean?" She let the thought hang. "We've got to work together, Lino. We can't bicker over this. We've both got our own problems, but Mom needs us, and I can't do much this far away. You can. You're going to have to do it."

Lino knew it was true, but he didn't like being pushed into corners. "I'll think about it," he said and hung up.

The cottage had not been renovated in the hundred years since it had been built. Lino liked that most about it. It evoked a feel, a spirit, a sense that it belonged. He felt none of those things about himself, even though forty-five years ago he'd been born twenty yards away in the red-shingled house.

Lino's father Vincent, like most Portuguese who settled in the area, fished Cape Cod's waters until his dragger went down, killing captain and crew in a violent fall storm off Stellwagon Bank. Lino was studying when his mother called with the news.

It was exam week at Boston College. Adilino Cardosa, the first male in his family not to fish for a living, closed his books, turned out the desk lamp and sat alone in the darkness. He saw clearly the seventy-foot *Amy Ann* floundering as his father tried to save his ship and crew. At the memorial mass, said at the church that was now reduced to ash, Lino heard only the wind shrieking through the winch cables; he saw waves the height of mountains; he saw the futility and fear in the men as their watery grave rolled them under.

Lino held back tears. The few that escaped were for his mother, who would live lost without her husband. Lino knew that as certainly as he knew he would graduate and marry Linda Maria Colas even though he had yet to propose. Some things were meant to be, like his new life in the cottage.

Lino moved out of his Gloucester house and loaded what little he needed in the back of his SUV. He then drove to Brown's Boatyard where the *Pico II* waited on its trailer. In five hours boat and man were parked in the shell-covered driveway of the family home in Provincetown's East End. He spent one night in the red house before confirming what he already knew: Staying under the same roof with his seventy-five-year-old mother would never work. She repeated conversations, asked the same answered questions again and again and wet herself at the dining room table. Lino knew about her mental lapses but not the physical. The next morning he was on the phone to social workers who put him in contact with a nurse's aide whom Mrs. Cardosa fired within the first week. Lino hired another, the stout, Irish Colleen Hurley, sixty years wise and wily. He gave her a key to the red house so Mrs. Cardosa couldn't lock Colleen out and promised her a bonus if she'd stay six months. Lino found great peace when Colleen survived the first thirty days.

Lino dropped his charter off at the landing on Fisherman's Wharf and backed his boat out between the other boats for hire that lined MacMillan Pier. Tourists could spend money traveling a few miles out to sea on whale watches or stay in the harbor for a few hours under sail. Still others came to Provincetown to fish. Most fishing boats that left MacMillan were bruisers. The large day boats carried dozens of fishers dangling lines over the anchored boat's sides in hopes of catching fluke and cod. The smaller charters carried four to six passengers plus crew on forty feet of sportfish capable of chasing down everything that swam, including thousand-pound tuna. Lino occupied the other extreme. He took only one passenger with fly fishing gear for either four- or six-hour trips out to Billingsgate Shoal or the Race or the shallows off Herring Cove or wherever his father taught him bass and blues could be found.

Lino made his father proud by learning quickly and well. In college there was never any doubt as to Lino's summer job. He would guide fishermen along the National Seashore in his father's four-wheel drive or take them to the flats in his father's skiff. It was in college that one charter asked if Lino had ever guided a fly fisher.

"No," Lino answered skeptically. "Should I?"

"You'd be the first in this area," the man said. "You should try it. It might change your life."

Lino took his advice, learning first how to cast saltwater flies to anticipate the frustrations and joys of his clients. Before long he was tying experimental flies and testing them at various depths and lighting conditions. Word traveled quickly among recreational fishers of Lino's dedication to the sport. Within one year he became the youngest and most sought-after fly fishing guide on the Outer Cape.

Back at his mooring Lino put away his gear in the lockboxes, then dropped the painter into the dinghy and rowed the fifty yards to shore. He pulled the dinghy above the high water mark and pushed it up onto the small dock. He carried the oars along a path lined with sea grass that led to Commercial Street. In his mother's drive he saw a neatly dressed, elderly man leaning against a large black car parked behind Colleen's little Honda. Lino crossed the street, wondering how a chauffeur could get so lost.

"Take a wrong turn?" Lino asked. "Not likely anyone here called for a driver."

The man smiled self-consciously. "You don't recognize me, do you?"

Lino took a long look. Something familiar in the round face and pale brown eyes nagged his memory, but he couldn't make the connection. "Sorry."

"It's the collar or lack of it." The man tugged at his open shirt. "I'm out of uniform," he said. "Katharine didn't remember me either."

"Mother doesn't remember much," Lino said, trying to place where he'd seen the man. "What can I do for you?"

"Quite a bit, if truth be told. Quite a bit." The man extended his hand and held it there until Lino leaned one oar against the car and accepted the greeting. "I'm Father Silva. Retired. Katharine and I had a nice visit. A bit strained, but I did some catching up with Colleen's help. I'd say your mother is at that stage that she requires a good personal attendant. Colleen seems to be that. It's also good of you to come back and spend time with your mother. She may not say as much, but she appreciates it. I can tell."

Lino picked up his oar. "Father Silva?" he mused.

"Coming back?"

"Some."

"No wonder," the priest said. "You and I left Provincetown at about the same time. It's easy to forget. How many years has it been?"

"Twenty-five, more or less."

"That's about right. I presided over your and your sister's first communions and your dad's memorial mass with his crew."

Lino blotted out the memory.

Silva half smiled. "You do remember some of it. You may not want to, but ..." The priest matched Lino's steps toward the cottage. "I drove down from Boston to see you."

"Me? Why?"

"To ask a favor. Strange, isn't it? You don't see someone for all that time, and then, out of the blue, he shows up and asks you to do something for him."

"Like what?" Lino asked, not sounding encouraging.

"You're quite right to be skeptical. Who wouldn't be?" Shoes crunching shells underfoot broke the awkward silence. "I understand you were in insurance for many years. Not sales but corporate investigation. Hauling in the crooks and thieves out to defraud Colas, Haggerty and Johnson. Your father-in-law's company, isn't it?"

"It is."

"One of the largest insurance firms in New England."

"In the country," Lino corrected.

Father Silva nodded. "Of course. Then, all of a sudden you quit and went back to fishing up in Gloucester near where you and your wife lived."

"A little guiding, that's all. I had the boat up there. I might as well use it."

"Quite a career change. One day you're traveling all over the world chasing crooks, the next you're in your boat chasing fish."

Lino shrugged.

"Do you mind if I ask why?"

"Family issues," Lino said flatly.

"Meaning your son. I left a message when I heard, but you never called back."

"There wasn't much to say."

"We all need someone to talk to from time to time. Especially when something so horrible ..."

"You never said why you drove down from Boston."

"I did. I want a favor. Nothing official from the Church, mind you. This is a personal favor for old time's sake. I assume you've kept up with the goings on regarding Father Jeremiah Dunn."

Lino shrugged. "I've heard rumors like everybody else. I didn't go looking for more."

"That's the favor," Father Silva said. "I want you to go looking."

"I'm a fishing guide. What free time I have belongs to my mother. I'm not interested in doing anything else."

"You'll be less interested when you hear that I'm not in a position to pay you."

"Then why should I even consider it?" Lino asked, genuinely curious.

"Because you are Vincent Cardosa's son."

Lino put the oars against the cottage porch. "Can't deny that," he said, opening the screen door. "Sorry you made the trip for nothing, Father, but I've had a long day and want nothing more than to mix myself a drink and relax."

"A fine idea," Father Silva said and followed him inside.

Three

The first floor of the cottage was open living space with a small kitchen along the back wall and a living-dining area in the front. A glass slider opened onto a small side garden that Lino tended intermittently. An outdoor shower was on the same side of the house as the garden. Two bedrooms and a bath were upstairs. The furnishings were typical renter's fare: A pull-out sofa and round Formica kitchen table for four. In one corner Lino had created a cramped office complete with computer, answering machine, a place for his fishing logs, fly tying vise and tying materials, and a marine radio that murmured weather updates. A small television sat unused in the opposite corner.

"What would you like?" Lino asked, annoyed that the priest had invited himself in.

"Scotch over ice. One cube is my preference."

Lino removed a bottle and two glasses from a kitchen shelf. He clanked a single cube into each and poured while Father Silva studied a photograph of Vincent Cardosa standing proudly at the docks in front of the *Amy Ann*.

"Did you know your father had a vision regarding the events that would take his life?"

Lino handed the priest his drink. "I can't say that I did."

"Thank you." Father Silva raised his glass in salute before taking a satisfying sip. "He did. He had a vision in which he saw every detail. The storm. The wall of waves. He knew he would die at sea. Yet, he kept going back out."

"Fishermen don't have much choice," Lino said. "They take risks to care for their families. In bad weather the risks go up, and bad weather is never far away, which is why he pushed Carol and me off to school. He used to say nothing bad could happen to us on dry land. He should have said nothing that would kill us as quickly as a sinking ship would happen on dry land."

"I understand things have been hard for you, Adilino. I'm sorry. Truly. If there is anything I can do …"

"There's nothing anyone can do." Lino sat wearily at the kitchen table and drank as the feelings of betrayal flooded in on him, bitter and raw. Adilino Cardosa, a practicing, faithful Catholic for over forty years, could not get past the feeling that God had betrayed him. His father's death and his son's headstone marked the harsh truth.

Father Silva crossed the room and sat opposite his reluctant host. "How long have you been back in Provincetown?"

Lino had arrived in mid-October, and it was now the middle of June. "Eight months," he said.

"Then you were here when that terrible business happened at my beloved St. Peter's. My most rewarding years as a parish priest were spent in that church. I wish I'd never been reassigned, but that's the life of a priest. I fell to my knees and wept when I heard it had burned." Father Silva steadied himself with a long pull of scotch, then said, "You must have heard about the bones that were found out on the dunes next to a cross. From the hind leg of a coyote, according to the authorities. I don't know how they can be so sure of such things. Some anthropologist in Siberia finds a two-inch fossil and based on that builds a hundred-foot dinosaur complete with sparkling eyes and shiny teeth." He shook his head. "A coyote, can you imagine?"

"They're all over the dunes," Lino said, "scrounging for scraps, trying to beat the sea gulls to the feast. My guess is that last winter a lot of coyotes starved to death."

"Or froze."

"Probably both."

Father Silva swirled the ice in his glass. "I wonder if a man died out there."

"What makes you think that?"

"The cross. The bit of cloth found with it. The cross had to get there somehow. Maybe the cloth was from a man's jacket, a priest's jacket."

"The State Police can tell you that," Lino said. "They've surely completed all their lab tests by now."

Father Silva bobbed his head. "The State Police don't confide in the likes of me. All I know comes from Tony Santos. You remember Tony. Can you imagine him now a sergeant on the Provincetown police force? A sergeant willing to share a few pieces of information with his old priest, and I'm thankful. God bless him."

"Did Tony tell you anything about the scrap of cloth?" Lino asked.

Father Silva nodded. "From a lightweight shirt or jacket sold by the thousands, is what he said. Absolutely worthless in terms of learning who it belonged to with any certainty. It may have belonged to Father Jerry, it may not have. But the cross is easy. It belongs to St. Peter the Apostle. I held it in my hands hundreds of times, if not thousands. The question is, how did it get out in the dunes?" The old priest waited for a long time, then said, "Aren't you the least bit curious?"

"You seem to be fascinated enough for the both of us."

"Fair enough," Father Silva admitted. "I likely am, so I'll tell you what I think happened. I think on the night of the fire, Father Dunn was forced out onto those dunes. It was the middle of January with the temperature below freezing. In the church he wore a light wool jacket that he didn't have time to change. Why didn't he dress more warmly for the freezing temperatures? A gun was aimed at him, that's why, the same gun used to rob the church of all its money. Father Jerry's life was threatened with that gun. When the money was stuffed into bags, he was forced into a waiting car outside the burning church and driven out to the secluded end of Herring Cove's parking lot. Once there, he was led out into the dunes, shot and left to die. The scavengers— the gulls and coyotes—picked at his corpse, pulling it apart. You can imagine in the middle of winter how ravenous the animals must have been. It wouldn't take long to eat the flesh, to drag chunks of that poor priest's body farther off into the dunes to eat later or down to the waterline where a crowd of gulls fought each other to pick the bones clean. The incoming tide swept away what remained, and the next snowstorm buried what was dragged across the sand. If I'm right about any of this, the cross was inside Father Jerry's jacket pocket when a coyote or wild dog tore it from his body. We have only God to thank that it was found."

"And God to thank that Father Jerry met such a terrible end?" Lino quipped. "I've always thought it odd that the man who survives a plane crash thanks God he's alive instead of blaming God for flying the plane into the mountain."

"Is that who you blame for your son's death, Adilino? God is not the one to blame."

"Who is?"

"Not the priest in Gloucester you accused of molesting your son, either."

"That little news item made it all the way to you, did it?"

"It wasn't a small news item to an innocent man, Lino. He volunteers one week at a summer camp your son attended, and you accuse him of something vile. You could have ruined his life."

"I accused everybody of everything back then. Besides, I came to my senses and withdrew the charge."

"And turned your back on the Church."

"How do you know that?"

"All news items, as you put it, about you make it to me, Lino. Keeping track of you was part of the promise I made to your father the night he told me how he would die."

Lino perked up. "How do you mean?"

"I mean I put my hand on your father's Bible and, at his request, swore that if he was no longer around to watch over you, I would. He feared that temper of yours would get you in trouble." Father Silva made the sign of the cross. "I have kept my word."

"You never before paid me a visit," Lino protested.

"I prayed for you."

"What about Carol?"

"Of course, but Carol was already married and raising her own family. You were just a student finding your way."

"Only to lose it, is that it? Is that why you're here to show me the path? Well, I'm not looking for any path. I like the one I'm on."

Father Silva finished his drink. "You don't need to convince me, you need to convince yourself."

"I have."

"And have ended up in your mother's cottage, bitter, lonely and angry."

"Why is that your business?" Lino shot back.

"I told you, I promised your father."

"Leave him out of this."

"I don't see that that's possible for either of us." The old priest stepped to the counter and poured himself another inch of scotch. He felt the warmth slide down his throat and said, "I knew this conversation wouldn't be easy, Lino. I understand how you must feel, but …"

"I don't think you have any idea how I feel," Lino said. "You have to have a son first."

"I didn't mean …."

"Then your son has to be ripped away. Only then can you experience the worst pain imaginable, the shock and horror of his death and the gnawing guilt you feel that you could have, should have, done something to prevent it. Compound that with the blame your wife lays at your feet every time she looks your way." Lino's eyes swept over the priest's pitying face. "That's my life now, Father. Morning, noon, night. The only time it lets up is when I'm on the water. There's irony there, because I'm riding on the same ocean that sank the *Amy Ann*. Hell of a life, isn't it?"

"What do you plan to do about it?" Father Silva asked.

"I'm doing it. What you see is what you get."

"You've always fought back, Lino. That's one of the qualities I've admired about you. You don't let the other man win until you've tried all."

"It's hard to fight when the opponent is inside. After a while you get tired of beating yourself up."

"Self-pity doesn't become you, Lino, especially when there's no need for it. There's a foe out there, an evil man who crept about in the dark to steal every penny before burning St. Peter's to the ground. Find the man who did it."

"Even if all the rumors are true, and it was Father Jerry?"

The old priest thought a moment, then said, "That would please you, wouldn't it? Father Jeremiah Dunn is both an arsonist and a thief. All right, set your sights on that. Find that miserable thief and craft one more reason to turn your back on God. If that's what you do find, Lino, I will stop interfering with your life. That's what you want, isn't it, to shut out everyone who cares about you and be left alone with your own misery?"

"I'd settle for being left alone."

"Fine." Stung, Father Silva put down his glass. "I guess I shouldn't have come, after all, but I had such high hopes that you would want to learn the truth."

"I told you, I don't care what happened to Jeremiah Dunn."

"Not Father Jerry, the truth about your son."

Lino's eyes flared. "It was low enough bringing up my father, definitely beneath you to use my son to get what you want."

"It isn't what I want, Adilino, it's what you want or, perhaps more to the point, what you need. Haven't you blamed your current state of affairs on Steven's suicide?"

Lino said nothing.

Father Silva crossed his arms in front of his chest. "In your eyes, the world would right itself if you knew what drove that poor soul to end his life. To some degree, when Steven killed himself, he also ended your life. Nothing can bring him back, but you can resurrect who you are, Adilino. You can live fully again if you want to, if you try, if you find the courage to dig for answers."

"Do you think I haven't tried? I spoke with Steven's friends and his teachers, I read every file on his computer, I retraced his steps down at Sweetbriar ..."

"In such a rage your anger blinded you."

"All I know is that Steven went to that summer camp for years and loved every minute. When he came home from his last stay, he wasn't the same boy. He'd changed in the worst way. Something happened to him, and I wanted to know what. I still do."

Father Silva nodded knowingly. "Do you know who was in charge of Camp Sweetbriar when Steven was last there?"

"If I did, I've put it out of my mind."

"Father Jerry."

The name settled on Lino like ice. He wracked his brain trying to remember, then said, "I may have been mad as hell, but I would not have forgotten that."

"Because you didn't look deeply enough," Father Silva scolded. "Sweetbriar is funded in large part by the Mary Alice Connelly Foundation, the rest is paid for by the Church. You were so intent on finding the Church at fault that you went after that innocent Gloucester priest."

"I know what I did," Lino snapped.

"What you did was not to look thoroughly at what was before you. Had you, you would have learned that Mary Alice Connelly was Father Jerry's sister."

"Was?"

"She lost her battle with cancer. May she rest in peace." The old priest made the sign of the cross. "If you were to find Father

Jerry, you might discover answers and, who knows, perhaps inner peace. Are you going to do me a kindness and look for Father Jerry?"

Lino looked evenly at the old priest and finished his drink without saying a word.

"Well, then, I have wasted my time, haven't I?" Father Silva pulled open the screen door. "I'll say goodbye to your mother on the way out."

Lino watched the screen door close and listened as the priest's footsteps ground into the crushed shells on the driveway. He heard Father's Silva knock on the back door of the red house. He heard Colleen's voice welcoming the priest inside. When all fell quiet, Lino sat in the stillness, his insides churning with the news Father Silva had relayed.

The only sound was the incoming tide and the squawk of gulls wheeling overhead.

Four

When Vincent Cardosa wasn't fishing, he was on the docks mending nets or back home at his workshop steaming frames and shaping planks for the small boat he was building for his son. He had no drawings or measurements, just the memory of the open workboats his own father took to sea from the fishing village of Cascais near Lisbon. The boats were double-ended and heavily built to withstand the power of the following seas that slammed them daily onto the Portuguese beaches.

Vincent had a different boat in mind for Adilino. He wanted to build a floating monument to everything he loved about the sea and his son. For two winters he spent long days in the workshop, cutting the oak and shaping it into the individual pieces. When all the wood was ready, he laid the keel, then attached the nearly vertical stem to the forefoot. He drilled holes and fastened every joint with bronze through-bolts.

Vincent worked with the skill of an artisan as he molded the hourglass transom and bolted it to the transom knee. It was as if the small boat had a voice that only Vincent could hear. He heard it so clearly that nothing could go wrong with either the design or the craftsmanship. He steam-bent the oak frames, starting with a small bilge angle to give the boat a flatter bottom so she'd draw no more than fifteen inches when cruising over the famous Cape Cod flats. When all the frames were bent and their curvature tweaked to produce a soft water entry, Vincent cedar-planked the hull.

Work on the inside was all done in teak, which over time would weather naturally to a silvery gray. Vincent laid the sole, then added a casting deck forward, a center console with a wraparound windshield, and an engine box for the lightweight inboard gas engine that would cruise the boat at twenty knots. He spent hours sanding bungs and fairing the gentle curves, not really wanting the project to end.

Finally, there was nothing left to do but paint the exterior. He selected traditional colors of Cascais boats: Mediterranean blue sides with a white boot top. He named her *Pico II* after the boat his father had built for him back in Portugal.

Lino loved the boat maybe even more than his father did. It was their connection, their entry into emotions never spoken. What need was there to say what never came easily for either? *Pico II* said it all for them in how lovingly she was built and how lovingly she was cared for. When Lino left Provincetown to take the job investigating insurance fraud, the boat went to Gloucester with him. When work crowded his brain so tightly sleep couldn't find room, he'd get out of bed, dress in work clothes, and drive down to the boatyard.

Wooden boats always need work, and the work on his wooden boat lessened the crowd in his mind. The day he found his son hanging by his neck in the basement of his home, Lino spent time alone on his boat. It was the only thing in the world he could trust, the only thing he was sure of except that something horrible had just happened and his life with Linda would never be the same. After a few months he gave notice at the insurance company and soon was out guiding again in the waters around Gloucester and Cape Ann. On good days he could almost convince himself that it was just like the old days in Provincetown. Nothing had ever changed when, in fact, everything had.

Lino collected his charter at MacMillan Pier and headed out around Long Point Lighthouse to fish the bay side of the beach. The early morning sky had turned murky, the wind from the east blew gently at ten knots. A light fog had the channel buoy's horn groaning like something half-human. *Pico II* rode the swells with the ease of a boat twice her size. The ride impressed Mr. Cutler, a man in his early sixties, who anticipated the water's movements and slightly bent his knees for balance.

"Nice boat," he said. "Never seen anything like it."

"She's one of a kind," Lino said, cutting the throttle and working close to the beach a hundred yards past the point. "What are you casting?"

"A red and white Deceiver killed them last weekend along the Rhode Island rocks."

"Might work," Lino said. "Not a lot of rocks on the bottom here."

"What do you suggest?"

"A chartreuse Clouser has been working well. Stripers can't resist."

Cutler pulled from his jacket a small plastic fly box. Inside were four neat rows of perfectly tied saltwater flies, a row of Clousers in the middle. "I spend the winter tying with a trip or two thrown in to the Bahamas chasing bones. It breaks up shoveling snow. My wife hates the Boston winters about as much as I do."

"You both had a lot to hate last year," Lino said, watching Cutler deftly attach the chartreuse Clouser to his leader with a precisely tied clinch knot.

Cutler snipped off the excess and said, "She likes fishing, but I couldn't get her to come to Provincetown, so I came by myself. First trip here. I've only spent one night, but it doesn't seem so bad."

Lino kept his attention on the birds resting on the water. "It's like every place, I guess."

Cutler choked on a laugh. "You've got to be kidding. Not every place is into the gay thing like Provincetown. You know the town's reputation. What am I saying? Of course you do, you live here. I'm here to fish, so I don't care one way or the other, but my wife was a little antsy about it. She didn't want to be around a bunch of women holding hands and men kissing each other and worse, so she decided to pass. She'll go with me someplace next weekend where men date women." Cutler stepped on the casting platform and stripped out a coil of line that fell at his feet as Lino moved the boat closer to shore.

"I'm going to put you fifteen feet in front of a patch of eel grass," Lino said. "Cast past ten feet or so and retrieve over the patch."

"How fast?" Cutler asked.

"Moderate. You want to skim the grass tops, not sink into them."

Cutler flicked out enough line so his eight-weight Thomas could go to work. He made one false cast, double hauled, then cast again. The fly landed in clear water over sand. When it sank a few feet, Cutler danced it along the tops of the grasses unabated. The tide had turned two hours ago and ran hard over the eel grass, bending it like wheat in a strong wind. Cutler cast again, more to the center of the patch, and hooked up. The rod bent slightly at the tip, a sure sign of a small spring schoolie.

Cutler worked the fish on the reel and directed it to the side of the boat. He leaned over the side and put his thumb in the fish's mouth. He unhooked it and held the fourteen-incher in admiration, its stripes running the length of its body starting out black before turning brown and ending up as cobalt blue at the edges.

"A beautiful fish," he said, releasing it back into the water. "They have looks and fight like hell. What more could you want?"

"Size," Lino said. A keeper had to be at least twenty-eight inches.

"Size doesn't really matter to me as long as we catch them. I never keep anything anyway. What I eat, I buy at the supermarket." Cutler checked his leader and looked warily at Lino. "Sorry if I offended you earlier, you know, about the gay thing. I don't even know you, and you might be ..."

"I'm not gay, Mr. Cutler," Lino said. "Don't worry. Like you, I'm married."

"Ahh," Cutler said relieved. "You can never tell nowadays, can you? Millionaires look like bums. Not that I mind one way or the other."

"That's a good way to be." Lino scanned the water for fish. "Everybody goes their own way."

"Suits me." Cutler followed Lino's eyes. "You see fish? I don't see much with this gray sky."

They were past the first patch of eel grass and over a second. Lino maneuvered the boat's bow into a wake produced by a lobster boat heading out. He steered back to the grass in the calmer water.

"There are three or four skimming the far edge of the grass," Lino said, pointing toward the birds who were now taking flight. "We'll drift by and see what happens."

Lino shifted into neutral and watched Cutler deliver his fly.

"Nice cast. Let her sink. They're about two feet down. A bigger one trails deeper, maybe three feet. See it?"

Cutler bent forward, scanning the area until he saw a shadow. He sped up his retrieve. One fish noticed and charged before turning away.

"You had a looker," Lino said.

Cutler cranked a back cast into the wind, powered the rod forward and watched as the line curled out in front of him. The fly flew a few feet in front of the larger fish, who turned with interest. Cutler let the fly sink before gradually hauling the line hand over hand toward the boat. The big striper followed and then, with one powerful thrust of its broom-shaped tail, struck. The thin rod quivered as if powered by a jolt of unwanted electricity. Line screamed off the reel, matched by Cutler's joyous outburst.

"Oh, yeah! Go daddy," he said, holding the rod high and slightly increasing the reel's drag. "Feels like a good one, captain. Twenty pounds, maybe more. You got good eyes."

Lino eased the boat forward to take some of the strain off the rod as Cutler tried to turn the fish. The big fish would have none of it.

"Guess he's not interested," Cutler said through a wide smile. The fight was a test for man and fish, a fight Cutler planned on winning.

But not as much as his prey. In a burst of swift power, the rod surged forward only to snap back trailing slack line.

"Damn!" Cutler looked back at Lino amazed. "Do you believe it? He's off."

"There'll be others," Lino said. "We've got the whole day."

Cutler looked back at the choppy water as he reeled in his line. "They're beautiful, they fight, and sometimes they win," he said, getting a new fly. "It's the way it should be."

"You're right," Lino said. "They test you. Every cast, every hookup is a challenge."

Cutler tied on the new fly. "I'm up for it," he said. "Big stripers one, Bob Cutler zero. Let's see if we can even the score."

Five

Shank Painter Road is a commercial strip connecting Bradford Street to Route 6. The Provincetown police station, a small, low, clapboard building sits along it midway. Lino didn't have a charter that morning, so he drove to the station early. He parked in the circular drive and got out. Inside, behind protective glass, a young female officer monitored incoming calls and dispatched necessary manpower for what sounded like a minor traffic accident out on the highway. A television mounted high on the wall above her flickered a morning news show.

Lino announced himself and was directed to the office behind him where Sergeant Anthony Santos stood beside a gray metal desk sorting through a thick stack of papers. Tony was a big man, Lino's height but fifty pounds heavier, with a slightly hound-ish sag to his jowls. He had a shy, cold smile on his square face. He studied Lino warily as he came through the door.

Tony dropped the papers on top of the desk and nodded a greeting. "Lino," he said without offering his hand. "Been a long time. I thought you'd stop by sooner to say hello to an old friend."

"Getting settled, you know." Lino shifted uncomfortably on his feet. "It takes a while."

"Sure it does," Tony said. "Have a seat."

"I'm fine. Won't be here that long."

"Suit yourself." Tony settled on the desk chair and leaned back, his hands clasped behind his head. "What can I do for you?"

"I'd like to ask a few questions about the disappearance of Father Jeremiah Dunn."

"You're all of a sudden curious?"

"You might say I'm doing someone a favor."

"And who might that be?"

"Does it matter?"

"If you want me to answer any questions, it does, unless you're asking on behalf of Colas, Haggerty and Johnson. If that's the case, I can't say a thing."

His curiosity piqued, Lino changed his mind and sat. "What's Colas, Haggerty and Johnson have to do with anything?"

"You really don't know?"

"Not a clue," Lino admitted.

"I suppose that could be true," Tony admitted. "You haven't worked there in over two years."

"I'm impressed, Tony. How do you know I even worked there at all?"

"Never would have until C, H and J became a pain in the ass." Tony put one hand on the papers in front of him and jabbed his index finger into the top page. "I've been reading up on your former company as ordered by Chief Bicknell. He doesn't take too kindly to the fact that Colas has refused to pay the insurance claim on St. Peter's. He sees it as a personal slap to our little town."

"Did Colas give a reason for holding back?"

"You're the hotshot insurance investigator, what do you think the reason is?"

"Past tense, Tony. Like you said, I haven't had anything to do with Colas in two years," Lino reminded him, adding, "But the reason for not paying any claim is pretty standard. Money never leaves the Colas, Haggerty and Johnson coffers until the investigation is officially closed."

"And you want to help us close it by finding out what happened to Father Jerry."

"That's right."

"Who's paying you?"

"No one. You might say I'm doing a favor for the old priest who used to threaten us with the fires of hell if we didn't stop giggling during catechism."

A burst of laughter reddened Tony's face. "That old meddler," Tony jeered. "Father Silva is a lovable pest everybody in the department ignores except me—and now, it appears, you."

"He is persuasive."

"And then some," Tony agreed. "What exactly does he want from you?"

"What everybody wants, find out what happened to the missing priest. I'd like to start in a more general way. What can you tell me about the man?"

"Officially nothing. Because we're old friends, I'll tell you a little, which is really all there is to tell. Father Jerry got assigned to St. Peter's just over five years ago and seemed to fit right in. You know how quirky our little town is, Lino. Everybody's welcome. Bikers, gays, fishermen. You name it. Provincetown rolls out the carpet. Some priests found that openness an adjustment."

"Not just priests," Lino offered. "I had a charter the other day whose wife stayed away because of that openness. But Father Jerry was a good match?"

"He was. He didn't pass judgment. He accepted his imperfect congregation as the perfect challenge. And another thing, he rolled up his sleeves and dug right in whenever something needed doing, which, in the long run, may not have been such a grand idea."

"Why's that?"

"The State Police ruled the fire suspicious. There were some questions about the basement electrical panel being overloaded. How could it not be? Last winter broke hundred-year-old records for cold and snow. When Father Jerry got cold, he plugged in another space heater instead of turning on the heat in the entire church. He thought he was doing the right thing by saving a little money."

"That doesn't prove he caused the fire," Lino said.

"No, not alone, it doesn't. Add the accelerant, and you've got a problem."

"What accelerant?"

"Father Jerry was painting his office in his spare time and left the paint thinner and turpentine in a box in the basement corner."

"How do you know that?"

"I helped with some of the painting," Tony admitted. "Several of us did when we saw the job Father Jerry was doing. He rolled up his sleeves all right, but it looked like he painted with them, too. Messy as hell. He needed a lot of help this time, and we gave it."

"Do you think he set the fire?"

"No. I can't imagine any priest doing that, Father Jerry included."

"Do you think he stole the money and ran off?"

Tony slightly shook his head. "I don't believe he did, but the alternative that someone did him harm is a worse thought. The honest answer is that like everyone else, I don't know what happened to him. The State Police and we are doing all we can to find the truth."

"What about the plane ticket to Rome?" Lino asked. "That suggests he was planning something."

"There were two tickets bought with his credit card and never claimed. Whatever he was planning likely didn't happen."

"What was the name on the second ticket?"

"Smith." Tony smiled sarcastically. "Catchy, isn't it? A name that leads nowhere."

"First name?"

"What does that matter?"

"Might give some indication as to his sexual preference. Do you think Father Jerry is gay?"

"Why would I think that?"

"You knew him. You saw how he behaved."

Tony lifted one arm. "You mean this?" He dropped a limp wrist. "Barking up the wrong tree, Lino. The man was a priest, period. No funny business that I ever saw or heard about."

"Even at Sweetbriar?"

Tony's expression brightened. "Well, well, you've done some homework, haven't you? What have you heard?"

"Just that he was somehow connected to Sweetbriar," Lino admitted.

"As an administrator. He basically ran the summer camp, hired the staff, scheduled the volunteers, helped organize the programs, that sort of thing. He wasn't down at the lake giving swimming lessons and feeling up the boys. Instead, you might say he was making sure his sister's money was being spent the way she wanted."

"How was that?"

Tony worked a mischievous smile. "Your son was a camper, Lino. You ought to know why you sent him to Sweetbriar. Good, clean fun for the kids with a strong, Catholic message tossed in for good measure."

"How did you know my son went to Sweetbriar?"

"Not once, but how many? Six summers was it?"

Lino nodded. "Six. Seems you're the one doing the homework."

"Just doing my job, Lino."

"How does that include me?"

"That run-in you had with the priest. You were charged with assault and battery. It's part of the record, Lino. Just following up, that's all."

"Make sure you note that the charges were eventually dropped. It was all a misunderstanding."

"So noted."

"Fair enough," Lino said, moving the conversation back to the missing priest. "What was the date on the tickets to Rome?"

"The night of the fire."

"When were the tickets purchased?"

"That same day."

"Any guesses as to why he didn't pick them up?"

"If he, indeed, bought the tickets," Tony said. "It could have been someone else making the priest look guilty."

"The illusive Smith, maybe?"

"Maybe, or the person or persons who walked off with the church's money and Father Jerry. I don't know, Lino. All I know is that like most of us, I miss listening to his sermons. Direct. Honest. Always full of hope in a mostly hopeless world. I walked out of St. Pete's feeling as if I'd just heard the voice of God. Your mother will tell you. I saw her there every Sunday. She never missed."

"Unfortunately, my mother doesn't remember anything all that well. If she did, I'd love to talk to her about Father Jerry."

"There are others who swear by him, not just me."

"Care to offer a name?"

"The Jackstones. Henry and Susan down in Wellfleet. I think Henry has calmed down by now. If not, Susan won't let him get a word in edgewise. Give them a call."

"Calmed down over what?"

"Henry will tell you. I don't want to steal his thunder."

"All right, Tony. Thanks." Lino stepped toward the door.

"Lino?" He turned back and looked into Tony's curious eyes. "Sorry to hear about your son."

Lino nodded and walked out.

From the second floor of the cottage, Lino looked out past the dunes at a setting sun that oozed light like blood in the streaking clouds. Behind him, through the open front windows, he heard the waves as loud as detonations breaking against the shore caused by the high tide and strong south winds gusting to thirty knots.

The rough weather forced him to cancel his afternoon charter, so Lino spent the time rummaging through the spare bedroom storage boxes and his mind. Somewhere in the cottage or in the red house his mother had packed away a box of personal photographs. He never anticipated her mental lapses, and now she couldn't remember exactly where she'd put them, but she was almost certain they were in one of the dozen or so cardboard boxes on the second floor of the cottage.

Lino had gone through all the boxes and not found what he was looking for. He made himself a drink and went back to the red house where Colleen stood at the kitchen sink washing the dinner dishes. Mrs. Cardosa, arms folded across her dark green sweater, her hands fidgeting, stood in the doorway to the living room.

"You didn't have any luck, did you?" she said, recognizing a hint of disappointment in her son's dark eyes. "I was afraid of that. You didn't find what you were looking for. Some boxes, am I right?"

"One box."

"One box of what, Lino?"

"Old pictures. I bumped into Tony Santos today. He reminded me of some high school photographs I'd stashed away. Friday night football games, some good times he and I had messing around out in the dune shacks. Made me curious, that's all, but it's probably for the best I didn't find them. Not good to look back, which goes for Tony Santos, too. I probably would have been better off not seeing him."

Mrs. Cardosa's eyes asked the question.

"He's a policeman now, Mother. As kids we used to raise hell all week and sit together like angels while Father Silva said Sunday mass. I'm sure you'd remember if you saw him," Lino said, not sure at all. "He's about my height. Heavier. He has the stamp of the Portuguese with his black eyes and black hair. Was one hell of a tough guy in school. The only guy he couldn't push around was me. I always thought he'd end up in jail instead of wearing the badge of the good guys."

"Good guys?" Katharine repeated.

"Just an expression for a cop." Lino sipped his scotch, knowing full well Katharine wasn't really paying attention. He talked, but no one listened. "How was your day, Mother? Did you manage to stay out of trouble?"

Katharine giggled at the thought. "I think so," she said, turning her attention to Colleen. "I didn't get into any trouble today, did I?"

"Not one bit," Colleen said, forcing the levity. "All we can hope is that tomorrow will be as fine."

"What did you two do?" Lino asked.

"Let's see." Mrs. Cardosa seemed lost in the throes of foreign travel. "What did we do?"

"We spent a good chunk of the day working in the garden."

"That's right. I think we planted the poppies. I love poppies."

"I know you do," Lino said, ignoring the fact that the poppies had not done well this year. They had dropped their deep orange pedals after only a few days.

"I think I'll go water them."

"Not tonight, Katharine," Colleen said. "First thing in the morning, we'll water everything."

Mrs. Cardosa cocked her head. "Is that all right, Lino, to wait?"

"It's fine," he said, feeling the weight of the conversation sap his energy. "You look tired, Mother. Why don't you get ready for bed?"

A flash of confusion crossed Katharine's face. She seemed not to know how.

"Come on, dear," Colleen said and led her toward the rear bedroom. When Colleen came back, she said, "We drove down to the hospital in Hyannis yesterday afternoon."

Lino felt a twinge of guilt when a charter conflicted with a run to Hyannis. "I know," Lino said. "How did it go?"

"Katharine said she doesn't need to see another doctor, that it's all a waste of time."

"Was it?"

"I don't think so. You and I might think she's losing more of her memory, but only her neurologist can say so with certainty."

"Sounds like she had more tests."

Colleen nodded. "Katharine hates them. Maybe hate is the wrong word. She's suspicious of all the questions. What's the point? Who cares if she can count backward by threes?"

Lino was with his mother the first time a doctor asked her to count. He saw her frustration when she stumbled and felt the glare from his mother's anger when he obeyed doctor's orders and didn't help her.

"When will we get the results?" he asked.

"Soon. A week or so. The doctor will call you directly." Colleen lowered her voice so Katharine could not possibly hear. "You know what poor results will mean, don't you, Lino? If Katharine gets more dependent, you're going to have to hire more help. I can't manage alone."

"I know that, too." Lino finished his drink. "You're doing a fine job, Colleen, a wonderful job. My sister and I appreciate it. We really do. Whatever it takes to get Mother what she needs so she can stay in her house, we'll do. If that's more help, you'll have more help. Don't worry, all right?"

Colleen pursed her lips. "All right," she said. "And, yourself? How are you doing with all this?"

"I'm fine," Lino said, repeating the words Katharine spoke whenever she could think of nothing else to say. "We'll get through it," he said and walked slowly to his mother's bedroom to kiss her goodnight.

Six

Lino felt more comfortable with repeat charters. They knew his routine, and Jack Toby knew the routine by heart: Be at the dock fifteen minutes before the charter begins; bring sunscreen, sunglasses, bottled water, warm clothes and gear. Jack, like many of Lino's customers, had fished on the *Pico II* in Gloucester and followed him to the Cape for a few days fishing.

"Top of the morning," Jack said, climbing onboard. "You look none the worse from the winter of hell you had down here."

"Nothing to it, but I did get a little worried when I couldn't find the boat under ten feet of snow." Lino shook Jack's hand warmly. "Good to see you."

Jack looked around the always spotless craft. "She's looking fine. Cape waters must agree with her."

"Built right here," Lino said proudly. "Every plank was shaped by my father's hands."

"Beautiful. Wish we could see you and your boat back in Gloucester. It's not the same up north without you leading us around. None of us are catching as many fish. Some of the guys wanted me to ask you to come back."

"Not a chance," Lino said, backing off the dock.

"That's what I figured. Guy getting a divorce wants to put as much distance between himself and trouble."

"That's part of it," Lino said.

"So, how's that all shaking out?"

Lino shrugged. "Our lawyers talk and run up the bills, but I understand we might be getting close to the end."

"Linda wants your balls in a vice?"

Lino chuckled. "You talk like a man with experience."

"Everybody goes through it once," Jack said with a sigh. "Me, I didn't learn my lesson. I went through it twice. As you can see," he patted his hefty stomach, "I survived. You will, too; a little light in the wallet, but you'll get through it. Anybody who can live through the death of his child can live through anything. She still blame you?"

"I think that's fair to say." Lino kept the engine's speed low through the anchorage protected by the breakwall and eased out into the expansive harbor. June was still early for most cruisers, and only a few guest moorings were occupied. "She certainly doesn't blame herself."

"Of course not. Everything's always the man's fault," Jack said, adjusting his pants up over his sagging belly. Jack's friends called him Jack Tubby. "That was the line used on me. I was the inconsiderate fuckhead who did nothing for our marriage but bring home the check. That we lived pretty damn fine means nothing when they want your ass out of the house. Women got short memories, but I've got a cure for that."

"Which is?"

"Salty air. Once you smell the sea air and look around at the beautiful views, you can forget some of that crap, you know? I don't think I ever told you, Lino, but I only took up fishing to get away from wife number one. She was on me hard, so I packed up and flew out to Montana to fish the trout streams. Stayed there for three weeks, about as close to heaven as I'll ever get."

"What about wife number two?" Lino asked playfully.

"She was worse. That's when I took up tossing flies in saltwater. If there's ever a wife number three, my guess is I'll soon be down in Costa Rica fishing the deep for marlin." Jack unzipped the cap on his rod case and slid out a two-piece, 9-weight Orvis. "But I'm not looking for wife number three, I'm looking for stripers. What have you got in mind for us?"

"The mouth of the Pamet."

Jack nodded. "I looked at a chart last night. Looks like a little river that could carry herring."

"It carries them right over the shoal just past the channel buoys," Lino said. "Stripers hold near the bottom, waiting for breakfast to drop in. We'll be waiting, too."

Jack held up a Clauser. "You still recommending this?"

"I am until it stops working."

"Then, let's see it work, old buddy," Jack said, connecting his rod.

As usual, Jack Toby was generous with his tip and offer to buy lunch. Lino accepted the tip for Jack's two keepers but took a rain check on the lunch. He wanted to get back on the mooring, shower and drive down to Wellfleet to talk with the Jackstones, who were leaving the Cape the next day for a few weeks in England.

Henry Jackstone, a retired investment banker from New York, agreed to talk to Lino at his summer house on the bayside. Lino knew the marshes and inlets there well. As a kid he'd learned how to sail a Sunfish and ride a boogie board in those protected waters. Neither held his interest for long.

Lino parked on the stone drive and walked up the curved, brick steps. Susan Jackstone, a woman in her early sixties, waited behind the screen to greet her visitor.

"You must be Mr. Cardosa," she said, her pink lipstick all smiles, her frosted blonde hair cut to frame her long, thin face. "Welcome." She eagerly shook Lino's hand. "Henry?" she called into the cavernous house that looked like it belonged more on a California hillside than among the pines of Cape Cod. "It's Mr. Cardosa."

Henry dressed like a yachtsman with worn Docksiders, no socks, beige cotton shorts and an open-neck white shirt. Neither of the Jackstones could be accused of weight problems; both were fit and trim, the picture of aging in style. Henry held out his hand. "Any trouble with Susan's directions?" His voice was cool, direct.

"None at all. I appreciate your seeing me on such short notice."

"Oh, we're happy to do anything we can do to help find Jerry." Her voice, in contrast to her husband's, was warm, bubbly.

Lino followed the couple through the living room and out onto a side deck that overlooked a glistening swimming pool. They sat around a glass table under the shade of a dark green umbrella. An overweight golden retriever lay sprawled in the nearby cut grass.

Susan said, "It's about time someone took the initiative to locate Father Jerry. All along, Henry and I have been convinced the authorities haven't done enough. It's a shame."

"Small-town thinking only takes you so far," Henry said like a man used to the unlimited resources of Manhattan.

"The State Police are also involved," Lino corrected. "Their crime labs are second to none."

"And where has that gotten us?" Henry scoffed. "Nowhere."

Susan poured glasses of iced tea. "You can tell we're a little frustrated."

"And angry," Henry added. "To be taken advantage of like that and by a priest. I never would have thought it possible."

"I thought you and Father Jerry were friends," Lino said, confused.

"I'm still his friend." Susan stiffened as if bracing for verbal blows from her husband that never came. "I'll always be here when he needs me."

"The man is a crook," Henry snapped.

Susan returned her husband's fierce stare. "Father Jerry doesn't have a mean bone in his body," she said firmly, "nor a dishonest one."

"The man," Henry said more loudly, "is the worst kind of crook imaginable. You never think the man wearing the collar in your own church is capable of doing the wrong thing. You can't sit in the pew on Sunday if that thought ever gets in your head.

His sermons would be a meaningless joke. You've got to have faith, and Father Jerry took that from me. Like I said, the worst kind of crook imaginable, the bastard."

"Henry." Susan blushed with embarrassment.

Henry set his jaw. "The bastard," he said again.

Susan forced an uncomfortable smile for Lino's benefit. "You can see we have a difference of opinion," she said.

"What we have is a missing fifty thousand dollars," Henry corrected. "That is a point on which we both agree. Correct?"

Susan nodded slightly, a painful admission. "Correct," she said, "but I'm sure there is a reasonable explanation."

"There is," Henry shot back. "He stole it and left Provincetown, and this kind man," he pointed to Lino, "is going to find him and get our money back. Isn't that right?"

"I don't know exactly what I'm going to do," Lino admitted. "This is the first I've heard about your money."

Henry nearly leapt from his chair. "The first you've heard? We filed a police report. We notified the diocese. How could you not have heard?"

"Keep your voice down, Henry."

He turned to his wife. "Susan, the only reason I agreed to see this man was because you said the church had finally gotten off its ass and was conducting its own investigation into our money."

"I know what I said."

"You mean it's not true? You lied?"

She held two fingers an inch apart. "This much," she said. "A little white one."

"Why?"

"So you would talk to Mr. Cardosa about finding Father Jerry. When he finds him, he will find our money."

"Unless he's already blown through it partying in South America."

"Father Jerry did not run off with that money, and you know it. He is not a thief," Susan said as if those words had tumbled from her lips hundreds of times before and fallen on deaf ears.

Lino asked them to explain about the money.

"It was a charitable donation to help the church repair some wiring," Henry said wearily. "That's all there was to it."

"That's not all, that's just the end." Susan brushed the hair from her eyes. "It would help if Mr. Cardosa knew the beginning of it. I was editing a parish cookbook—as a fundraiser, you understand. Even though we live here in Wellfleet half the year, we always go to church at St. Peter's. We like the change of scenery."

"The bottom line," Henry quipped, "is that Jerry Dunn loved to eat, and Susan loves to cook. That's the bottom line."

"It was a passion of his, yes, but Henry isn't implying that Father Jerry was a glutton. On the contrary, Father Jerry was a master cook, and he liked what I did with the cookbook. We got to talking, and one thing led to another, until soon he was a frequent guest in our house trying out recipes."

"How long had this been going on?"

"Three, maybe four years," Henry said. "One night not long ago, the three of us sat around talking about St. Peter's and the condition it was in. Susan and I have done pretty well for ourselves and have been generous to various charities, so I wasn't completely surprised when Jerry asked if we'd make a donation to improve the church's electrical service."

"The fifty thousand dollars," Lino said.

"That's right. Susan and I talked it over and wrote out a check. Less than a week later, St. Peter's lay in ashes, and Father Jerry was gone after cleaning out the church's account with our money in it."

"Any idea how much that was in total?" Lino asked.

"Nearly a hundred thousand dollars. Father Jerry had close to fifty thousand coming in from an emergency fund the diocese kept."

"Then why didn't he pay an electrician out of existing church funds?" Lino asked.

"I asked that very question," Henry said. "Jerry told me that he had a seasonal contract to heat the church and the rectory and for snow removal for the parking lot. He said that because of the severity of the winter, once he paid those bills, he'd be about broke. I had no reason to doubt him."

"I still don't," Susan chimed. "I don't have Henry's sixth sense for reading people, but I know he has one. He's spent his life in commercial banking, agreeing to loans in the millions of dollars. It isn't just a credit rating that gets the loan approved, it's what Henry sees in people's eyes. He saw that same honesty in Father Jerry's, or he never would have agreed to help."

"I made a mistake."

"No, you didn't, Henry. You didn't see Father Jerry as a cheat, because he isn't one."

"Then what happened?" Lino asked.

Susan's confidence sagged. "I don't know. He had no family since his sister died a few years ago. He had no special friends that we know of. At least, he never brought anyone to the house."

"Except what's-his-name."

"Who?"

"I don't remember the name." Henry looked questioningly at Susan. "You remember. A tall guy built like a marathoner with one arm. He was renting a vacation house down here for a couple of weeks, and Jerry brought him over for drinks. He couldn't wait to leave, as I recall. Had a memorable last name that I can't remember. Canopy? Calliope?"

"Oh, of course, I remember. Callegari. Francesco Callegari."

"That's the one. Wasn't much of a conversationalist."

"He was uncomfortable," Susan reminded her husband, "nervous."

"Do you remember anything else about him?" Lino asked. "Where he lives? What he does?"

"He teaches history somewhere in Boston. At a university, I think," Susan said. "We told all that to the police."

"Anyone else come to mind?" Lino asked. "Any special friends Father Jerry might have mentioned?"

Henry shook his head. "None."

"I don't think he had many," Susan added. "That's what makes all this so sad. People who didn't know him make him out as some fiend, some criminal, when he's neither. When you find him, you'll see for yourself."

"What makes you think he's still alive?" Lino asked.

"I've prayed that he is," Susan said. "I know my prayers will be answered."

"I'm not so sure they will be," Henry said, getting to his feet, "but one way or another I'd like some resolution. Alive. Dead."

"Henry, stop."

Henry shrugged, then led the way back through the house. "We'll be staying at the Savoy in London for ten days if you need to contact us, Mr. Cardosa."

"With good news," Susan chimed in, "news that you've found Jerry."

"And, our fifty thousand."

Seven

Lino's sister Carol told people her brother was lucky when it came to finding fish. She never saw him working through his logbook, analyzing different tides, water temperatures, bottom structures that changed frequently during the violent storms on the Outer Cape. Even as a summer guide during college, Lino believed in minimizing the odds to maximize his client's catch. It was something his father had told him. Study everything— daylight, darkness, wind, season, tide, current, bait—to see how they affect the catch. "I do that after every trip, and I'm captain of a dragger," Vincent had told him. "You're in a small boat, casting a rod with a small fly. It's a huge ocean, Lino. You need every advantage you can get."

When Lino returned to Provincetown he buried himself in information. What he couldn't learn firsthand he read about, including how fish used sound, smell and sight. He observed feeding behaviors and a fish's reaction to monofilament versus fluorocarbon line. He experimented with different fly patterns, designing variations and tying his own until his fingers ached. When he could tie no more, he went back to his log, poring over entries, looking for that single fact he'd not registered before, looking for another advantage, looking for details that would jam his brain and keep out the horrible image of his son.

But sometimes no level of trivia (Fish do not need external ears because their body tissue is the same density as water so sound in the water passes through their body into an inner ear; fish use nostrils exclusively for smell, not for breathing; fish eyes can rotate one hundred eighty degrees without head movement) could keep out the jagged image of the sixteen-year-old boy wearing Tevas and chinos and a pale blue shirt hanging lifelessly from a rope tied around his broken neck.

Steven Vincent Cardosa left no note, which was in keeping with his generally quiet way. He studied every night to maintain an A average. He went to the movies on weekends and to the occasional school dance. He experimented once or twice with beer, which made him sick. He smoked a cigarette, or at least half of one, before throwing it away. He had a girlfriend who called the house daily. When not away at summer camp, he and his friends played baseball or lined up as caddies at the country club to make some extra cash.

Traveling on business, Lino frequently talked about his son at the airport bar if the occasion arose. His pride charged the air. Every parent should have such a boy who sat down at Sunday dinner and talked about the week past and the week ahead.

"We're a good family," Lino would say, almost embarrassed at his fine fortune. "We're blessed and say our prayers for those not so lucky."

Then the luck ran out like a runaway freighter Lino saw coming but could not stop. The changes in the boy happened so quickly that Linda and Lino thought their son must have found a drug he did enjoy.

"Steven, I want you to know that you can tell your father anything," Lino pleaded one night after his son had attempted to shave his head, resulting in a ragged, bloody scalp. "What would you like to tell me?"

"Nothing." Steven's unforgiving dark eyes shifted from his father to his mother. "I don't want to tell you anything."

"There must be something," Linda said. "You certainly can't be an usher in my cousin's wedding Saturday looking like that. Is that why you did this? You wanted out of the wedding?"

"I don't know what I want." Steven ran one hand over the rough edges of his head. "I don't even want this haircut."

"It'll grow back," Lino tried to reassure him, "but there's a lesson in that, Steve. Steven, are you listening to me? Sometimes you, me, everybody does something that's irreversible. Sometimes you can't take it back like that time in the backyard when you shot the field mouse with the BB gun. No matter how much you wanted to, you couldn't give back the life. Remember? In an instant everything changed. You want to be careful, Stevie. Do you understand what I'm saying? Don't rush into anything like you did with that mouse. Think about it long and hard and ask God for guidance, okay? God is there for you, just like your mom and dad."

A thin smile crossed Steven's lips. Though barely perceptible, it startled Lino and Linda. They spoke about it after their son had gone upstairs to bed.

"He scares me," Linda admitted. "That look. I don't like it."

"Growing pains," Lino said, equally concerned but not admitting it. "What do you want to do?"

"I'll call the doctor in the morning."

The doctor ran tests that proved Steven to be in good health. Physically there was nothing wrong. He referred Linda to a psychiatrist who spent an hour with Steven every Monday after school for six weeks.

"A mild depression is not that uncommon nowadays," the doctor told Lino and Linda in his office. "It's unfortunate, but it's the world we live in, or I should say, the world our children live in. Some of them require a little assistance, a mood elevator until they sort things out."

"What things?" Lino asked, stuck on the cause of his son's problems. Lino wanted to understand them, to attack them, to solve them. "Did Steven tell you what was bothering him?"

"It's not something he's specific about, no. It's a general malaise, dissatisfaction with everything, including who he is, who you are, the expectations at school, the pressures on his life. He's got a severe case of growing pains."

Lino felt the hair dance across the back of his neck. "What do you mean who we are?" he repeated, trying to make sense of such a simple, troubling statement. "There's nothing wrong with who we are."

"I'm not saying there is," the doctor reassured. "It's what your son thinks that matters."

"All kids go through that," Linda offered as if the emotional valley Steven stumbled through suddenly made sense. Even if it didn't, she knew one thing for sure: She didn't want her son on pills. She had gone that route with her depressed mother and knew she couldn't tolerate the blank looks, the haunting indifference from her son. She couldn't bear watching him turn into a distant stranger living in her home. "You're saying he'll grow out of this, is that right, Doctor? I mean on a scale of one to ten, we're not talking ten, are we?"

"No." He looked at his notes. "We're certainly not there yet, but the mind is unpredictable. None of us knows for sure how your son will handle the next few months. We need to keep an eye on him, a close eye."

"Of course," Lino said, "but I want to go back to the cause of all this. You don't simply wake up one morning and find the world closing in."

"Some people do," the doctor admitted.

"But not my son," Lino blurted, "not our son. Something happened to him, and I want to know why he can't handle it."

"Nothing happened," Linda countered, startled at the resentment in her own voice. "Let's not concern ourselves with what happened, let's work on making Stevie better, okay? Besides, what difference does it make? We have a situation we have to deal with now." Her cold, blue eyes bore in on her husband. "Let's deal with it, all right?"

Lino checked his frustration. To him, problems had identifiable causes. That was his job at Colas when an insurance claim rang false: Find the cause and turn the criminal over to the authorities for prosecution.

"All right," Lino finally said. "I know my wife isn't in favor of this, but what if we try the medication you mentioned to elevate his mood?" Lino asked the doctor. "Not as a cure, but as something to help Steven get on with his life until he gets better."

"That is my recommendation."

"What are the risks?" Lino asked.

"Aspirin has risks," the doctor said. "All medications have side effects. Mood elevators are no different. I suggest starting with a small dose, and we'll see how Steven responds. If he has trouble tolerating it, we'll try another until we find what works."

Linda bristled. "You make it sound like an experiment."

"Within a tightly controlled range, it is," the doctor admitted. "We have ample research to demonstrate that antidepressants do produce improvements, but everyone responds differently. We won't know about your son until we try."

"What's the alternative?" Linda asked, her mother still on her mind.

"We help him through with more Monday sessions and hope he doesn't get worse," the doctor said. "Why don't you think about it? Talk it over with Steven, and then let me know if you'd like me to phone in a prescription."

The family talk was strained. Steven wanted nothing to do with capitalistic pharmaceutical companies increasing their profits by poisoning his system. Linda followed Steven's lead and spent hours searching the internet and printing out articles from medical journals with titles like *Missing Childhoods and Prescription Drugs* and *Numbing Down, The Lost Years of Teens.* Lino read the articles. He followed their arguments and discussed their merits with his wife. After all the talk Lino agreed to keep peace in the family and not to insist on the pills.

"All right, we'll wait," he said, knowing in his heart that Steven knew no peace, that he needed medication. "Maybe he'll snap out of it."

"He might," Linda said, hopeful. "He just needs a little more time to get his balance, that's all. Just a little more time."

"How much time?" Lino wanted to know.

"Six months or until something happens."

The "something" appeared a few weeks later. In wide letters painted three feet high across all four white walls of the living room, Steven had painted "Stop it! Stop! Stop it! Stop it! Stop!" He used black paint and a roller. Splashes and drops ran down the furniture and dried into the carpet. When Lino got home from work, he found Linda sitting on the floor in the middle of the room, her eyes red and glassy from crying.

Lino felt struck, stomped hard in the gut as he jerked the phone from its cradle.

"He doesn't know what he's doing." Linda's voice was a hoarse whisper. "He's sick."

"Where is he?"

"In his room."

"I want him on those pills before he paints the whole fucking house black." Lino found the doctor's number scribbled on a pad of paper and punched it in.

Ever since the graffiti, Lino steeled himself for the worst when he entered his house. He inhaled deep, long breaths and stretched himself to his fullest height. When he pulled open the door, he peeked in before stepping across the threshold. On the day he found Steven, the living room was clear, even inviting. The walls had been repainted, the furniture and carpets replaced. He almost sat but knew he had to check on his son. That was part of the new regime. Come home, make sure Steven was upstairs doing his homework. Make sure he was out of trouble. No variations.

Upstairs in Steven's empty room, Lino found an open textbook. A good sign. He checked the bathroom and guest rooms. All empty. On the stairs he called Steven's name and waited for a reply. The silent house sent a chill through him. He hurried down the steps and called out again.

"Steven? Steve? Where are you? Dad's home. Steve?"

In the kitchen a half-open Pepsi sat warm on the counter. The door to the garage was ajar.

"You hiding in the garage?" Lino asked, afraid he was not.

"Playing games on your old man?" He almost choked on the words, knowing how false they sounded even to him.

Lino pushed open the garage door and saw that coiled line for the *Pico II* was missing from its peg. A knot swelled in Lino's throat as the air seeped out of him. He could barely stand, so strong was the certainty that Steve was gone, dead.

"Dear God." Lino made the sign of the cross as the air jumped from his lungs in short bursts. "Please. Please. Please. Please, oh, please, oh, please. Let him be all right. I'll do whatever you want. Give me a sign, and I'll do it, I swear. Just let Stevie be all right. He's just a confused kid. Please, let him be all right. Deal?" Lino looked toward the heavens. "Why don't You answer me? Why?" he snapped.

Lino sucked in breath so deeply that he spun lightheaded back into the kitchen. He steadied himself, then stepped in front of the basement door.

He opened it. The lights were on.

"Steve? I'm not in the mood for games, you understand? That's enough. You just come on up, and we'll forget this ever happened, but you've got to come up now."

The only thing moving was Lino's stomach. He swallowed back the bile and forced himself down the steps. The knocked-over chair came first into view, then a nylon sandal. Slowly, Lino let his eyes drift upward to the hanging stillness.

"No, God, no." He collapsed on the stairs, his muscles gone to water as tears welled into his eyes. "You were going to help him. You were going to make him all right."

In a burst of anger so primal, Lino slammed the wall next to him, his fists punching through the sheetrock. "We made a deal. You were going to make him all right! What happened, huh? *What the fuck happened?"*

Lino's hoarse and harsh voice roared through the house.

Eight

The last weekend in June always brought with it the Portuguese Festival and the annual blessing of the fleet. This year the weather was clear, the breeze light and variable. A perfect day for a charter, but Lino kept the *Pico II* on its mooring. To fish on the day of the blessing was a sign of disrespect. The day was festive, a party, a joyous coming together of those who made their living from the sea. Many a captain who ignored tradition and went out found his nets cut or gears jammed soon thereafter.

Lino opened the back door of the red house and followed Colleen into the living room where Katharine, dressed in a rose-colored summer suit, sat on the sofa in front of the coffee table covered with old newspapers. When she saw her son, her eyes glistened.

"I found the box, Adilino," she said proudly. "I found the box you were looking for. It wasn't in the cottage after all."

Lino put down his coffee cup and scooped up clippings describing snippets of his past: "Adilino Cardosa leads P-town Fishermen to League Championship." "Cardosa and Santos Crush Plymouth in Title Game." "Cardosa State Wrestling Champ Cardosa Signs Letter of Intent to BC." "Cardosa Wrestles Big East Title from Syracuse." Lino sat next to his mother and picked up a yellowed photograph of Tony Santos in pads and cleats, his arms bear-hugging Lino in the end zone. Lino put down the brittle papers, embarrassed that he had wanted to see them in the first place.

"You did a good job, Mom." Lino put one arm around her thin shoulders. "A great job."

"The box was in the basement," she said, "under a table in the corner. Colleen took out every article and showed me. They're all about you."

"A long time ago."

"Would you like to see each one?"

"Not today. Some other time maybe."

Katharine cocked her head. "Is it the wrong box?"

"It's the right box, but there isn't time today. Colleen said you wanted to be early for mass."

"I did?" Katharine scrunched her brow as if forcing a thought into clearer focus. Her confused gaze drifted to Colleen. "Help me."

"The blessing of the fleet, Katharine," Colleen said. "With the church gone, it's being held on the wharf. You're all dressed for it, remember? You wanted to get there soon for a good seat, and Lino promised to take us."

With his mother beside him and Colleen in the back seat, Lino drove at walking speed down Commercial Street past countless old, captains' houses with well-tended gardens in lush bloom. Everyone in town seemed headed for the blessing. Lino managed not to hit anyone in crowded Lopes Square and dropped Colleen and his mother at the beginning of Fisherman's Pier. The mass would take place in the old wooden warehouse at the far end. Even from here Lino could see that Portuguese flags decorated the makeshift church, and the ten-foot-high loading doors had been opened to make the cool ocean air and views of Long Point part of the service.

"Aren't you coming?" Katharine asked.

Lino shook his head. "I'll be nearby. Don't worry, I'll make sure you get home."

Katharine's mood saddened. "You'll miss the bishop, Adilino. That's how important the blessing is. A bishop always blesses the fleet." She saw her son's stubbornness and turned to Colleen. "I don't think he's coming."

Colleen took Katharine's arm and helped her to her feet. "It's all right." She closed the door with a thud. "We'll save him a seat in case he changes his mind."

"Good idea," Lino said, not wanting to dampen his mother's excitement any further.

An unmanned machine spit out a ticket and swung open the gate leading to the town parking lot. Lino parked on the MacMillan Pier side. A dozen or so lobster boats bobbed in their slips under the weight of preparations for the party following the blessing. Farther down the pier, draggers rafted three deep, dress and Portuguese flags fluttering in the breeze. These were strong, old workboats, built mostly of wood with rusted iron winches bolted to their decks. Their hulls, painted in dark greens and blues and black, bore proud names painted white on bows and across transoms. Lino read the names as he walked: *Ancora Praia, Antonio Jorge, Three of Us, Second Effort, Terra Nova, Chico-Jess, Richard Arnold.* He still could not get used to the fact that the *Amy Ann* was not part of the celebration.

Lino's father had lived for the blessing. It was like a badge for him, a protective shield keeping trouble at a distance. Vincent had believed that deep within his soul. When the bishop leaned out over the water from his sacred platform and caught Vincent Cardosa's eye as he blessed the *Amy Ann*, Vincent knew God would care for him and his men. He had faith that the ceremony, the pageantry and the blessing made him worthy, like St. Peter himself, to serve God and fish the seas. And if he was worthy in God's eyes, Vincent believed he would be resurrected from the hells that lurked below the surface of the water. Hells driven upward by the wind. Hells building mountains out of dark, cold water. Hells driving men crazy with their piercing sounds. Hells that nothing could stop. Nothing.

"Hey, Adilino," the voice said, "you look like the weight of the world is on your back." Raymond Olivera, Captain Ray to his friends, closed one meaty fist and mockingly connected a haymaker to Lino's jaw. "Snap out of it, man. It's a day to relax, be with family. Whatever's bothering you, forget it. If you can't, wash it away. You want a beer?"

Lino glanced at his watch. It was just now ten-thirty. "It's a little early," he said.

"Makes it all the more special," Ray responded. "Come on, I've got plenty on board."

They strode past the harbormaster's office, past the rows of chairs creating a reviewing stand for dignitaries who'd come down to participate in the blessing. Before St. Peter's burned, a long procession, complete with a huge statue of St. Peter riding a wooden platform carried on the shoulders of parishioners, left the church following the mass and wound its way to the pier for the blessing. Today, the procession would still occur but would lead only from the wharf to the pier.

Lino and Ray climbed down iron rungs to the deck of the *Ocean Blue,* an eighty-five-foot dragger. Captain Ray opened a cooler shoved up against the wheelhouse and removed two ice-cold Buds. He popped the tops and handed one to Lino.

"To what ails you," Ray said and waited until Lino had committed. Ray joined in, drank half in one long gulp and said, "So, what is it, Lino? What's bothering you?"

"Nothing, Ray, nothing."

"That might work for somebody you take out for a day's fishing but not somebody who watched you grow up. What's the problem? Money? If it is, you're like everybody else trying to make a living on the water."

"No, no, money's good."

"I'll remember that next time I need a loan." Ray laughed at his own joke. "The whole family's coming aboard after mass. Joey and his brood, Sam and his, my wife, everybody. You're welcome to join in, Lino. Bring your mom, fine lady that she is. Be like old times when your dad was alive."

"Thanks, Ray. I mean it, but I don't think so."

"How's she doing, anyway?"

"Not bad. Some days are better than others."

"She's lost weight."

"A few pounds. She's got an Irish cook trying to change that."

"You living in the house?"

Lino sipped his beer. "No, the cottage."

"Good move. A man moving back with his parents is not a good thing. I speak from experience with Sammy. After his divorce, his mother and I said, 'Come on home, relax a while, clear your head.' After a week I understood why his wife threw him out. I wanted to do the same thing, and he's my own son."

"Why didn't you?"

"His mother wouldn't allow it. Instead, she got Father Jerry involved. Sort of a counselor, you might say. Every time I turned around, the priest was in my house talking to Sammy about taking control of his life. 'Stare down the demons,' Father Jerry used to say. 'Stare down the demons, take back your life.' Whatever he said worked. Sammy got a good job down at Bay Sails repairing outboards, got remarried, and now has two kids." Ray beamed. "You're looking at a grandfather, Lino, five times over."

Lino raised his beer in toast. "Congratulations."

"Me? I did nothing. Half the credit goes to my wife for raising two sons who never got into bad trouble. The other half goes to Father Jerry. He set Sammy straight when I never could."

"I take it you liked the priest," Lino offered.

Ray's brows crinkled across his broad forehead. "What," he asked, "you didn't?"

"I never met him," Lino admitted.

"How can that be?"

Lino shrugged. "Never crossed paths, that's all."

"You stopped going to church, didn't you?" Ray pulled in a deep breath and let it out with a sigh. "I hate to admit it, Lino, but I did, too. My father would roll in his grave if he knew. I feel bad about that, real bad. In my own living room Father Jerry, the man who'd just straightened out my boy, accused me of giving up on the church, of turning my back on it."

"Did you?"

"Maybe." Ray finished his beer and crushed the can with one hand. "Or maybe I just turned my back on Father Jerry." He reached in the cooler and grabbed another Bud.

Lino's interest in the conversation shot up a notch. "Why?" he asked.

"Like I said, he was in my house all the time. The more I was around him, the more I didn't like him or trust him. I don't know, Lino, it's a hard thing to put my finger on. All I can tell you is that one Sunday I was sitting near the back of St. Pete's like I always did, listening to Father Jerry's sermon but not believing a word of it. I never went back to St. Pete's until all that remained were ashes. I stood right where the altar used to be and felt the ground had been purified, that a portion of evil had been driven out by the fire." Ray swallowed more beer. "Crazy, isn't it?"

"Maybe," Lino admitted, not knowing what to make of it. "What about him bothered you?" he asked.

"That's the thing, I don't know. Maybe the part about staring down your demons. Sammy had them, no doubt. He had enough to share, what with his drinking and chasing women, but Father Jerry? He was fighting his own, I could tell."

"How?"

"The way he talked to Sammy about suffering. You know how it is, Lino. The voice of experience has a certain ring. Father Jerry's voice sounded real different when he talked about what it is to suffer. He'd been there, no doubt. His demons made him an expert."

"Any idea what his demons were?" Lino asked.

Captain shook his head. "I don't know, but whatever they were, they were eating him alive."

"You mean he was losing the battle?"

"He wasn't winning, that's for sure," Ray said. "Now you'll think I'm really crazy."

"Try me."

Ray shifted nervously on his feet. "The fire in the church, I know who started it."

"Have you told the police?'

"I haven't told anybody."

"Why not?"

"Like I said, they'll think I've lost my mind." Ray swallowed more beer, then looked Lino straight into his eyes. "God started it. He burned His own church to the ground."

"A bold charge, Ray. Why would He do that?"

"To destroy the demons that Father Jerry couldn't fight alone."

"What happened to Father Jerry while this was going on?"

"He walked away, a man wrapped in the comfort of peace."

"Did this walk have a destination?" Lino asked skeptically.

"Where no one will ever find him, Lino. His whereabouts will remain an eternal mystery, because that's the way God wants it." Ray looked toward the heavens, then reached for Lino's beer. "You're not drinking fast enough, Lino. Your beer's hot."

"Thinking," Lino confessed.

"About?" Ray opened the cooler and took out two cold cans.

"Fireballs raining down from the sky."

"You joke, Lino, but I walked the grounds of the church after the fire. The demons were gone. I swear it. But hey, I told you you'd think I was crazy. Maybe I am." Ray laughed and handed Lino his beer. "Let's forget these foolish ramblings and get this party rolling, what do you say?"

Nine

With the last refrain of "Ave Maria" coming from the warehouse, the procession moved slowly down Fisherman's Wharf, turned right past the Plymouth and Brockton bus stop and inched its way up MacMillan Pier. The visiting bishop set the pace, followed by Portuguese dancers, twirling in their black and red native costumes, while the four hundred or so parishioners followed like solemn lemmings. Lino spotted his mother and Colleen in the middle of the pack and waved as they went by.

Out in the harbor boats were dropping mooring lines and heading inside the breakwall to queue up. Draggers were blessed first, lobster boats second, pleasure craft third, followed by the Coast Guard and Harbormaster's boats. Lino guessed nearly a hundred festively decorated vessels took part. Captain Ray's *Ocean Blue,* his family and friends now on board, led the way past the reviewing station as soon as the bishop was in place. Controlled chaos ruled the day under beautiful blue skies.

"Gonna be a lot of hangovers in the morning," Tony Santos said, motioning toward the action on the water. "It's one hell of a big party. Mardi Gras at sea. Why aren't you out there, Lino?"

"Hey, Tony," Lino said absently. "I'm spending the day chauffeuring my mother."

"The dutiful son."

"Something like that."

Tony loosened his tie and unbuttoned the top button of his dress shirt while a girl of ten in a pretty yellow dress ran up and tugged at the pants of his suit. Tony feigned surprise. "What are you doing here?" he teased. "You hustle back to grammy and stay close to your mom, okay?"

The girl shook her head in such a full arch her dress swayed.

Tony bent lower to look into her wide, dark eyes. "I'll be there in five minutes. I've got to talk to my old friend here. It's police business, honey."

"Mom said it's your day off."

"I know it is, but you run along anyway. Now shoo." Tony turned her toward the milling crowd. "Five minutes," he repeated and nudged her forward. Soon the yellow dress and shiny patent leather shoes were lost in the friendly crowd. "Kids," Tony said in mock despair. "Three girls. Who would've thought I'd be the father of three girls? Not that I'm complaining, but deep down, every man prays for a son." Tony caught himself. "I shouldn't have said that, Lino. Sorry."

"It's all right. It's over."

"How long has it been?"

"A little over two years."

"I take it your wife's not here with you."

Lino shook his head. "We're in the process of settling up, going our separate ways."

"Sure. Must be tough, I mean, the whole thing." Tony slipped out of his suit coat and slung it over one shoulder. "But now it all makes more sense. I mean, I was wondering what really brought you back to Provincetown."

"I seem to be a popular topic of conversation at the police station," Lino offered. "Must have been a slow day."

"As a matter of fact it was a busy day a week or two after the fire. Chief Bicknell was going through one of his lists, and your name popped up."

"Oh?"

"Nothing serious really. I chalked it up to no stone unturned, you know what I mean? You can't be a small town police department taking orders from the State Police and not come up with some of your own ideas," Tony said, inching along. "At least it wasn't something that I couldn't deal with right then and there."

"Deal with what, Tony?"

"Your being back in town for a short while before Father Jerry vanishes and St. Peter's burns."

Lino stopped in his tracks. "You mean I was a suspect?"

"Not really, no," Tony covered, "but that business with the priest in Gloucester made Bicknell curious."

"I made a mistake, all right? I was connecting dots, hunting for an explanation for my son's death. He'd gone off to church camp, the same camp he'd gone to every summer since I don't know when, only this time when he came home, he wasn't the same. The priest at a church a mile from our house, Father George Donovan, was one of the camp counselors. I went to speak with him."

"The police report said you struck the man," Tony corrected.

"It was a heated conversation."

"Why did Father Donovan drop assault charges against you?"

Lino shrugged. "It was a condition of my leaving town. I wasn't thinking too clearly around that time. Linda and I were fighting, I couldn't keep my mind on my work. Nothing was going right. Everything was a blur, and when I woke up, I was back where I started here in Provincetown. For the record, Tony, I had nothing to do with the church fire or Father Dunn's disappearance."

"I never thought you did. It was just Bicknell being Bicknell. He's very thorough, very by the book."

"Should I go speak to him?" Lino asked.

Tony shook his head. "That conversation happened a few months back, Lino. I wouldn't dig up the past. By the same token I wouldn't make a nuisance of myself doing any more legwork for Father Silva. I'll fill him in if anything needs filling in. So do me a favor and keep a low profile around Bicknell, if you catch my drift."

"I catch it," Lino said and stepped around a family taking pictures of a juggler on stilts. "I'll fly under his radar."

"Stealth. I like it," Tony said, his attention on the yellow dress running toward him.

"Five minutes, Dad. You don't want to miss the other boats. Mom says to come on."

"Mom's the boss, Lino. Got to go."

"One thing before you do," Lino said. "Captain Ray spoke of Father Dunn's demons."

"Captain Ray talks too much, but I can't write him a ticket for that. You don't believe him, do you?"

"About lightning bolts from heaven? No."

"What else is there?"

"The demons. They don't seem to fit with the 'voice of God.' Were you aware of any of Father Jerry's demons floating in the rafters of St. Peter's?"

"Never saw a one," Tony said, leaning closer to Lino and lowering his voice. "This is the kind of conversation Bicknell would not like to get wind of, the rumors, the crazy chatter. Keep all that to yourself, and stay out of Bicknell's way. Do that, and everything should work out fine."

"Stealth," Lino repeated and watched Tony and his daughter fade into the crowd. Along the way Tony offered a greeting to Katharine Cardosa, who was firmly attached to Colleen's arm.

"Who was that?" Katharine asked as Lino took her other arm.

"The man in the newspaper clippings you found in the box. That's Sergeant Anthony Santos. We went to school together," Lino said.

"Where?"

"Here." Lino looked into his mother's eyes searching for a connection to his past. When he didn't find one, he asked, "Want me to go get the car?"

"It's such a fine morning. We should walk." She looked up at her son. "Are you in trouble with the police, Adilino?"

"No trouble, no," he said.

"Then what did the man in the newspaper clippings want?"

"He asked me to do him a favor."

"Like Father Silva," Katharine chimed. "He told me he wanted you to help him with something."

"When did you see Father Silva?" Lino asked.

"He never misses the blessing," Katharine said. "He sat in the chair we saved for you. I told Father Silva you'd be honored to help him. Your father would want that, too."

"I know," Lino said.

Katharine let out a satisfying breath. "The doors of heaven will open wide for you, Adilino. You help your priest, and they will open wide."

"Does it matter that he's retired?"

Katharine looked blindsided. "Who's retired?"

"Father Silva."

"When did that happen?" Katharine asked. "I didn't even know he'd left St. Peter's. Are you sure, Adilino?"

"Positive."

"Why didn't someone tell me?" Katharine shook her head. "My mind, I ..."

"It's all right," Lino said.

"I don't know that it is." A cloud of worry settled over Katharine's expression. "I don't really know anything at all anymore."

Ten

The sun's first light sparkled across the still harbor, revealing a Provincetown floating in its own dreamy reflection. Lino sat at his desk in front of his fly-tying vise, winding black thread over the shank of a number 4 Mustad hook. When finished, he cut an oval, six-inch piece of silver tinsel and wound it on the underside of the hook, stopping an eighth of an inch in front of the curve. The long, untied end of the tinsel extended beyond the hook's bend.

Lino reached for a small pinch of yellow polar bear hair, which he tied beside the tinsel with a few wraps and a half hitch. He held bright orange hackle fibers below the yellow hair and anchored them in place with the thread. Next he took a ring-necked pheasant feather and pulled the webbed fibers from the base of the quill. He held two sets on top of the hook and with the precision of a surgeon slid them along the side of the shank facing each other. He then made several turns of the thread so that the feathers looked like wings. In front of the wings Lino wrapped deer hair across the length of the shank, wrapped it forward and tied it off. He sealed the last knot with a drop of Zap-A-Gap into which he set two eyes. Once dried, he put the streamer into the box with the others and got ready to pick up his charter.

The morning mist hung over the water like smoke as Lino rowed his dinghy to the boat and climbed aboard. He stowed his gear before putting the key into the ignition. The engine fired and purred like a big cat. Lino dropped the mooring lines and guided the *Pico II* through a few dozen lobster pots and over to the courtesy dock on Fisherman's. Lino watched as thirty-five-year-old Alex Winters climbed confidently aboard. She put her rod case and travel pack down and offered her hand.

"I've seen that look," she said, enjoying the surprise. "You were expecting a man. Am I right?"

Lino returned her smile. "You are, but the fish don't mind."

"The question is, do you?" She pulled her long hair into a ponytail and slipped a red-billed fisherman's cap over it. The red matched her waterproof jacket that stopped at the top of her faded and pressed blue jeans.

"Not at all," Lino said honestly, backing away from the dock. "It's just that when I spoke to your secretary about the booking, she ..."

" ... followed instructions." Alex picked up her rod and removed the cloth cover from the eight-weight St. Croix. She fit the two pieces together, insuring a snug fit before taking a large arbor Scientific Angler from its reel case. As she tightened the reel in its seat, she said, "It's not that I'm ashamed of being a woman. It's just that if a guide thinks a man is showing up, he's more likely to plan our trip to the best spots."

"As opposed to?" Lino asked.

"As opposed to assuming a woman can't handle a fly rod." Alex slid the leader through the guides. "Why waste the best fishery on an amateur? I pay what the boys pay and want the same chances at good fish that they get. I don't charter to take a boat ride." She smiled mischievously at Lino. "Besides, I'm a better fisher than they are, and in most cases I throw a better party. I own a catering business back in Boston. If you ever need one ..."

"I'll call you," Lino said, amused by her confidence.

The sun rising full behind the dunes caught Alex's attention. "Beautiful, isn't it? I'll have to admit that your working conditions are better than mine. I'd trade mornings like this for a noisy kitchen any day."

"No trade," Lino said. "I've spent enough time in offices to last me."

"Doing what?"

Lino returned the wave of a lobster boat captain on his way out. "What everybody does, pushing paper, playing phone tag, waiting in airports."

"You're defining my life." Alex laughed. "Not the airports so much but the rest of it." She opened a fly box and removed a green, bug-eyed popper. "Any chance for some top-water action? I love seeing the strike."

Lino nodded. "The water temperature is up a few degrees. The blues are hitting on top, the big stripers have settled on the bottom."

"How big are the blues?"

"Five to seven pounds. Some bigger."

Alex's smile glistened like the sun. "Wouldn't I love to get into one of those. Fantastic." She pulled a wire leader from her jacket pocket and tied it on. "So," she said, "you got tired of the papers and the phones and the airports and gave it all up for this?"

"More or less."

"Something like that has crossed my mind," Alex said. "My husband's, too. He's an accountant. We're looking around for options, but nothing has compelled us to walk away from the grind. We might be working when we're seventy, who knows?"

"Is your husband in P-town?" Lino asked.

Alex nodded. "He is. He's out on the bike trails."

"He doesn't fish?"

She shook her head. "Doesn't like the water. I'm the opposite. If it has to do with water, count me in, but it wouldn't matter anyway. You only take one fisher out at a time. Why is that?"

"One boat, one captain, one fly-fisher. Keeps everything simple."

"You must lose out on a lot of money. Most boats take up to three rods, don't they?"

"They do, but I'm not interested," Lino said, passing the breakwall and pushing down on the throttle. "Besides, no matter how good you are in wind, it's too easy to tangle fly lines, and tangled fly lines catch nothing. Out here there's always wind, except early in the morning and late at night."

"Suits me." Alex wound the popper to the wire leader. "Besides, a little time away from my husband is a good thing. Makes him appreciate me more." Rigged, Alex was ready. "So where to?"

Lino pointed behind Long Point Lighthouse to two sandy mounds approximately one hundred yards apart. The locals called them the sisters because the knobs looked like breasts. He positioned the *Pico II* between them and angled in close to a bar jutting fifty feet out from shore, creating a small rip.

"The blues stalk that spit," Lino said, pointing. "Bait fish wash over it and get confused in the turbulence. They don't stand much of a chance with hungry blues and stripers around."

Alex stripped some line. "Let's hope they're hungry," she said and stepped forward onto the casting platform. She cast well in the cool air, jerking the popper along the surface of the churning water. She cast again, varying her retrieve and allowing the popper to drift longer in the current. "They're not starving," she said, working the rod like a professional. "Any advice?"

"You're doing fine," Lino said, moving the boat deeper into the swirling water which sped around the *Pico II* as if she were a rock. "Try the other side of the rip. Let the lure drift farther over the bar, then yank it in with as much speed as you can."

Alex did as told. Five feet from the boat on a fast retrieve, a blue slammed the plug. The powerful fish took one leap in the air, flashing its silver underside, and took off on a run. The St. Croix bent in an arch when the big fish headed for the bottom. In five minutes Alex fought the fish to the top where it jumped again, thrashing its big head and trying to spit the plug.

"Looks like a ten pounder," Lino said, his Boga Grip in hand, but the fish wasn't done. Another run and another five minutes later, Lino had the hook removed and a relieved customer admiring her catch. "Just under ten," Lino said, reading the scale. "Nice job."

"Thank you. I could use some smoked blue fish pâté for one of my clients next week. Okay if we keep him?"

"You're the boss," Lino answered and put the fish in the fish box as Alex looked at the shredded popper.

"They have teeth like razors, don't they?"

"They'll take your finger right off," Lino agreed and opened his newly created box of streamers. He handed Alex one. "It won't float, but a fast retrieve will keep it just below the surface."

"Thanks. I've never seen one quite like it. Is this your design?"

"An experiment." Lino turned the boat back into the rip. "Always looking for a variation that will attract the big ones."

Alex wired on the fly. "Same speed as before?" she asked.

"Same speed," Lino said and watched his creation sail across the water at the end of a nearly perfect cast.

After a late lunch of a pulled pork sandwich and a Red Stripe beer at Mac's Shack, Lino drove back to his cottage and showered. At three o'clock, right on schedule, Dr. Allen Coldwell, Katharine's neurologist called with her test results.

"Mr. Cardosa?"

"That's right."

"It's not often I do this over the phone, but I can appreciate that it's difficult for you to come to my office. I'll send you a written evaluation by next week, but as I said earlier to you, I think you need to understand the issues involving your mother so you can start thinking about making some alternative plans."

Already Lino didn't like the sound of things. "All right," he said.

"The tests, as expected, show a substantial loss of memory compared to the previous results. Her ability to associate common household items has degenerated as well as her sense of time and place. For example, she could not tell me who the current president of the Unites States is. When asked to look at a series of shapes—a circle, a square, a triangle and a rectangle—she could not say which one had no angles."

The doctor kept speaking, but Lino tuned out. He would never remember the tests, and he certainly didn't need them to know that his mother's mind was failing. He witnessed it on a daily basis. The issue for him and his sister was that they wanted their mother in her house until that was no longer possible. Katharine loved the red house. She loved her garden. She was comfortable pulling weeds, raking leaves and watering plants that had long ago died. She knew the rooms, the furniture, the slant of the old floors, the smells, the cracks in the plaster. She belonged there. She didn't belong in a shared, sterile room in a hospital bed with raised metal railings and chatty nurses stopping by with their hourly interruptions.

Coldwell droned on. "This is not to say that your mother's faculties are going to switch off overnight. She certainly has moments when she's quite lucid, but those moments are further and further apart. Her decline will take time, but you need to recognize, Mr. Cardosa, that the degradation is certain."

"How much time?" Lino asked.

"We have no way of telling precisely. What we can say with confidence is that at this stage, your mother should not be living alone."

"She has Colleen," Lino offered. "Colleen brought her to your last appointment."

"I realize that," Dr. Coldwell said. "I spoke with her about your mother's living situation. She said she's with your mother most of every day, and she spends three, maybe four, nights a week sleeping over."

"That's about right," Lino said. "Colleen needs some time to herself. I watch mother when Colleen is away, or I get someone else to come around if I'm out on a charter."

"In the future that won't do," Dr. Coldwell said. "She needs watching around the clock by someone as conscientious and professional as Colleen."

Lino knew that was coming, but hearing it from Katharine's doctor made it more real, more urgent.

Coldwell continued. "I don't like being so blunt, Mr. Cardosa, but your mother can't distinguish a book of matches from a book to read. Any day, she might get confused and burn the house down with her in it. That's my primary concern."

"I don't think she's that bad," Lino defended.

"No? Over the past six months Colleen reported three occasions when your mother walked off and got lost, one fall without consequence, one fall with cuts to the forehead, one fall with bruises to your mother's right arm and hip, and the usual wetting without an understanding that she's not in the bathroom. I'm afraid it is that bad."

Uneasiness swelled in Lino's stomach. "What do you recommend?" he asked.

"You need to have a conversation with your mother. You need to explain to her that she needs more people around providing more care. She needs to understand that she'll never be alone in her own house ever again. You need to talk with her about that," Coldwell said. "You need to make sure she understands."

"That's the point, isn't it?" Lino said. "She doesn't understand much anymore. Some, but I'm not sure how much."

"Still, you need to have that conversation with her. How much she'll take from it, I can't say, but it wouldn't be fair to her not to try."

"None of this is fair, is it?" Lino said. "What's fair about your mind rotting away?"

"Nothing," Dr. Coldwell agreed. "I know this is hard, Mr. Cardosa. The hospital will provide assistance for your family, if you're interested. Group therapy. Sharing your difficulties with others. Sometimes talking to someone who's going through the same thing can be beneficial. Would you like me to send along some information about those services with your mother's report?"

"I don't think so," Lino said. He'd said the same thing to a social worker who wanted him to join a group and speak about his son's death. What was there to say about such an event other than the pain was unimaginable and constant? The thought of talking about it to strangers literally took away Lino's breath and left him speechless.

"Mr. Cardosa, are you still there?"

"Sorry. Yes, I'm here, and no, I don't want any information about therapy. I'm not very good in groups," Lino told the doctor and put down the phone.

Eleven

Lino left a message for Carol about their mother's test results and Dr. Coldwell's recommendation for more help. He then searched for the business card of Pro-Care, the agency that had recommended Colleen. He was about to call when the phone rang. He put his scotch aside and answered it.

"Lino?" The husky voice belonged to Jack Moore, the Boston attorney representing Lino in the divorce action. Jack, a two-pack-a-day smoker, had built a successful practice out of failed marriages. "Did I catch you at a bad time?"

"Just looking for a phone number," Lino said. "I need to hire more help for my mother."

"The Irish woman not working out?"

"She's working out fine. I'm going to call her agency and ask for a clone."

"I like that," Jack said over a raspy laugh. "I could use two of me, too. Not enough hours in the day keeping track of your wife's next moves."

"What's she up to now?"

"Tightening the vise."

"What else is new?"

"Her lawyer." Lino could hear Jack exhale smoke. "She's got a new one, Mark Solomon. Every heard of him?"

"Never," Lino said.

"Maybe he came aboard after you left the company. Solomon is your father-in-law's personal counsel. He's bright, tough and heartless, as evidenced by the settlement proposal he faxed over this afternoon. It includes a plot evaluation of your mother's land in Provincetown, which is just large enough for legal subdivision."

"I don't like the sound of this," Lino said, feeling his blood rise.

"You shouldn't. Town zoning would allow the owner to sell the red house separately from the cottage. Instead of one property there could be two, and once the cottage is expanded into a full-sized, multi-bedroom unit with all the high-end amenities, it might be worth one million more than the red house."

"What the hell are you talking about?"

"Something close to four million dollars. That's Solomon's estimate. He says your wife is entitled to a piece of the action."

Lino gulped an inch of his scotch. "I hope you told him to go to hell."

"Not in so many words."

"Why beat around the bush?"

"We don't want the enemy even more hostile, which is why I want to talk to you. Linda's previous attorney and I had everything under control. A few details here and there, and we would have settled. Then without warning he's gone, Solomon is in, and we're looking down the wrong end of a loaded cannon." Jack inhaled and blew more smoke into the phone. "What I want to know is, what happened to get Mark Solomon involved?"

"Why ask me?"

"Because, old friend, you are the one with the temper."

"I'm innocent, Jack."

"Well, it certainly wasn't me," Jack mused. "When was the last time you talked with Edwin?"

"About a year ago, just before I moved down here," Lino said, remembering clearly the day his father-in-law's dark green Jag had pulled into Brown's Boatyard. Edwin Colas was a medium-built man with black, wavy hair and smooth skin. Linda used to say that if her father hadn't spent all his energy making millions in the insurance business, he could have been a movie star.

Edwin had moved toward the *Pico II* like a man on a mission. "Lino," he said, his chest swelling then falling, the pent-up tension escaping on his breath. "Linda called upset. You know I've kept away from your troubles, but I can't anymore. She said you are leaving."

"That's what you do when your wife kicks you out." Lino put the wrench down on top of the boat's engine and wiped the grease from his hands. "There doesn't seem to be a reason to fight it anymore, Edwin. We can't make it work. I'm sorry."

"What if you came back to the company, stepped back into your old job, huh? Forget the boat, forget the fishing. What if you came back and gave it another try? You were the best, Lino. I always told you that."

"Did Linda ask you to come down here?"

Edwin looked struck. "Linda? No. This was my idea entirely. If you had a real job, there'd be a reason to stick around, work things out, wouldn't there?"

"I'm afraid your daughter's not interested," Lino said evenly. "Maybe this time I'm not either."

"I know you've suffered a terrible tragedy. All of us have. You've got to give it more time, Lino. You and Linda are good together. I can see that. You two can't rush into this."

"More than a year since Steven died is hardly rushing. Besides, we've tried everything we can think of to stick together. There are just some things you can't survive. Another day, another year won't make any difference."

"That's giving up," Edwin said, struggling for another approach. "I didn't build my business by giving up. I stayed in there and fought. That's what you've got to do. Think of it from my perspective for one second, Lino. What did I tell you when you came to my house and asked for my only child's hand in marriage?"

"You said you regretted not having a son, and now you would have one."

"That's right, Lino. Word for word, that's what I said. And didn't I always treat you like my son?"

"Always," Lino admitted. "I appreciated it very much."

"Then do me a favor, huh? It will be hard, I know, but do me this one favor: Stay. Work things out with Linda." He put his hand on the *Pico II*. "Forget this old boat, huh? You and I are done with boats." Edwin managed a slight smile, feeling he was making progress. "I never told you this, Lino, but before I entered college, I changed my name from Ernesto to Edwin. Ernesto Colas born near the New Bedford fishing docks. I left that life behind, just like you." When Lino said nothing Edwin admitted the central, painful truth that drove him here. "I lost my only grandson when Steven died," he said, his voice slow and heavy. "I don't want to lose you, too."

Jack's raspy voice interrupted Lino's memory. "Are you listening to a word I'm saying?" Jack barked.

"Sorry," Lino said.

"See if you can't come up with the answer as to why Edwin's suddenly involved."

"I think I know," Lino answered. "Edwin took Steven's death very hard. The breakup of our marriage only made things worse. The second anniversary of Steven's suicide will be in a few weeks. Turning the screws might be Edwin's way of commemorating if he thought it would make me suffer."

"That might be it, it might not," Jack said. "Give it more thought. There might be another reason he's involved, and I want to know what it is. Are you ready for the worst? I saved it for last."

"Do I want to hear it?"

"No," Jack said matter of factly. "In addition to the Provincetown property, Solomon listed your boat as part of the settlement."

Lino nearly gagged. "Can they do that?"

"They did it."

"Now what?

"Now it's our turn to take the gloves off."

When Lino had problems in college, he'd head to the gym and work out until a solution poured from his sweat. Now he headed to the beach.

Lino rigged up and let the air down in his SUV's tires. He waited at the cottage until midnight before driving the half-mile down Route 6 to the turnoff at Pilgrim Lake. He took a left at the fork and slowed to a crawl when the tarmac turned to soft sand. He shifted into four-wheel drive, and in minutes was on the beach at High Head, watching the tide fall in the sliver of a new moon.

He drove past a line of surfcasters and stopped when there was no one else around. Sitting on the back of his truck, he pulled on a pair of waders. He clipped his stripping basket around his waist, picked up his custom nine-weight, a gift from his father, and walked to the water's edge. The wind was at his back, steady out of the south at ten knots. The early morning fog was crawling back in but holding off shore at fifty yards. The rhythmic waves at about two feet high curled to the shore and broke in a wash of white foam.

Lino used to fish this spot while watching the *Amy Ann* ride the swells along with the other boats of the fishing fleet. It was a special place for him, a place that calmed and provided serenity.

Lino whipped the rod, letting line flow through the guides and out the rod tip. With fifty feet out he followed his cast into the water and hauled line into the basket. The sea rolled to his waist. When he was younger he used to wonder where the waves started or if the moist, salty air he breathed had been breath in lungs before. Those days he'd let his mind turn inward and drift, interrupted only by an awareness of arm movement, rod load and the unfurling line dropping a perfectly tied fly at the end of the cast. There was no strain, no fatigue. One movement flowed gently into the other like a form of yoga practiced alone on the beach. Lino saw it as blissful isolation, a chance to watch the sun rise and the moon fall, a chance to let nature soothe his wounds with warm winds and cool seas.

Lino stripped more line and cast again. He tucked the reel under one arm and retrieved with two hands, following the line to the fly. He made another cast and another, gathering distance each time. Wash from a passing ship so far out he could not see it pushed him back, but his casts continued in slow, controlled motions almost mechanical in their perfection.

Lino wasn't sure how much time had passed. Enough for the fog to cover him and the wind to die. He was casting blindly, effortlessly. That his fly hit water was an act of faith, since he could see only to the end of his rod, which in an instant bent to the breaking point.

Lino could tell by the strength of the pull that the fish was big and going parallel to the beach. Lino followed, keeping his rod tip skyward to maximize its resistance. The waves washed away the sand under his feet, and he nearly fell. He stumbled upright and kept pace along the shore. The thin line in his reel connected sea and soul, life and death. He pulled back and took in line trying to slow and turn his catch. The fish didn't turn. Instead the battle seemed to propel him forward, giving the fish more energy.

Lino adjusted the reel's drag and let his prey run another hundred yards, dragging line with each thrust of its tail. Gradually, Lino sensed weariness, a slower rush toward freedom. He backed out of the water and up onto the bank, reeling line in slowly as the rod brought the fish to him. He heard it first, splashing and tossing its massive head. Lino reeled quickly, keeping the line tight as he hurried back into the wash and grabbed the fish by the bottom jaw. He worked quickly to remove the hook, then after one appreciative look at what was surely a thirty pounder, Lino slid his catch back into the water. He held the fish's tail, moving him back and forth, forcing water through the gills. It took several seconds, but the revived bass broke free and swam off, taking with him, for at least that moment, some of Lino's worries.

Twelve

Lino fished alone on the beach until sunrise, then drove back to the cottage. He made breakfast of bacon, toast and coffee before taking a hot shower. When he'd dressed and climbed down the stairs, Father Silva was peering through the screen door just about to knock.

"A little early for you to be out, isn't it?" Lino asked, letting the priest inside.

"I don't sleep much," the priest admitted. "I stayed over with friends after the blessing and did some ground work for you."

"I don't want you to do any ground work for me. I move ahead in my own direction and at my own pace. Coffee?" he asked at the stove. "It has to be black. I don't use sugar or cream."

"Black is fine. Aren't you going to ask what I discovered?"

Lino took two cups from the cupboard. "Didn't you hear? No help. Besides, Tony spoke to me yesterday. He wants me stop looking into the disappearance of Father Dunn. He doesn't want me to help you."

"Oh?" Father Silva seemed genuinely surprised. "How did you answer?"

"Stealth."

"Meaning?"

"The police won't see what I'm doing," Lino said, handing the priest his coffee.

"I'm grateful, Lino, as I hope you will be when I tell you what I learned. It wasn't that I did all that much, really. In fact, this little tidbit rather fell in my lap. Robert Connelly is vacationing in South Orleans."

Lino cocked his head. "Who?"

"Connelly," Father Silva repeated, "Mary Alice's husband or, more accurately, widower. The people I spent the night with, they spotted Robert in Little Pleasant Bay on a boat. Loves to sail from what I was told. He'll be here for another week or so."

Lino tasted his coffee and winced at the bitterness. "Mary Alice of Sweetbriar fame?"

"That's right. She's a central figure in this in a roundabout sort of way. If Mary Alice hadn't been diagnosed with throat cancer, and Father Jerry hadn't requested a medical transfer to a parish closer to her treatments at Mass General in Boston, I probably never would have met him or Mary Alice or Robert Connelly. A nice, if rather unusual, family."

"How so?"

Father Silva sipped his coffee, then put the cup on the table, deciding how to answer. "I've been thinking about that," he said. "Who among them was stranger, the fastidious and straight-laced Robert? The strong and forthright Mary Alice? How they ever got together, one wonders. Or the man caught in the middle, Father Jerry? I'm not certain I have that answer yet and likely will never have it since two of the three are not around to add to the conversation. But Robert is, and I feel in my bones that he can help us sort out what happened to Father Jerry."

"I'm sure the police have already spoken with him," Lino suggested. "If Connelly had useful information, it's been processed."

"Are you saying you aren't going to speak with him? It will save you a drive to Boston."

Lino shook his head. "No, I'm saying that his information may not be as productive as you hope."

"You need to be tenacious, Lino. Never take no for the final answer. That's how I dealt with Mr. Colas. I kept phoning the man until he spoke with me."

A surge of dread raced through Lino. "You spoke with Edwin?" he asked, now certain as to why his father-in-law had hired Mark Solomon.

"I did." Father Silva's chest puffed with pride. "I do like dealing directly with the man in charge. Was I wrong to do that?"

"When did you speak with Edwin?"

"A week or so ago."

"Damn," Lino muttered.

Father Silva's shoulders sagged. "I did do something wrong, didn't I?"

"What did you and Edwin talk about?" Lino prodded.

"I don't remember exactly," the priest said. "I remember the secretary was not too inclined to let me get through to Mr. Colas when I first phoned. I had already planned to drive down here to see you, so you were certainly on my mind. It wouldn't surprise me at all if I used your name to get Mr. Colas to take my call. Or maybe I mentioned the insurance on St. Peter's not being paid. One or the other."

"Or both?"

"Possibly."

"Who told you that Colas, Haggerty and Johnson held the policy on the church?"

"I saw a folder on Tony's desk and asked about it. I said I thought it disgraceful that a company would not pay. What's the world coming to?"

Lino tossed the rest of his coffee in the sink. "Did my divorce from Edwin's daughter come up by any chance?"

Father Silva shook his head. "Not with Mr. Colas, no. A few days later another man called me."

A prickle of heat danced along Lino's spine. "Mark Solomon?"

"That sounds right. Solomon, yes. Pushy type. I almost hung up."

"But you didn't," Lino said knowingly.

"Not when he said he was helping you and Linda resolve your marital issues. You're to be commended, Lino. Reconciliation is always preferable to divorce."

"Solomon told you we were reconciling?"

"He did, yes. He said everything was going to be fine now that he was on board."

"Fine for Linda and her father, maybe."

Father Silva cocked his head. "Sorry?"

"Not as sorry as I am," Lino admitted.

"You definitely make me feel as if I've done something wrong. Have I?"

"You might have helped unleash Solomon."

"The king?"

"The lawyer." Lino stepped toward Father Silva and put one arm around his shoulders as he led him to the door. "Thanks for the tip about Connelly, but remember, no more help."

"I promise."

Robert Connelly's vacation house was on Paw Wah Pond, a small, tidal basin that fed into Little Pleasant Bay in South Orleans. At low tide there was just enough water in the channel for Connelly to maneuver his eighteen-foot Marshall Cat back to the private dock where Lino waited. He grabbed the bow line and helped Connelly tie up behind a twenty-one-foot Boston Whaler powerboat. Only when the sailboat was secure did Connelly, a man Lino's age but much taller and with the body of a swimmer, exchange introductions.

"Nice sail?" Lino asked.

"Very. No place better to own a catboat. Of course, we take the Whaler out when we want to get somewhere fast."

"We?"

"Friends I rent from," Connelly said, closing that door. "Do you sail?"

"I've done a little."

Connelly nodded. "It's my weakness," he admitted, his pale blue eyes sparkling. "Mary Alice and I owned a Concordia yawl we sailed up in Maine for years. Wonderful times. When she got sick, we put that aside. I've been moving down in boat size ever since. Next thing you know, I'll be floating little toy boats in the bathtub." He laughed at his own humor and picked up a water hose. "You don't mind if I clean up while we talk?"

"Not at all."

Connelly pulled the hose on deck and began spraying off the salt. "My secretary said you wanted information about my brother-in-law." Connelly shook his head, mystified. "Terrible business, isn't it? Absolutely horrible that he died out on the dunes like that, and no one ever found his remains."

"Why do you believe he's dead?"

"He would have called if he were still alive, made contact somehow. We saw each other frequently whenever I was here on the Cape. " Connelly worked the spray down one side of the boat and up the other before opening a hatch and pulling out a bucket and brush. "He and Mary Alice were extremely close. Their mother died of cancer in her early sixties. Within a year their father died of what Mary Alice described as a broken heart. After that Mary Alice became both parents and sister to her brother. She felt responsible for him." Connelly splashed some Fantastic into the bucket and started scrubbing the decks. "Jerry paid back her kindness during the last months of her life. He was remarkably strong. I couldn't have gotten through her passing without him. He was incredible. Day, night, you name it. When she left the hospital and came home with private nurses, Jerry was at her side constantly. I am still grateful for that."

"How long have you known him?" Lino asked.

"Thirty years, easy," Connelly said. "I met Jerry when he was an undergraduate. I was doing graduate work at Harvard in the School of Design and had just started dating Mary Alice. She introduced us."

"Do you remember your first impressions?"

"Of Jerry? Sure. Jerry was open-minded, serious, kind and full of limitless energy. I was envious of that. He'd go to class, study much of the night, then meet up with friends and hit the

Boston clubs. He could run full tilt on a few hours of sleep."

"Sounds like you're defining the typical college student," Lino offered.

"In some ways, I guess, but the typical college student doesn't end up being a priest."

"Did that surprise you?" Lino asked, picking up the hose and rinsing the soap from the forward deck.

Connelly thought a moment. "In the very beginning I think it did. It wasn't a surprise for Mary Alice as much as it was a dream, a wish fulfilled."

"She wanted him to become a priest?"

"Not just Mary Alice," Connelly said. "The entire family was intensely religious. That was one of the qualities I admired about her. In a world gone a bit lax with everything, Mary Alice strived daily to be the best person she could be. She went to mass daily, read the Bible and put into practice the best teachings of the Catholic Church by starting her foundation."

"Sweetbriar Camp," Lino offered.

Connelly looked up from his scrubbing. "You've heard of Sweetbriar?"

"Yes."

"It was the cornerstone of her philanthropy but by no means the only organization she supported. If it had to do with children establishing a strong sense of morals mixed with intellectual curiosity and a few games tossed in, Mary Alice was likely writing a check."

"With your approval?"

"Of course," Connelly chuckled. "To be frank it was my money, and in case you are interested, in the ten years since Mary Alice's death, all of her selected organizations continue to receive full funding. Nothing has changed and won't as long as I am still alive."

At Connelly's direction Lino sprayed more water into the plastic bucket. "I understand Father Jerry worked at Sweetbriar."

"He did as an administrator. He was good at it, too. Hiring

counselors, advertising the camp dates, registering the children, all of it. It seems like fun and games, but a lot of planning goes into a productive camp. Jerry put in the hours of planning and was given a title and salary to do it."

"What was his title?"

Connelly shrugged. "I don't remember, something like administrative director or some such. And before you ask, the salary was minuscule, fifteen thousand more or less for a few months effort. He earned every penny and gave much of it back in the form of scholarships to families who couldn't afford to send their children to Sweetbriar."

"Doesn't sound like the kind of man who would rob his own church, does it?"

"That's what I told the State Police months ago. Don't waste your time looking for my brother-in-law as if he were a thief, look for him as someone who's been abducted or murdered. That sort of investigation might get you somewhere," Connelly said emphatically.

"Did you provide any names to the State Police of people who might want to abduct or harm him?"

Connelly shook his head. "How could I? Jerry Dunn was a parish priest with a heart as wide and deep as the Atlantic Ocean. Who could want to hurt a man like that?"

"And burn down his church," Lino reminded.

"Mary Alice would weep in her grave if she knew what some monster did to her brother's church. Burn it to the ground? Why?" Connelly shook his head, baffled. "It would be like Jerry giving some student a bad grade and the kid coming back at night and burning down the college. I guess it's a good thing he got out of that profession."

"I didn't know he taught," Lino admitted.

Connelly stepped into the cockpit and resumed scrubbing there. "Not for long," he said. "He was working on his masters in English while teaching introductory survey classes in the English department at Simmons College. He stayed on for a while after he got his degree, but in his late twenties he decided he wanted something different and quit the classroom. Within a year he was a seminarian."

"Did you ever meet any of Father Jerry's friends?"

"Sure. Not that he had all that many, but that's true for most of us, isn't it? I can count on one hand the number of acquaintances I'd call real friends."

"I was thinking more of friends from Simmons. A Frank Callegari, maybe. I understand he was a professor somewhere in Boston."

"Francesco?" Connelly said surprised. "He wasn't at the college. Frank was a seminarian. That's where he and Jerry met. Mary Alice and I had them over to the house several times. Why do you ask?"

"I'm just trying to learn what I can about your brother-in-law. The best way to do that is to speak with everyone I can who knew him. Callegari was identified as a friend and history professor teaching in Boston."

"It's possible," Connelly admitted. "All that was a very long time ago, or so it seems. Frank could have had a change of heart and moved on to another profession. I don't really know."

"When was the last time you saw Father Jerry?"

"The last time I was scheduled to see him was the night of the fire. I'd promised to drive up to the church and help Jerry finish some painting project he'd started, but something came up and I had to cancel. I've always wondered how things might have turned out if I'd gone." Connelly put his scrub brush down and thought a moment. "But the last time I did see Jerry was sometime around Christmas, a few weeks before the fire. He was in Boston for some shopping. We had dinner together, and I insisted that he stay over. The last time that spare bedroom was used was when I set it up for Mary Alice's care at home. Even though another one of those horrible winter storms was forecast, Jerry didn't want to stay."

"Too many painful memories in that room?"

"Jerry liked driving. He liked it better when he drove alone at night. He said it relaxed him. When he was helping me out with Mary Alice, he'd get in his car and drive for hours. It cleared his mind and gave him a little distance. It wasn't easy watching his sister die over the course of a year. It was very hard on him—for all of us, really. Even the nursing staff I hired had a tougher time than usual."

"Why was that?" Lino asked.

"Because Father Jerry touched their hearts like the older priest never did."

"What older priest?"

"The one who told you where to find me."

"Father Silva?"

"Yes. Toward the end of Mary Alice's life, he came to the house at Father Jerry's request. He sat with Mary Alice. During her last days she was very difficult. All the drugs, the pain. She had a difficult time making herself understood. Father Silva showed tremendous patience."

Connelly sprayed the final rinse himself, then turned off the water. Lino followed him up a small hill to where a shingled house sat, offering views of the pond and the bay.

"All that driving," Lino mused. "Do you know where Father Jerry went?"

"Inside himself," Connelly said. "Headlights on high beam out there in the night, looking."

"For what?"

"Clarity. Faith is not logical. Sometimes life's events challenge one's conviction."

"Are you suggesting that Father Jerry had a crisis of faith?"

"I'm saying Father Jerry was human and reacted as such to his sister's illness. If he found a moment's peace behind the wheel, I said let him drive."

Thirteen

Pro-Care's office was tucked behind a coffee shop next to the Wellfleet Post Office on Route 6. Lino parked in the large lot and entered. A receptionist looked up from her keyboard and gazed over her half-glasses.

"Mr. Cardosa?"

"That's right. I'm a little early."

"That's all the better," boomed Ruth Keller's voice from the next office. In seconds a middle-aged woman with blonde hair stiff with spray and the pudgy face of an elderly baby stood in the doorway, her hand extended. "Good to see you again. Come in and have a seat, please," Ruth said and settled in behind her desk. Lino sat across from her. "I'm delighted Colleen is working out to your satisfaction."

"She's perfect," Lino said. "That's why I want someone just like her to share twenty-four hour coverage, seven days a week."

Ruth opened the folder in front of her. "The rate goes up for overnights, but you already know that, and up again on weekends."

"My sister and I talked that over last night. Money isn't the issue. The issue is to get someone like Colleen to help provide my mother with seamless care."

"Of course," she said, looking at the folder's contents. "You're making a wise move, Mr. Cardosa. Staying ahead of the curve in these matters is much better for everyone. It gives us time to plan, to select the most appropriate candidates. Will you personally be interviewing everyone, same as last time?"

"Yes."

"Very good." Ruth's eyes stayed on the paperwork. "You want someone with experience. Someone who can stay overnight. Someone with a car who can escort your mother to doctors' appointments, shopping and the like."

"Someone she'll get along with," Lino added.

"Yes, of course." Ruth looked up sympathetically. "It's common for the elderly to be protective and suspicious. We see that all the time and train our staff to expect less than a warm welcome." She turned a page. "I've pulled a few names already," she said, glancing at her notes. "One in particular you might find promising. He's retired here on the Cape but was a nurse in Boston for several years. He comes with excellent references." She looked back at Lino. "How would you feel about a man staying in the same house with your mother?"

"I'd have to think about that," Lino admitted. "More importantly, how would my mother deal with it? Then there is Colleen to consider. I don't want to do anything that would upset either of them."

"Certainly not," Ruth said. "Maybe it would be best if we reviewed the female options first."

"Fine, let's start there," Lino said and listened to qualifications of three other candidates.

"What do you think?" Ruth asked when she had finished her summary. "Do any sound interesting?"

"All of them, but let's start with the first two."

"Joan Hawkins and Claire Talbert," Ruth said, writing their names and phone numbers for Lino. "I'd like to go back to Roger Langsford again. Would you consider doing a telephone interview at least? Talk to him for a bit. I don't want to seem that I am pushing you, Mr. Cardosa, but in all my years in this business, I have honestly never seen anyone with such glowing credentials. I'm positive he would present no problems for Colleen."

"It wouldn't hurt, I suppose," Lino said reluctantly.

"Fine." Ruth added his number to the list and handed Lino the paper. "I'll notify each that you'll be in touch within the next twenty-four hours. When you make your selection ..."

"I'll let you know."

The morning turned into one of those hazy, hot and humid afternoons with a light, south wind so moist it made lungs feel heavy. The *Pico II* cut through the water on the way to Race Point, home of some of the finest fishing anywhere. Tom Neal, a short, squat man, stood beside Lino on the ride out so Lino could hear every word, even though Lino tried not to listen.

Neal's voice rode up and down with the swells. He was a married man, unhappily so. He felt like he lived in prison. His own house was a cell. He came to Provincetown looking for action, know what I mean? Any action. All the action. It made no difference. He was eager and ready to add more notches to his gun. To his pistol. To his wang. To his whatever. Put the word out. Tom is here. Tom Neal, the newly revitalized Viagra man of action is here to conquer. Taking no prisoners. Going all out. Going twenty-four hours a day until his pistol runs out of bullets. Yee-haw!

The shout sent needles along Lino's spine. He cringed and slowed the boat a half-mile from the Race. Tom Neal was not worthy of prime fishing grounds, Lino thought, and maneuvered his boat past a line of lobster pots. Several boats trolled near the pot line, indicating fish. Lino drove past them two hundred yards and farther out from shore. When he cut back on the throttle, he was the only boat around. The *Pico II* bobbed in fishing no-man's-land. Lino never let a bore cast among his dignified fish.

"This it?" Tom looked around, perplexed. "Nobody's here."

"That's the point," Lino said. "No one else knows this particular spot but me. More action for you."

"Primo," Neal beamed, picking up his fly rod. He pulled line into a pile on deck and started working the fly with a few false casts. His movements were jerky, the loop of his backcasts flat because his rod tip dipped too low. He glanced over his shoulder at Lino, a proud, foolish smile covering his lips. "Pretty fine, huh? Private lessons."

"I can tell."

"Two weeks worth. I want to be ready. Going to Florida this winter. Taking a new babe. Go down for the grand slam, you know. Bones, tarpon, permit. I think I ought to be able to do that, don't you? Work on my distance a little, you know. Get the fly out there a little more. Let it float to the water. Don't want to scare the little puppies, you know. Fish are skittery."

"So I've heard," Lino said, watching the first real cast flutter harmlessly twenty feet from the bow.

Neal bent at the knees and hauled in, braced for a sudden monster strike. "Nothing that time," he said and mauled another cast. "You sure there are fish out here?"

"Where there's water, there are fish."

"I suppose." He hauled in again. "You do any fishing? I mean, on your own time."

"Some."

"I wasn't sure, you know. I mean you look at this boat, and you can't really tell."

"How's that?"

"I don't know," Neal said, kicking the gunwale with his new boat shoe. "This old thing's about to fall apart, isn't it? Who goes out in a wooden boat nowadays? Fiberglass shouts success, trust me on that. If you can't afford it, maybe you could class things up a bit by smearing some glass around here and there. Might be a start and good for business," Neal said, posing like a runway model in his new fishing garb. "Looks are everything, right? I got this entire outfit mail order from Flyfish.com. Rod and reel, too. You got to have the look."

"Right," Lino said. "Very important." He tapped a finger on the instrument panel, waited until Neal noticed, then tapped again. "But this is a bad look."

"What is?"

"This gauge."

"Engine overheating?"

"Captain's overheating. We're going back," Lino said.

"We just got here."

"Can't risk it."

"Can't risk what?"

"The safety of a charter, Mr. Neal. At this moment you are in danger of going over the side."

"Why?" Neal looked around clearly frightened. "Rogue waves?"

"Rogue captain. Might go out of control at any minute."

"You're nuts."

Lino spun the *Pico II* one hundred and eighty degrees. "Consider it a free boat ride, my treat."

"Hey, I came here to fish."

"Find someone else to take you."

"Hey, you owe me an explanation."

"If I told you, you wouldn't understand."

Neal gritted his teeth. "Try me."

"All right," Lino said. "Fly-fishing is an exclusive club, Mr. Neal. It isn't about the look or the cost of the equipment, it's about equalizing the hunt. Each fly is small and single-hooked, no treble hooks like the surfcasters toss. When I fish, I file off the barb so the fish can toss the fly if the line is not kept taught. Fly-fishing is thinking and observing and striving for the perfect cast, because the fish, perfect in its own right, deserves perfection in the fly's presentation. That's the beauty of the sport, Mr. Neal. I gladly share that beauty with people who understand it. It's clear to me you don't. Now I'll take you back to the dock."

"But ..."

"Not another word if you wish to remain dry."

Back at the mooring Lino scrubbed his boat doubly hard, washing the scent of Tom Neal over the side. When he was done he opened his cell phone and made a call to the private number of Edwin Colas.

"Hello, Edwin. This is Lino. I don't want this conversation anymore than you do, but I think we need to talk."

"I take it you've heard from Mr. Solomon," Edwin said coolly.

"I did. There's no need for you to get involved in Linda's and my affairs."

"You don't know what I need, Lino. You can't imagine."

"I want you to stay out of this."

"This is not about what you want."

"What is it about?"

"It's personal, Lino. I asked you to come back to work for me. I asked you be patient with Linda, go slow, solve your differences. You took none of my advice. You ignored me. You came into our lives with all the promise in the world. What you gave in return is heartache."

"You still blame me, don't you? Just like your daughter, you blame me. Had I come back to work for you, would that feeling ever have changed? Had Linda and I clawed away at each other for another few years, would you have stopped blaming me? We both know the answer, Edwin. We all loved Steven, but that love wasn't enough to keep him alive. I did not kill my son," Lino seethed, "but his death killed my marriage. What more is there to say?"

"I'm going to use that boat of yours for firewood. That's what more there is to say. I'm going to build the biggest goddamned bonfire and burn everything your mother hasn't moved from her house on the day I have her and you evicted." Edwin slammed down his phone.

Fourteen

Lino's son surprised him. Steven had the options for his twelfth birthday present of Red Sox baseball at Fenway Park, hiking to the top of Mount Monadnock in New Hampshire, or taking the fast ferry to Provincetown. He chose the boat ride and the hour-and-a-half trip over calm seas and the super special birthday cake grandma Katharine promised.

Katharine was an expert at baking gooey chocolate layers the consistency of fudge brownies. Steven's favorite frosting was lemon, which Katharine whipped full of tart zest and juice. She assembled the three-decker and carefully troweled the creamy frosting onto the top and sides. Then she took softened chocolate into her pastry bag and wrote across the top, "Happy #12 to my best boy, Stevie." Katharine finished it off with candles and anxious moments waiting until her son and his family knocked on her front door.

That day the air was clean, sharp and full of September's crispness. The sun was warming by the time the big ferry rounded the green channel marker off Long Point and sped through the harbor. Once docked at MacMillan Pier, Steve led all the passengers off and waited anxiously until his parents ambled down the ramp.

"You guys are so slow," Steve said.

Linda nudged Lino and smiled playfully. "Your father's getting old, Stevie, old and slow."

"Right." Lino wrapped one arm around her small waist. "Not so old I can't take care of you, Missy."

"Oh, yeah?"

"Yeah."

Steve grabbed his mother's hands and pulled her free. "Will you two come on? Grandma's waiting."

They walked three abreast to Commercial Street, then single file on the narrow sidewalk toward the red house. Steve darted up ahead, weaving in and out of the dawdling crowds, making a game of it with his arms out like a fighter plane. Linda stopped in front of a jewelry store specializing in estate stones and settings. A pair of pearl earrings in the window caught her eye.

"Nice," she said to Lino. "You always say I look ravishing in pearls."

He kissed her on the cheek. "Pearls and nothing else."

"Stop."

"I can't. I'm in love with you." He kissed her again, this time meaning it.

"Not here in public."

"This is Provincetown. You can do anything here."

She kissed him back then pulled away with a mischievous grin. "Anything? Shall we give them a thrill right here in the street?"

"Them, hell. Give me the thrill."

"You'll have to wait," she said, kissing him again.

"I don't know that I want to."

Her eyes widened in mock dismay. "You're impossible, but pearls are my weakness. Do you know who else is having a birthday soon?"

"Not a clue," Lino teased.

"I'll give you one guess."

Lino furrowed his brow and narrowed his eyes, straining for an answer. When Linda poked him in the ribs, he burst out laughing.

"You?" he said in mock surprise. "You're kidding. I thought you were twenty-nine forever." He rubbed his temples. "But my mind's not what it used to be. Must be my old age showing," Lino said, faking a limp. "May not make it to grandma's. You might have to carry me."

"Right." She sped off toward their son, who had stopped in front of an art gallery, waiting impatiently.

Lino caught up. "Think you might want to be an artist someday? Paint pictures, chisel sculptures out of marble for a living?"

Steve looked at his parents. "I dunno. I never thought about it."

"You should," Lino said. "Think about all the options. A successful man is not the one with all the toys, he's the one with all the options."

Linda put her arm around the boy. "Doctor, lawyer, artist. You can do anything, Stevie. Whatever you want, you'll be wonderful at it."

"Whatever I want?"

"Whatever you want," she repeated.

"I want grandma's chocolate cake," he said and raced off toward the red house.

"You never come around unless you've had a crummy day."

"Not true," Lino defended.

"Then let me modify." Diane handed him his wine and sat back down on her deck chair. "A crummy day or a charter cancels."

"Today I cancelled the charter," Lino said, "or more precisely, I cut it short."

"Why?"

"Because I didn't want to be away from you another second."

"I'll believe that lie."

"Thank you."

Diane brushed her shoulder length blond hair away from her shimmering hazel eyes. She lived a few blocks down from the red house in a sprawling, shingled manse built on pilings. At high tide the deck sat out over the water, leaving the impression you were living on a raft floating leisurely out to sea.

Diane's studio was on the second floor, where she painted what she saw out the ten-foot-high windows. The sea was in all her work, and recently so was *Pico II* and Lino. She saw him in early April when she'd opened up her house for the summer and was immediately interested in this fisherman and his strange-looking boat.

"How's your mother?" Diane asked.

"She misses you as much as I do."

Diane peered over her sunglasses. "Now that lie I don't believe," she said, looking into Lino's eyes. "Like me, Katharine would rather run her own affairs. I feel bad that she can't."

"Her doctor wants round-the-clock care," Lino admitted.

"Really? You'll have a hard time finding another Colleen," Diane said.

"Why don't you apply?" Lino teased. "Mother likes you."

"Katharine's a sweetheart," Diane conceded, "but unless you have it on good authority that the art market is about to collapse, I'll stick with painting for my living."

"Could be a mistake."

"That's what my father used to say to me right after I dropped out of college and enrolled in art school. He thought I was crazy. He thought I was crazy when I bought this house in Provincetown, too. Half my time here, half my time in New York. What kind of life is that?"

"What kind is it?" Lino asked, tasting his wine.

"Invigorating. Never dull. When I started out all I wanted was to get a few canvases in a show. Then I wanted a show of my own. Then I wanted a show of my own in New York. Then I wanted the critics to notice and the patrons to line up, checkbooks in hand. Whatever I had was never enough, which my father reminds me is why I've been divorced three times."

"Their loss," Lino quipped. "My gain."

"I'd say we both gain, Lino. If I have one complaint, it's that you're getting a little thin. My men need meat on their bones, or

I toss them back. I suggest we have another glass of wine and walk into town without a reservation and see who'll feed us."

"And then?"

"Is this one of the nights Colleen stays with Katharine?"

"It is," Lino said.

"Good, then you can stay with me."

Fifteen

The next morning Lino opened the door to the red house and picked up Colleen's overnight bag. "How'd last night go?" he asked.

"She fell asleep on the couch watching television. When I woke her for bed, she didn't want to budge."

Lino peeked in the living room.

"She's not there," Colleen said. "I helped her with her shower. She's getting dressed."

"You look tired."

"A little. My old bones don't do well all night on a couch. Your mother's either. She's a little cranky."

"I know it's hard," Lino said, "but the good news is help is on the way."

Colleen exhaled a sigh. "No offense, Mr. Cardosa, but I hope it's more than just you and your well-intentioned friends. Your mother needs …"

"I know," Lino said. "She needs watching, and you need help doing it. I'm going to make some calls this morning to set up some interviews. You won't have to do this alone much longer."

Colleen let the information settle. "I take it you got discouraging news from Doctor Coldwell."

"Sobering news," Lino admitted. "The test results aren't optimistic. We need to be ready for a downturn, and that means twenty-four-hour care, seven days a week, just like you indicated."

"Have you told Katharine yet?"

Lino shook his head. "I've been putting it off, but it's on my list for this morning."

"What's on your list?" Katharine asked, walking stiffly into the kitchen.

"A chat," Lino said, handing Colleen her bag. "You get some rest, I'll see you tomorrow morning." Lino held the screen door. When Colleen was in her car, Lino said, "Nice woman. We're lucky to have her."

"I suppose," Katharine said, a distance in her voice, "although for the life of me, I don't know why she's here."

"To help you. To help both of us, really."

Katharine opened the refrigerator and looked inside, her eyes searching.

"What can't you find?" Lino finally asked.

She closed the door. "I don't know what I was looking for. Does that ever happen to you, you're hungry for something, but you can't explain what it is?"

"Sometimes."

Katharine slowly eased down into a chair at the kitchen table.

"Would you like me to fix you something?" Lino asked.

She shook her head. "I'm not hungry. Being around that woman ..."

"Colleen."

"Being around that woman takes my appetite away. It's a wonder I'm not skin and bones. I think I should fire her."

"Not a good idea, Mother."

"Why not?"

"I told you, we need her help."

Katharine's expression shifted from puzzlement to concern. "What's wrong with you?"

"Nothing's wrong with me."

"Same with me," Katharine said, fidgeting to her feet. She shuffled to the stove, picked up the tea kettle and put it under the faucet. As she turned on the water, she said, "That woman made me sleep on the couch last night. She wouldn't let me in the bedroom until the sun came up."

"You need to take the lid off."

"What?"

"The lid. No water's getting into the pot, because the lid's on."

Katharine turned off the water and put the kettle on the stove. She fumbled with one of the knobs until flames rose from a burner, then slid the empty kettle onto the fire. Dr. Coldwell's words about burning the house down echoed in Lino's mind.

Lino shut off the burner. "I've got an idea," he began. "Any time you want something from the kitchen, you should ask for it. You shouldn't be in here messing around by yourself. Now what would you like?"

"To be left alone."

"That's not possible anymore."

"When I fire that woman it will be." Again Katharine sat at the table, her bony fingers intertwined in front of her. She looked only at her hands. "I don't like people in my house. They see things and make up lies, and before you know it, you're not in your house any longer. Someone comes and takes you away."

Lino sat next to her. "Is that what you think is going to happen?"

"I don't think, I know. Mrs. Grafton three doors down. Her husband died, and in no time she was gone. Her whole life in that house, and the terrible part is that she never wanted to leave. It was her home, Adilino. They take old people from their homes. Ask Mrs. Grafton, she'll tell you how old people are treated."

"That's not going to happen to you."

Katharine's eyes drifted from her hands to her son. "I can't be sure."

"You can be. As long as I'm here, you can be sure."

"How?"

Lino took a paper from his shirt pocket and put it in front of his mother. "See these names? I'm going to talk to each one of them. I'm going to find someone to help Colleen and me, so you can stay right here in your house for as long as you want."

Katharine's look hardened. "Why do you need more people here? I don't want them."

"But Doctor Coldwell does. He says you can't be alone anymore."

"That's another thing, Adilino, all these doctors. Colleen tells them about me. She makes up more lies and tells the doctors. I've been in the room and heard her. It's embarrassing, the lies she tells. You should get rid of her. Get rid of all of them. If I ever get sick, I'll reconsider."

"It's not a physical thing, mother. It's your memory. You know something's not quite right. You know you have trouble remembering things."

"I know I forget," she admitted, "but it's not something to worry over."

"You may not worry, but others do. Me. Carol. We don't want anything to happen to you."

"What could happen?"

"Any number of things. The fact is you can't live alone any longer. Someone has to be with you all the time."

"That's a lie." Katharine's cheeks flashed red. "Who made the decision that I can't be by myself? That woman?"

"It's not a lie," Lino said calmly. "We have Doctor Coldwell's test results. It's a fact we have to live with, that's all. If you want to stay in the house, you can't be alone."

Katharine leaned back in her chair, her anger and frustration rising. "I see. When did you take their side, Adilino? When did you turn against your own mother?"

Lino felt the blow. "That's not fair," he said. "I came home, didn't I?"

"I never understood why."

"Because you need help," he snapped and immediately regretted the harshness in his voice. He reached out to take her hands, but she pulled them away. "Let's not fight over this, all right? Let's just do what we have to."

With great effort Katharine pushed herself up to her feet, turned and walked toward the living room.

Lino couldn't bear her sadness. "Mother, please."

She passed the threshold and was gone. When Lino heard sounds from the television, he wiped the anxious sweat from his hands and sat uncomfortably under the weight of irrational guilt. He'd known when he came back there would be moments like this, but knowing they were out there just beyond his vision didn't prepare him fully for when they slipped into view. What he saw was his mother's pain, her hurt, as if Lino himself reached inside her chest and cut out a part of her heart.

He pulled in a deep breath. When he let it out he said over the blaring TV, "I'm going to make those calls now."

Silence.

He stood and walked into the living room. Katharine lay curled in a ball on the couch, her head propped up on pillows, her eyes open to the flickering lights on the set. Lino put a blanket over her.

"I'm going to make some calls."

"I know."

When he kissed her cheek, he noticed she'd been crying. "It'll be all right."

"I hope so, Adilino. I can only hope."

Back in the kitchen Lino picked up the list of names. He left a message for Joan Hawkins; then spoke with Claire Talbert, who had already accepted a new assignment. Roger Langsford's phone was busy. While Lino waited for the line to clear, he dialed Boston Information and asked for the phone number of Francesco Callegari.

Lino punched in the number. A man answered on the third ring.

"Professor Callegari?"

"Yes. Who is this?"

Lino told him and said, "I understand you and Jerry Dunn were in the seminary together."

Callegari's voice jumped. "You found Jerry?"

"Afraid not, but I've just started looking. I'd like to speak with you about him if that's possible."

"Of course. Whatever I can do to help, I will. I'm free this afternoon."

"I'm afraid I'm not," Lino said.

"That's too bad," Callegari said. "I'm going to be away at a conference starting tomorrow, and after that free time won't come easily."

Lino thought a moment, then checked his watch. If he could find someone to watch Katharine for a few hours, he could catch the morning ferry to Boston and be back in Provincetown in the late afternoon. "I need to call you back," Lino said and phoned Diane. "I need to ask a favor," he said and explained the situation. "Would you mind watching mother again?"

"All night with you, followed by a few hours with your mother? What a family treat," Diane beamed.

Lino thanked her, then phoned the professor back and arranged to meet at the hotel bar across from the Long Wharf ferry dock.

Sixteen

Lino stepped off the Boston Harbor ferry, across the gangway and into the Long Wharf Marriott where he took the escalator to the second floor bar. Professor Callegari was easy to spot among the business clientele finishing an early lunch. He sat at the back corner table, wearing thick, black-rimmed glasses and a tweed jacket over an open-collared shirt. The left arm of the shirt and jacket were tucked neatly into the jacket's pocket and pinned. When Lino approached, Callegari closed the book he was reading and greeted Lino warmly.

As they took their seats, Callegari said, "It's the only advantage of having one arm. I'm easy to spot in a crowd. It's one of those things you have to address right from the beginning, or people don't know how to deal with it."

"How'd it happen?" Lino asked, appreciating the professor's frankness.

"I fell off my bicycle as a child. A slight scratch led to a massive infection. There wasn't much choice if I was to live. The arm had to come off." A waiter came by and took their coffee orders. When he'd left Callegari said, "A quirk of fate or bad luck or something else."

"Such as?"

Callegari shrugged. "I didn't know really. My father was the one with answers. As a small boy he came to America from Italy with his parents and spent his whole adult life in North Cambridge, repairing city bus engines. He was an excellent mechanic. They used to say he had the ear. One listen to an ailing engine, and he knew the problem. When I lost my arm, my father listened to God and said it was a sign from above. I had been chosen."

"To?" Lino asked.

"To become a priest, of course."

"And you believed him?"

A slight smile crossed the professor's lips. "As a boy, no. I was too angry. All I could think was that I'd never play baseball again, but we were a religious family and believed everything in life had a purpose, even if we didn't understand it. Later, when I was trying to decide what I wanted to do for the rest of my life, I considered a life in the church. Besides," Callegari admitted, "I didn't want to disappoint my father. Does that make any sense to you?"

"It makes a lot of sense," Lino acknowledged. "It sounds like our fathers were a lot alike. They had plans for each of us. My dad was a Portuguese fisherman who wanted to keep me off the sea."

"Did he succeed?"

"For the most part."

"That must make your father very happy."

"I'll never know," Lino said. "He died when his boat went down. He never saw how I turned out, but I like to think he would have been happy. Did your father live to see you start the seminary?"

Callegari nodded with a smile. "He was so proud when I was accepted, he put my mother in the car and drove me to the front door. Do you know much about Weston Seminary?"

"I'm afraid I don't," Lino admitted.

"It's a lovely compound on several acres in a small town twenty minutes or so from Boston. There's a chapel, a dining hall, classrooms, residences, everything one might expect in a small college, because that's what it is essentially, a place to live and to learn about God and priestly duties. It's all very communal, all very transparent, because that is what a priest's life is. Seminarians eat together, worship together, make decisions in committees. Life is out in the open for all to see, which is what the priests teaching us wanted. They wanted to see how we fit in, how we might succeed in the priesthood if ordained."

"How old were you?" Lino asked as their coffees arrived.

"Thirty-one. You have to be thirty or thereabouts to get accepted. By then you've lived enough to know something of life and what you want from it." Callegari smiled modestly. "At least that's the assumption. Many of us were more lost than found."

"Jerry Dunn included?"

"In some ways." The professor studied Lino for the first time. "You said on the phone you were not with the police, but you didn't say what your interest is in all this."

Lino explained his background with Colas, Haggerty and Johnson and his connection to Father Silva. "Let's just say I'm doing a retired priest a favor."

"Fair enough."

Lino drank some of his coffee. "You were talking about Jerry."

"Oh, yes. When he came to the seminary, he was a bundle of contradictions, pious yet irreverent, devoted to his studies yet lax. I thought at first he wouldn't last one year at Weston, which I suppose is not all that surprising. It's the hardest of the four. So many adjustments, so much time to think seriously about what you're really doing with the rest of your life. It's a wonder more seminarians don't change their minds and quit."

"Why did you?" Lino asked.

The professor sipped his coffee and said, "It was a very difficult decision, because I knew how disappointed my father would be, but I felt I had no choice. The calling wasn't there. I hadn't been chosen for anything except to slip on sand and fall off my bike. There was no heavenly sign like my father wanted to believe. It was a simple earthly accident caused by a boy riding too fast. That's what I went home and explained to my father."

"You say that like you lied to him."

"Not a lie but not the entire truth either," Callegari admitted. "Nor were my father's expectations the sole reason I applied to the seminary. There was a woman in my life back then, a beautiful, loving woman who wanted to marry me. I turned away from her for the reason I always turned away: my empty sleeve. I could never get past the feeling that anyone who cared was really only feeling sorry for me, confusing love with pity. I didn't want to wake up some morning in an empty bed and learn that I had been right. So I took the easy way out and ran away to the seminary." He held up his hand to show his wedding band. "Fortunately," he said, grinning, "she waited, and I came to my senses before it was too late."

"Congratulations," Lino said.

"Thank you."

"Would you say Jerry Dunn was also running from something?"

"I know he was," Callegari said evenly.

"Do you know what?" Lino pressed.

The professor straightened his back and filled his lungs with air. When he let it out, he leaned forward on the table as if about to tell a secret.

"Jerry and I were friends. At Weston we lived across the hall from one another and spent many nights talking until the sun came up. We talked openly about many of our reservations regarding our lives as priests. One of those reservations was the ability to remain celibate. I knew I couldn't do it or didn't want to."

"And Jerry?"

Callegari drank more of his coffee. "I hesitate, because I swore I'd never mention this, and I've already broken that promise once. I wonder if I'll feel any better about doing so the second time."

Lino knew not to press, to let the man across from him struggle with his own doubt.

Finally Callegari broke the silence. "The only reason I even considered revealing this the first time was because Jerry is gone. Maybe what I know will help find him."

"It might. It probably won't do any harm either."

"Exactly what I thought." Callegari made his decision and visibly relaxed. "All right," he began. "There is no secret gay men are part of the priesthood. That sexual inclination in no way diminishes their desire for a spiritual life. I mean, it's not as if someone wakes up one morning and decides to be gay. It just happens, and it happens to men whose love of God is absolute. If they embrace the vow of celibacy, as most do, the issue becomes irrelevant."

"I understand," Lino said.

"Good. That's very important. Celibacy makes sexual orientation a moot point. However, a small percentage of gay men enter the priesthood because of the all-male lifestyle—not to act perversely, mind you, but because of the nurturing comfort found there. A small percentage of those enter in hopes of finding strength so they can battle an evil they feel lurks inside them. Jerry was in that last camp."

"You know that Jerry Dunn was gay?" Lino asked without emotion.

"Without a doubt."

"How can you be sure?"

"He told me." Calligari's eyes lowered to the table. "He told me how much he hated himself for being homosexual and how disappointed his parents would be, looking down on him from the heavens. He saw it as the ultimate moral weakness, and it tormented him. He saw a life in the church as a way of harnessing God's strength to add to his own in the fight against his sexuality."

"That seems a harsh view of himself."

"I told him the same thing. He shouldn't be so critical, so callous about who he was. He should live his life the way he felt most comfortable."

"What did he say to that?" Lino asked.

"He said that was impossible."

"Did he explain why?"

Calligari shook his head. "No. When I told him I was confronting a similar crisis and was leaving the seminary for a woman, a flash of anger flared in his eyes for an instant, then he became impassive, a man without emotion. He said he was happy for me. Envious. Then he turned around and walked away. That was the last time I saw him until last fall at the Jackstones."

"How did that come about?" Lino asked.

"My wife and I rented a cottage on the Cape for a few weeks' vacation. I knew Father Jerry was pastor at St. Peter's. We went to a mass, and on the way out of the church I introduced Jerry to my wife. He seemed delighted to meet her. It was all very warm and friendly, as I'd hoped it might be. We gave him our number at the cottage in case he wanted to come over for a drink. The night he was free, my wife had already made plans to see old friends. I squeezed out for an hour and met up with Jerry at the Jackstones. I wouldn't have gone, but after all those years I wanted some sort of closure with him. That was a mistake."

"Why?" Lino asked.

"The conversation was mostly about raising money for St. Peter's. Mrs. Jackstone did her best to include me, but I could see I was in the wrong place. I finished my drink, got in my car and met up with my wife and her friends. That was the last time I saw Father Jerry."

"Did Jerry have lovers?"

"I know of only one."

"Someone you met?"

Callegari shook his head. "No. Jerry mentioned someone he was involved with while teaching at Simmons. It ended horribly."

"Did he explain what happened?" Lino asked.

"He didn't provide details, no. He said only that he would never go through that again. He was done. Finished."

"Did he name the person?"

"Lee something or something Lee. That's all he ever referred to him as: Lee."

"A student?"

Callegari thought a moment. "It's possible. Jerry was quite young then himself, so it could have been. It could also have been someone on the faculty. Sorry I can't be of more help on that front."

"Don't be sorry, professor, you've been very helpful. All I've got to do is find Lee."

"Why?" Callegari asked. "That was years ago."

"People change their minds. Maybe Lee and Jerry Dunn got back together. Maybe that reunion is behind all of this. I'll find Lee and maybe learn the truth." Lino slid out from the booth and stood. "You mentioned I was not the first person you told about Father Jerry being gay. Who else did you confide in?"

"The Provincetown police officer, Sergeant Anthony Santos."

"Really?" Lino mused, remembering his conversation with Tony at the police station. *Was Father Jerry gay? No*, Tony had said. Why did he lie? Lino wondered and put ten dollars on the table. "Can I rely on you if I need more information?"

"Of course, and good luck."

On the way out Lino stopped in the hotel's lobby and looked up the Simmons College main number. He stepped out into bright afternoon sunlight and dialed it. When the operator answered, he asked to speak to Professor Lee in the English Department.

There was none.

"Maybe I've got the wrong department," Lino said and waited.

"I'm sorry," the operator said. "We have no listing for a Professor Lee in any department."

"What if he moved on?" Lino asked.

"You'd have to ask human resources for that information."

"And if I want information about a student?"

"The office of the registrar," the operator said.

Lino thanked her and ended the call.

Seventeen

According to the résumé Joan Hawkins handed Lino, she was fifty-eight, married with three grown children, trained in Alzheimer's care and experienced as a live-in care provider. She listed references, past employers, other skills, like being able to drive a standard shift, and the fact that she lived close by in Truro.

Lino liked her immediately. He put her vitae aside and asked if she had any further questions of him.

"I can think of none," she said pleasantly. "Besides, I don't want to intrude on your time." She glanced at her wristwatch. "Didn't you say you had another appointment in a few minutes?"

"A charter," Lino corrected. "I'm not interviewing anyone else for this position. If you'd like it, and you can work out a schedule with Colleen that provides the coverage Mother needs, the job is yours."

"Thank you." Mrs. Hawkins did not appear surprised. "I'm sure we can work out those details."

"Excellent." Lino felt as if a giant anchor had dropped from his neck. "I guess the only thing to do is go meet Mother and Colleen."

Lino stood and opened the cottage door. He followed Mrs. Hawkins out and sprang ahead to let her into the red house, where Colleen waited with a grim look.

"What's the problem?" Lino asked, his heart sinking.

"It's Katharine." Colleen rolled her eyes toward the ceiling.

"Don't tell me."

"I'm afraid so. She's barricaded herself in your old bedroom again."

"What for this time?"

"She said I've turned against her."

"What?"

"You, too. She doesn't want to see either one of us again," Colleen said. "You and I are now the enemy."

"Where'd she get that crazy idea?" Lino asked, exasperated.

"From Mrs. Grafton."

"Oh, Christ," Lino said, wishing he hadn't said that in front of Mrs. Hawkins. He turned to her. "I'm sorry about this. My mother's twisted a few things in her mind. Mrs. Grafton was a neighbor who hasn't been around in years."

"It's perfectly understandable," Mrs. Hawkins said. "Maybe if I went up and had a chat with your mother. A different voice sometimes works wonders."

A new confidence swelled inside Lino. "Would you?"

Mrs. Hawkins grinned broadly. "I can give it a try."

"That would be wonderful, if you would," Lino said.

Colleen led Mrs. Hawkins to the stairs, and they both went up together. Lino stayed back, wishing he could somehow trade places with his California sister who enjoyed the insulation from family problems that distance and money provide. What selfish pleasantry was entertaining Carol while their mother stomped on the floor and shouted for everyone to go away?

Lino took Katharine's loud and angry advice and stepped out onto the driveway. The morning sun shone like a laser in the windless air. Across the street on the beach children chased after seagulls while parents trotted along behind, taking pictures. Farther out, couples waded in the shallow water, enjoying the serenity only warm sun and sand create.

Upstairs, through an open window, Mrs. Hawkins could be heard coaxing Mrs. Cardosa. Mrs. Hawkins' soft, yet strong, voice reminded Lino of someone trying to reason with a child, but Katharine would not be reasoned out of her mood. Lino knew that. He'd lived through similar contentious moments with her. She grew more fierce, more unswerving, with each reasoned attempt at calming her.

Lino walked to the cottage to get the keys to his boat, silently thanking his mother for providing an excellent test for Mrs. Hawkins' abilities. When he got back to the red house, he asked Colleen how things were going upstairs.

"She's still trying to get Katharine to come out. She hasn't given up, I'll give her that much."

"Will you be all right until I get back?" Lino asked.

"Of course. I don't know about Mrs. Hawkins."

Lino worked a smile. "We'll compare notes when I finish with my charter."

Starting in late June when the water has been warmed by the sun, the striper catch thinned out with schoolies moving into cooler water farther north. The remaining bigger bass went deeper and got much harder to attract. These big bass were smarter, masters of their own freedom and more easily spooked. They were bigger and older, because they'd learned how to survive marauding seals and pesky fishermen. But fishermen adapted, too, creating chum slicks out of cheap cat food, frozen clams or ground mackerel to tempt the fish up from the depths. The truly zealous fisherman fished at night and lit the chum below the surface with waterproof lights, attracting squid and stripers alike. On a good trip the lit food streaming down current made the catch easy, like fishing in a barrel.

Carl Adkins, a forty-year-old car dealer from southern Maine, would never resort to such trickery. Nor would he charter with anyone who did. He was a purist, a fisher looking for a fair fight he would be proud to win. He climbed aboard the *Pico II*, put his rod down and shook his friend's hand with a sturdy grip.

"You're looking well, Lino."

"That makes two of us, Carl. Good to see you again."

Adkins nodded agreement. "This is like being out at the end of the world," Carl said, taking in the view of the harbor as Lino motored through it. "It's also a much harder place for me to get to than Gloucester, but I'm sure you're going to make it worth the drive."

"I'll do my best."

"You always do," Adkins replied with a grin.

"The action's a little spotty," Lino admitted. "They're here but deep. You're skilled enough to pull one to the boat, if you brought your sinking line."

"Just like you advised."

"The good thing is that what you catch this time of year is usually big."

Adkins reached in his carryall and pulled out three reels, one a brand new Abel. "Been dying to try this. She's loaded with sink, one hundred and twenty-nine grains. Ought to go right to the bottom. How deep?"

"Fifty feet to one hundred," Lino said, powering up and steering around a tacking sailboat.

They rounded Long Point in a gentle north wind that flattened the seas all the way to Race Point. Some captains argued the best striper fishing on the Cape was at the Race where the current churned over the bar at ten knots. Big fish settled low in the speeding current, waiting for the fast moving water to deliver lunch. There were always boats there. Most trolled live eels close to shore; a few cast spinning rods. A fly fisher rarely made an appearance, because the heavy boat traffic made it nearly impossible to haul back a cast before the line got shredded in another boat's prop. Sinking line solved that problem and put the fly down near the bottom where the fish waited.

Just before the bar Lino cut speed and fell in line behind a trolling boat. When they passed over the bar, Lino turned to the inside of the other boat and closer to shore. Here the current churned the dark green water into powerful rips. A small boat with an inexperienced captain could easily be swamped.

As Carl finished rigging up Lino said, "Anywhere in here could be a winner."

Carl stepped to the casting platform and pulled free enough weighted line to make one back cast before shooting the fly into the boil. Boat speed and line weight combined to sink the line one foot every two seconds, dragging with it twelve feet of tapered leader and a yellow and black Deceiver.

Carl waited long enough for the line to hit bottom, then hauled in slowly. Lino stayed close to shore a hundred yards past the Coast Guard station at Race Point Lighthouse. There he turned around and retraced his track. Carl worked his casts like a professional and came up empty.

Lino took a fly from his pocket fly box and said, "You may want to try this."

"What the hell is it?"

"Something new," Lino admitted, handing over what looked like a pink Clauser, only it had big black doll eyes and extra long pink feathers trailing at the back. "I've been experimenting."

Carl tied it on. "You're always experimenting. Most of the time, you dream up a winner. What do they do, come to you in your sleep?"

Lino chuckled. "My dreams aren't that interesting."

Carl was ready to cast. "How should I work it?"

"Bob and drift," Lino said. "A slight pull and let her drift back. Do that all the way in. She'll act just like a squid."

"You're the boss," Carl said and put the new fly in the churning water. When the line hit bottom, Carl jerked the lure as Lino suggested. On the fifth bob and drift, the fight was on. Line spun from Carl's new reel as the rod bent. Carl tightened the drag and pulled the rod back slightly to test the size of the fish.

"Feels like a good one, Lino," Carl said, excitement riding his voice, "a real good one. Hope you brought more of those flies."

Three flies later, after five twenty-pound bass had been caught and released, Lino tied the *Pico II* to its mooring and rowed the dinghy back to shore. Across the street he saw Katharine and Colleen working in the yard. On her knees,

Katharine concentrated on the weeds she was about to pull while Colleen dragged the watering hose into place. She saw Lino and stopped.

"How'd it go with Mrs. Hawkins?" he asked, his voice low so his mother could not hear.

"I'll give you one guess," Colleen said. "The poor woman couldn't get out of the house fast enough."

"I was afraid of that," Lino admitted. "Maybe we need a man on board."

"A man?"

Lino nodded. "He's the last name on Pro-Care's list."

"Are you sure that Katharine would like that?" Colleen asked skeptically.

"It might not matter," Lino said. "I mean, she doesn't really like anyone at the moment. The other question is with you."

"It wouldn't bother me, if that's what you're asking."

"That's what I'm asking," Lino said. "He's a retired nurse. You three would be in close quarters. I don't want to do anything that might make matters worse."

"I say we find out," Colleen said. "I don't know that we have much choice."

"None," a resigned Lino admitted. "I'll give him a call."

Eighteen

Lino added notes about the day's fishing to his logbook while finishing lunch. He put the dishes away, then called Roger Langsford, who'd just come in from a swim. Of course, he'd like to discuss the possibility of a job. Considering the scene that greeted Mrs. Hawkings, Lino suggested he not come to the house but instead meet close by for a drink at Fanizzi's Restaurant. Langsford said he would clean up and be there in an hour.

Lino put down the phone and booted up his computer. The Simmons College website listed the full-time faculty by department. Lino scrolled through the list and, just as the college operator had said, found no one with the first or last name of Lee. He looked up the phone number of the Human Resource Office and thought about calling to ask if anyone there would research their employment records, but knew he had too little information to expect their help.

"How far back did Mr. Dunn teach here?"

"Good question. Over twenty years ago."

"And what was the name you are after?"

"Lee something. Something Lee. And no, I don't know the department he taught in. I don't know if he taught. He might have been a student."

Click.

Lino ran through the faculty names one more time. In the English department, the closest Lee was Leland Ricks. With nothing to lose Lino wrote Ricks an e-mail, explaining that he was looking into the disappearance of Father Jeremiah Dunn and wondered if that name meant anything. If so, could he spare some time to talk.

In minutes Ricks responded. "There's nothing to talk about," he wrote.

"There is, if you're Jerry Dunn's Lee." Lino added his phone number and sent his reply before walking the few blocks down Commercial Street to the restaurant.

A slim man of medium height, wearing a tight-fitting olive tee-shirt and khaki shorts, waited uneasily inside the front door. He pushed his wire-rimmed glasses higher on his nose. "Mr. Cardosa?" He shook Lino's hand. "I'm Roger. Roger Langsford."

His grip was overly firm as if trying to prove a manly point. From the deep, tanned lines fanning out around Langsford's blue eyes and the slight sag of his jowls, Lino guessed his age to be well into his sixties.

"Thank you for coming," Lino said as the hostess came over from the bar.

She looked disappointed. "Your mom's not with you this trip?"

"Not this trip," Lino admitted. "She's more interested in her dahlias right now than going out."

"Give her my best, all right?" She led them to a table with a water view and put down menus. "Enjoy."

The waitress was right behind. "Something to drink to get you started?"

"Bass Ale for me. Nothing to eat."

"Seltzer with lemon," Roger said, one hand adjusting the diamond stud in his right ear.

She grabbed the menus and bounded off.

"So where do you swim?" Lino asked, breaking ice.

"My friend in Wellfleet has a pool. I take advantage of it when he's away. It's part of my reward for taking care of his houseplants and dogs, two Scottish terriers with more energy than you can imagine." Roger shifted uncomfortably in his seat. "You'll excuse me if I seem a bit nervous, but the fact is, I am a bit nervous."

"You shouldn't be," Lino offered.

"I shouldn't be in the position I'm in. That's the whole trouble. I retired down here to be with friends and enjoy myself, but you can't enjoy yourself once you realize retirement costs more than you calculated. You start to scrimp and count pennies. I'm not an extravagant person, but I've never scrimped and counted pennies in my entire life. I don't want to start now, but for a man my age there's not much opportunity for year-round employment down here on the Cape. Certainly not in my field and certainly not part-time, as I believe is the case with your position." The drinks came, and Roger drank half of his immediately. When the waitress was out of earshot, Roger whispered, " I certainly don't want to be a waiter, but you likely know that after reading my cover letter and résumé I left with Ruth at Pro-Care."

"I never saw either," Lino admitted. "The fact is, Mr. Langsford …"

"Roger, please."

Lino nodded. "The fact is, Roger, I never thought we'd have this interview. There were two qualified women ahead of you on the list."

"I see." Langsford didn't hide his disappointment. "What changed your mind?"

"One had already taken a position, and the other my mother didn't like."

"So I'm the last man standing."

"You're the only man standing."

Roger wiped the water droplets from the outside of his glass before taking a short sip. "I didn't think to bring an extra copy of my résumé," he finally said.

"That's all right," Lino said. "I got enough information from Ruth. I understand you were a nurse."

"That's right. I spent my entire thirty-six year nursing career at Mass General. I started out in ER and ended up in cardiac. I'm proud to say I lasted much longer than many of the women. Nothing against women, you understand. Had my genes lined up the way they should have, I would have been one." He looked sheepishly at Lino. "You don't have anything against gays, do you?"

"Nothing at all."

A stream of air gushed from Roger's lips. "Whew," he said, wiping imaginary sweat from his brow. "You never know. Even in this day and age when almost anything goes, there are still people who would not hire a caregiver like me. Which is too bad for them, because I'm very good at what I do. Patients love me, and I have the references to prove it."

"Ruth Keller said she'd never seen anyone with such glowing credentials," Lino confessed.

Langsford seemed taken by surprise. "Ruth said that?"

"She did."

"I'll have to send her a little thank you note. Kindness demands a reward, even kindness generated by the truth."

"What about patients who don't love you?" Lino asked, explaining his mother's eccentricities. "I'm afraid at the moment my mother doesn't like anyone, especially not Mrs. Hawkins."

Langsford's brows scrunched in a question. "The last candidate your mother didn't warm to?"

"That's right."

"Is your mother violent?"

"No."

"That's the key. Violent patients tend to hurt themselves more than anyone else. As long as she's not violent, we'll get along." Langsford drank more of his seltzer, then said, "The way you describe your mother, she needs more than part-time assistance."

"There will be two of you," Lino said and told him about Colleen.

"She sounds wonderful," Langsford admitted. "We might make quite a pair."

"Then you're still interested?"

"I guess the question really is, are you interested in me?"

"I'm warming to the idea," Lino admitted, mildly surprised that he was. "You mentioned your friend with the pool and taking care of his houseplants. What do you know about gardening in general?"

"Dirt under the nails. Calluses on the hands. The basics. Why?"

"I want mother to give you a chance, and I don't think she will if I introduce you as a nurse coming to look after her. I was thinking of a little deception."

"Such as?" Langsford asked, intrigued.

"Mother has always wanted help with her garden. It's too much for her to keep up nowadays. Early in the spring when I wasn't busy, I did what I could, and Colleen pitches in when she can. Still, it's not really enough to stay ahead of the weeds. I think it might be a good idea to introduce you as her new gardener. What would you say to that?"

Langsford smiled knowingly. "I'd say your mother doesn't want strangers running around her house telling her what to do. She doesn't want this to happen, does she?"

"No, but her doctor says we have no choice."

"Then we'll make it work, Mr. Cardosa. Whatever it takes—gardening, baking, candlestick-making—we'll make it work if you'll give me a chance."

"We'll need to work a schedule out with Colleen."

"Fine."

"And we'll need to come up with a good explanation as to why a gardener is spending the night."

"I'll have to think about that one."

"Me, too," Lino said, adding, "How soon can you start?"

When Lino got back to his cottage after running the *Pico II* down to the fuel dock to fill her tanks, a small bouquet of yellow and orange nasturtiums sat in a mustard jar in the center of the kitchen table. The note under it, written in Katharine's wobbly hand, read, "We should not fight, Adilino. It is not a good thing. Make the phone calls you have to make, then say ten Hail Marys tonight before you go to bed. The Lord and I will forgive you. Mother."

Lino put down the note. A prayer hadn't crossed his lips since Steven tied the rope around his neck and stepped from the chair. Where was God that instant? Where was the voice of restraint, of reason? Where was God's wisdom rushing into Steven's sick, turbulent mind? Was He waiting to see what Steven would really do? No. God knows all. He didn't have to wait. He knew the poor boy was going to kill himself and let it happen. Why He did had gnawed at Lino every hour of every day. Where is the sense in it? Where is the logic? How is a parent to understand such a horrible act?

The only answer is that God turned His back. Lino did the same to God. An eye for an eye.

Lino twirled the ice in his glass and sipped his scotch, savoring the cool temperature and warmth of the alcohol. It was like a controlled burn sliding down inside him. It felt wonderful.

A timer jangled. Lino drained the potatoes, made a simple pan sauce of butter and wine for the chicken, dressed the salad and ate in silence. It wasn't restaurant quality, but many restaurants weren't either. He cleaned the table and washed the dishes while finishing his wine. He checked his logbook for tomorrow morning's charter and switched on NOAA's weather forecast. While listening, Lino cut some Mylar tubing for a variation he wanted to tie of the famous Mickey Finn Streamer. He'd just slipped the Mylar over the hook when the phone rang.

"I'd like to speak to a Mr. Cardosa," the official-sounding voice said.

"That's me."

"I'm not used to being harassed, Mr. Cardosa."

"Who is this?"

"Leland Ricks."

"You're overreacting, professor. One e-mail ..."

"One e-mail, one thousand e-mails doesn't matter. What matters is the reference to Jerry Dunn, and I don't want to talk about him. We haven't spoken in years."

"About the time he went into the seminary?"

"That's right." Lino heard the pain in the professor's voice. "You'll have to track someone else down who might know more about Jerry than I do."

"That's the point," Lino said. "I'm not sure there is anyone else." Silence. "You still there, professor?"

"Yes. Even if there weren't others, what you're talking about happened years ago. I've forgotten all about it."

"None of us forgets love affairs," Lino said, "the good parts or the bad. They stay with us forever. I only need a few minutes of your time. Name the place, and I'll be there. Professor Ricks? A few minutes. What have you got to lose?"

Another long silence followed. "Tomorrow morning," Ricks said reluctantly. "I'll do it then, before I change my mind."

Nineteen

Leland Ricks gave Lino one option. He would meet him at ten o'clock in the morning for one hour so as to be done with all this foolishness. He never wanted to speak of Jerry Dunn or hear about him again. Lino agreed and called his good friend Hal Rossi down in Orleans. Hal owned and operated Nauset Charters, a tackle shop and charter business. Hal was a first class fisherman and a world class fly tier. He was also Lino's backup.

"Need some help, Hal," Lino said. "Got an appointment in Boston I can't get out of and a charter I don't want to cancel."

"More business with your mother?" Hal asked.

Lino took the easy way out and lied. "Afraid so."

"You've always got to take care of your mother. That's priority. When's the charter?"

"Tomorrow morning at six."

"Jesus," Hal said. "That's gonna be tough, but I can probably switch a few guides around. I've got two groups going out in the trucks to fish North Beach. I'll get Luke to take my group, then I'll swing up to P-town. I'll take my boat, if you don't mind," Hal asked.

"Whatever makes it happen," Lino said. "I know it's short notice."

"Hey, my engine conking out this spring was short notice. Did I ever thank you for all the help getting me back up and running?"

"A hundred times. Can you cover?"

"Count me in."

"Thanks, Hal." Lino put down the phone. From the window he could see bluish light flicker from the television in the red house. He walked over.

Katharine lay stretched out under a gold and green afghan she'd crocheted years ago. Her feet were propped on the ottoman, her head back and to one side, her eyes closed, passing for dead. Colleen got up and moved away like a cat.

Lino stayed by the door. "I've got to go into Boston tomorrow for a meeting. The ferries don't leave early enough, so I'm driving, but I didn't want to leave without telling you the good news. Help is on the way in the name of one Roger Langsford."

Colleen's eyes shone like beams. "He took the job?"

Lino nodded. "I came by to tell you around dinner time, but you two were out."

"Grocery shopping," Colleen said. "Katharine wanted blueberries for her ice cream. When does Roger start?"

"Monday at the latest. He's got house-sitting responsibilities until then. Lay out a schedule that works best for you. We'll make sure Roger works around it."

Katharine stirred.

"I wouldn't mention anything to Mother, if I were you."

"Not a word," Colleen said, pinching her fingers and pulling an imaginary zipper across her pursed lips. "Aren't you the least bit afraid of another Mrs. Hawkins disaster?"

"Not this time," Lino said. "Roger's going to be a welcomed surprise."

"Mind telling me how?"

"Who's there? Hello?" Katharine's voice carried the sounds of sleep.

"I'll tell you later," Lino said, "but trust me, Roger will work out."

Normally, the drive to Boston from Provincetown is two and a half hours. Coming off the Cape and going into the city during the morning rush can often add another hour, but Lino had no choice if he was going to make his appointment with Leland Ricks.

Lino parked in a space on the corner of Newbury and Exeter streets and walked down one block to Commonwealth Avenue. Ricks' apartment was in the middle of the block toward Dartmouth Street. Lino climbed the gray-painted concrete stairs and was looking for the apartment number when the buzzer sounded, releasing the electronic door lock. Lino entered the marble foyer as a door on the left opened. Framed in the doorway stood a man in his fifties, tall, no fat on him. He'd obviously spent a lot of time working out in a gym.

He flicked suspicious eyes over Lino and said, "I saw you come up the stairs. I'm Leland Ricks. I take it you can prove who you are?"

Lino presented his driver's license.

Ricks handed it back. "Now that I know who you are, I want to know why you are."

Lino explained the favor he was doing for Father Silva.

"Tracking down the missing is the job for the police, isn't it?"

"It is," Lino admitted. "I'm also looking for answers relating to my son's suicide."

That answer took Ricks by surprise. He moved aside slowly. "Let's get this over with, shall we?"

Lino stepped into the living room, which was so neat and clean it looked as if no one had ever set a drink on the polished, wooden furniture. The only personal touch was a collection of porcelain, wood and bronze armadillos of various sizes. They crowded the mantle and the window sills. They grouped on lamp stands and along one edge of the coffee table. Five shelves in a glass case contained hundreds of miniatures.

"I've been told," Ricks said self-consciously, "that I own the largest private collection in the world."

"I can imagine," Lino said, glancing at the oil painting behind the sofa. An armadillo's beady black eyes looked back at him. "Curious animal," he said, not knowing what else to say.

"Very curious," Ricks agreed, "and thick skinned. That's what attracts me to them. You can't survive in this world without thick skin." Ricks took a seat on the sofa. "Sit if you like."

Lino sat in the cream-colored, overstuffed chair across from Ricks. Through the bay window he could see joggers dodging an elderly couple walking their golden retriever. For the first time he was aware of faint music in the background and the voice of Sinatra.

"Recognize that tune?"

"I can't name it, if that's what you mean," Lino answered.

"'Fools Rush In' with the Tommy Dorsey band. It was one of Jerry's favorites. When I want to feel completely ghastly, I play it." Ricks crossed one leg over the other and straightened the crease in his slacks with a slight tug. "Your bringing up Jerry brought back a universe of feelings. That's why I decided to meet with you today. I don't want those horrid feelings lingering. I want them in the open and out the door with you when you leave. Out, out, out. Finished. Don't call me again. Do you understand?"

"I do," Lino said.

"All right then." Ricks' head tilted slightly back, making him look down his nose at Lino. "How did you learn about me?"

Lino explained his conversation with Callegari. "They shared a lot in the seminary," Lino added.

"Sex in the shower, no doubt," Ricks said bitingly.

"Callegari is straight."

"All the more challenging. I once took it upon myself to steal an attractive young man away from his wife. Of course, I was much younger then and quite something to look at. A bit of a dasher, you might say. A dandy."

"Did you succeed?" Lino asked.

Ricks seemed offended. "I never had it any other way. I was like a lion in the African wild. I spotted my prey, stalked it until ready, then attacked."

"Is that what happened with Jerry Dunn?"

"No, sweet little Jerry was different. He'd run if confronted with the possibilities of life with another man."

"How did you pick up on that?" Lino asked.

"It was easy. Jerry didn't know he was gay. He'd had suspicions, I'm sure, doubts about his masculinity while growing up. All gay men do, but not all react to those uncertainties the same way. Some, like me, embrace those possibilities. Others, like little Jerry Dunn, dread who and what they are. Those anxieties were written all over his handsome, diminutive face."

"How did you meet?"

"Jerry had just joined the Simmons faculty when I saw him at one of our interminable department meetings. He was so new to it all, he actually paid attention as our chairman rambled on about one thing or another. Nobody heard a word except Jerry, who sat there like a choir boy, eyes wide, antennae out, pulling in every stray moonbeam. I offered to sort through the politics of campus life for him. He accepted, and we went out for a drink."

"How did he respond to you?"

"Professionally. We were colleagues getting to know one another. We weren't lovers until many months later. On weekends we'd get away to Newport or Provincetown. Our first summer together, we rented a place in P-town for a month. It was wonderful, if one word could describe our time together: wonderful."

"Did you live together here in Boston?"

Ricks shook his head. "No. Jerry insisted on being discreet. It was not my way, mind you, but if I wanted to be with Jerry, I had to follow his rule. Weekends away, fine. A Provincetown vacation, splendid. But here in Boston? No. Here it was church every Sunday for him, not me. I'm not Catholic."

"Why the Boston secrecy?" Lino asked.

"Jerry's sister and her husband lived here. Jerry didn't want them finding out until he was ready to tell them."

"How long did your relationship last?"

"About two years. One year, eleven months and four days to be exact." Ricks exhaled a deep breath and seemed to deflate. "This was long before the trend in gay marriages, but I think, had we stayed together, marriage would have been a distinct possibility. Mr. and Mrs. Leland Ricks. That has a nice ring to it, don't you think?"

Lino didn't answer. "What happened?"

Ricks sank back in the down cushions as if distancing himself from the truth. Finally he said, "His sister happened, Mary Alice, the queen of Catholic propriety."

"She found out about your relationship?"

"She didn't find out, no. Jerry finally got the courage to tell her. He was thirty, a college teacher living a gay life in the closet. He wanted her to know who he really was. He wanted her to accept him so he could take the next step and be honest with everyone else. He wanted to come out." Ricks shifted in his seat. "It was a colossal mistake."

"How so?"

"They were not on the same wavelength. Have you ever experienced some momentous thrill in your life that you simply had to tell your best friend about? Your facelift wiped away fifteen years of wrinkles, not ten. You're ready to explode with the joyous news and call your friend on such a high your nose bleeds, only your friend ruins the moment by killing the mood. His dog died. He has a hangnail. He's in a bitchy mood, because his soufflé flopped, and your thrill is reduced to an apology for even calling the bastard. Mary Alice was Jerry's bastard."

"What happened?"

"She heard the words, but she didn't understand them. She couldn't have a brother who was homosexual. It didn't fit who she was. Can you imagine she actually said that? Her brother's being gay didn't fit who she was! And who she was was her foundation and all it stood for with its Boston propriety and wholesome summer camps for children. Children," Ricks repeated as if struck by a memory. "What did you say your last name was?"

"Cardosa."

"Why does that name ring a bell? Ah, yes, your son was at Sweetbriar before he took his own life."

"You have quite a memory."

"I keep up with Sweetbriar. It's an interest of mine like armadillos."

"Why is that?"

"I kept hoping Jerry would have the courage to stand up to his sister and shut it down. He never did," Ricks said, his thoughts drifting to something else. "Did your son ever mention any out-of-the-ordinary camp games?"

"Such as?" Lino asked warily.

"The cruelest kind. Children blindfold someone they want to torment, then walk them into the woods holding a paper bag. The poor child is to stand there holding the bag until a furry little playmate jumps inside. Only there isn't any furry playmate. There is nothing but darkness when the child removes the blindfold and sees that he's lost. He fears he'll never find his way back. He panics. He screams, but no one hears."

"You tell the story like it happened to you."

"I do, don't I?"

"Did it?"

"No, but I am familiar with a variation of that game played in the gay world. A man watches the game a short distance away. When the child removes the blindfold and cries out in fear, the man becomes a trusted friend. A guide back to the camp. A confidant to the tortured little soul. There will be other walks in the woods, swims in the lake, hands held on walks back to camp, a kiss, maybe."

Lino felt his stomach clinch. "Were you the lonely man in the woods?"

"No."

"Jerry Dunn?"

"Don't be ridiculous. We heard the stories, same as others in the gay world heard them. You don't keep things like that secret for long."

"Were children raped?" Lino asked afraid of the answer.

"Of course."

"How many?"

"I don't know."

"Why didn't you go to the police?"

"With what? We didn't have names, we didn't have dates, we had only a story and a place: Sweetbriar."

"Did Mary Alice know?"

"Yes," Ricks said. "Jerry told her. She was stricken, shocked. She said she would take care of it."

"When was this?" Lino asked.

"Years ago. Jerry and I were still seeing each other."

"Why didn't Mary Alice close the camp?"

"Because she had her social standing to uphold. She couldn't admit that such a vile thing occurred at one of her camps. It was that same social standing that had her pronounce me an old fag who'd taken advantage of her brother. She would forgive Jerry's indiscretion once, but she would never hear of such behavior again in her house. She turned her own brother away until he promised to come to his senses. Her reaction nearly killed Jerry. When he didn't fight for us, for me, it nearly killed me. He slunk off and in a matter of months was in the seminary, where he could cleanse his soul."

Lino felt strangely sorry for Ricks, adding, "Mary Alice died, you know."

"There's justice after all," Ricks said bitingly. "I went to one of Jerry's sermons after he'd come back to Boston to be closer to her. I fell in line with the other parishioners and shook his hand as I left the church. That was all there was left between us, a perfunctory handshake out in the open for all to see. That was the last time I saw him."

"I suppose the police have spoken to you about all this."

Ricks nodded. "Of course."

"Provincetown or State?"

"I don't remember. State, I think, he had that odd looking hat on with the flat brim. Didn't even take it off in the apartment. Peasant."

"And you provided him with an alibi?"

"Do you think I took Father Jerry out to the dunes and killed him after I burned his church? A spurned, spiteful lover gets his revenge?"

"Did you?"

"No," Ricks said, "and I have numerous unimpeachable witnesses who will tell you where I was the night hell visited Provincetown. I was on the dais at the college along with dozens of others presenting the Community Award of Excellence to the mayor of our fine city."

Twenty

Lino felt his insides tighten like hammered wire as he followed Father Silva's directions through Cambridge and into Somerville where St. Catherine's of Genoa stood at the top of Spring Hill. He drove to the back of the drive and parked at the rear of the rectory that looked like a French chateau. The elderly man in casual dress, raking flat the cedar mulch around the base of clipped holly bushes, was Father Silva.

"I see you found it with no trouble," the priest said, his attention on his work. "I have a room upstairs, but to earn my keep, so to speak, I volunteer for whatever needs doing. Idle hands, you understand."

"I doubt your hands are ever idle," Lino said, still a little troubled.

"What's the problem, Lino? You said you learned something that bothered you. Something Robert Connelly mentioned?"

"Something Leland Ricks mentioned."

"Who?"

Lino reached over and took the rake. "Leland Ricks. Does that name mean anything to you?"

Father Silva considered it, then said, "Not that I recall."

"What about Francesco Callegari?"

Father Silva shook his head. "A name I would certainly remember, but no, I've not heard of him either. Why?"

"Callegari quit the seminary while Jerry Dunn was there."

"Not all hear the calling as deeply as they must."

"Tony Santos had also spoken with Callegari."

"I would chalk that up to good police work, don't you think? Tony's sniffing out all possible leads. Bravo for him."

"Callegari told Tony something troubling about Jerry Dunn that I wonder if you're keeping to yourself to protect a fellow priest."

"Such as?"

"Father Dunn's sexual preference."

Father Silva retook the rake and smoothed a rough patch with the tines. "Father Jerry is not gay, if that is where this conversation is leading," the priest said stiffly. "Many years ago a young man, a confused young man named Jeremiah Dunn, experimented with a lifestyle. He realized after conversations with his devout sister that he was dying in sin and changed his ways to rise to a new life in Christ. The Lord forgives all, Adilino, even those who temporarily turn their backs on Him."

Lino ignored the dig. "How did you find out about Dunn's sexual preference?"

Father Silva's back straightened. "I told you, many years back a confused young man ..."

Lino raised his hands in submission. "I heard. Any idea why Tony would not tell the truth?"

"About?"

"Knowing that Father Dunn is gay."

"You have a hard head, do you know that? It's probably what makes you good at your profession, which is why I shall have to put up with it. As to your question, I can't imagine why Sergeant Santos did not tell the truth," the priest said testily. "Maybe he didn't hear the question, or maybe, like me, he makes the critical distinction between a young man's experiment and a grown priest's adopted and committed lifestyle of celibacy. To put it another way, a priest has no sexual preference. Tony knows that."

"Tony heard my question and lied when he answered it," Lino said and asked again how Father Silva knew about Jerry Dunn's past.

"The way a priest knows most things, Adilino. I once heard Father Jerry's confession."

"Only once?"

"I was only asked by Mary Alice once to provide that service. She insisted on it. Father Jerry and I complied, but what difference does any of this make?" the flustered priest asked.

"It might help explain the motive for Dunn's disappearance," Lino answered.

"And what might that be?"

"Blackmail. Someone could have found out about Father Jerry's past and the rumors surrounding Sweetbriar and demanded money to keep quiet."

"What rumors about Sweetbriar?" Father Silva wanted to know.

"Child abuse."

Father Silva was quiet for the longest time. "To read the papers," he finally said, "you would think that all priests care about is preying on the young. None of the good ever comes out."

"You're supposed to be good. Besides," Lino added, "I never said a priest was the abuser."

"No, but in this day and age that's where the conversation would go, isn't it?"

"Probably."

"No doubt about it. You need to keep that in mind, Lino. When you speak of Sweetbriar and those ancient rumors, you are speaking of a different time, a different way of seeing the world."

"Why the history lesson?" Lino asked.

"Because mistakes were made."

Lino's heart pounded. "Then you did know something," Lino pressed. "What?"

"What Mary Alice wanted known. She was in charge, remember. There were rumors followed quickly by reassurances that the situation had been dealt with. People wanted the ugliness to go away, and Mary Alice made that happen without the involvement of the authorities. Once the camp returned to normal, no one dug deeper to learn the truth, in part because some feared a priest may have been involved."

"Did you have that fear?"

Father Silva nodded. "I never buried my head in the sand, Lino. We religious fail like everyone else. In those days, even if it were true that a priest was involved, that information might have been swept under the rug. I'm sorry for it, but that's how things were done."

"Were the guilty parties ever named?"

"Not that I know of."

"How did Mary Alice keep things quiet?"

"Payments were arranged for the aggrieved families in return for their promise of silence," Father Silva said. "I heard the payments were substantial and the families could take it without guilt, saying they were protecting their child from a long and traumatizing legal battle."

"Nice and neat," Lino said bitterly. "When you found out Steven was going to Sweetbriar, why didn't you tell me what was going on there?"

"Because nothing was going on there when Steven attended camp."

"How do you know that?"

"Father Jerry was in charge of Sweetbriar for many years, the years Steven was a camper. Father Jerry told me that those years were uneventful. I know he told the truth."

"Why?"

"Because he confided in me during confession. A priest would never lie during confession, especially Father Jerry." Father Silva took a step toward the rectory. "I think it best if I show you something, Lino. Come along. Come."

Lino followed through a side entrance and up a set of narrow stairs to the second floor where Father Silva opened an unlocked wooden door and stepped inside. His room contained a single bed, a desk and two straight-backed chairs. Father Silva pulled one of the chairs out from under the desk and sat. Lino occupied the other as Father Silva opened the top drawer of his desk and removed a manila folder. He set it squarely in front of him and opened it, then handed Lino one small sheet of paper.

Lino struggled with the nearly incomprehensible writing. "What is this?" Lino finally asked.

"It's the writing of a very disoriented, very ill woman," Father Silva answered, pointing at what looked like the scribbles of a child. "Mary Alice was on a feeding tube by then. Poor thing couldn't swallow, and her voice gushed out in hoarse waves. I tried, but I couldn't understand her. She thought it best if she wrote down what she wanted to say, but as you can see, that wasn't much help either."

Lino handed back the paper. "What do you think she wanted you to know?"

"I'm not really certain. I didn't admit that to her, of course. I wanted to help Mary Alice die in peace. Interrogating her didn't seem the best way to achieve that," Father Silva said, handing Lino a second sheet. "This one is a little clearer, a little more understandable."

Before Lino looked at the paper in his hand, he asked Father Silva why he had these documents and not Mary Alice's husband.

"She didn't want Robert to know about these. She wanted this kept secret. The only people she showed these to were her brother and me."

"Any idea why she kept them from Robert?"

"According to Father Jerry, she kept many things from Robert, or more accurately, she didn't include him in conversations. She made decisions and issued orders, orders that were obeyed, I might add."

"Sounds like a tough lady," Lino admitted.

"Yes, but not tough enough to survive her disease. She fought to the end and wanted very much to explain something with her notes on these pages, but she was very ill, and what with the drugs and the pain, she didn't make a lot of sense. For all I know she may have said things she didn't even mean. For example, when I told her that I'd heard Father Jerry's confession, she got quite agitated."

"But she asked that you hear Father Jerry's confession."

"That's what I thought, yes."

"And now deathbed secrets kept from her husband?" Lino said, waving the paper.

"So it appears, and unless someone can make out the writing, it's a secret from us all."

Lino looked at the four words scrawled along the jagged line that sloped down the page like stairs. The letters were larger on this sheet, making the decipher easier. "What's this supposed to mean?"

"That's what we wondered." Father Silva anticipated Lino's question. "Father Jerry and I worked on it for hours."

Lino took a stab at the writing. "Note. Doze. Rest. Sick."

Father Silva nodded approval. "You got one."

"Doze?"

"Sick."

"What are the other three?"

"Nose. Dare. Rest. Of course we're guessing," Father Silva admitted.

"That's it?" Lino asked, thinking. "'Sick' and 'rest' make sense. Mary Alice was no doubt exhausted. Who wouldn't want rest under those circumstances? Did she offer anything else?"

"No. I read the words back to her, and she signaled for a nurse. A day later she died."

"Not much to work with, is it?"

Father Silva shook his head. "Buried with the poor woman, I'm afraid." He put the papers inside the folder and closed it. "Let me fix you some lunch. You look like you could use a boost."

"I've got to get back to Provincetown."

Father Silva stood. "I won't take no for an answer. Come on, young man, this way. Might find a bit of scotch to go along with it. Come along."

"No, no."

Father Silva stopped at the door. "This way."

"On one condition. Let me borrow Mary Alice's papers."

"Think you can make something of them?"

"I can try."

Father Silva handed them over.

Twenty-One

It was early evening when Lino pulled into the driveway of the red house. He knew something was not right when he saw a distressed Diane standing near the kitchen door, her arms folded across her chest. He parked and jumped out of his SUV.

"What's wrong?" he asked.

"Katharine's gone off on her own," Diane said.

Lino's heart sank. "Run away?"

"I'm afraid so."

"Where's Colleen?"

Diane motioned past the cottage toward Bradford Street. "She's following the dune trail. She said Katharine took it once before when she wandered off."

"Damn," Lino grumbled. "She also took off along the beach once and toward town once, and once she hid in the woods behind the cottage. Did anybody check there?"

"I did as soon as Colleen called me."

"Why didn't someone call me?" Lino shot back. "I could have been here sooner."

Diane reached out and put her steadying hands on Lino's shoulders. "I know you're upset, but Colleen thought she'd find Katharine before you got home. She's been gone less than an hour. Colleen asked that I stay in the house in case your mom comes back on her own." Diane held a reassuring smile until she'd coaxed the hint of one from Lino. "That's better," she said. "We'll find her."

Lino nodded. "I think I'll walk into town and look there. Can you stay? Please?"

"Of course."

Lino started off, then turned around. "I've hired someone to help Colleen."

"She told me."

"His name is Roger Langsford. His phone number is on my desk in the cottage. Would you give him a call, and tell him we can't wait any longer for him to start? He needs to be here tomorrow."

"I'll do it." Diane stepped close and kissed Lino on the cheek. "Don't worry."

"I'll do my best," Lino said and walked down the drive.

Provincetown's street layout is like a ladder. Two miles of the nearly straight Commercial and Bradford streets make up the rails, and dozens of small side streets make up the rungs. Bradford doesn't have an East End sidewalk, so Lino started walking to the center of town on Commercial, thinking his mother might have done the same.

He looked up the side streets, some little more than sandy lanes containing a few tiny cottages built decades ago by Portuguese fisherman. In bad weather they'd haul their dories through the sand right up to their front doors. The bay was only fifty feet away. This had been Lino's play world when he was a kid. Pirates. Cowboys. Firemen. Adventure everywhere. Carol and her young girlfriends needed rescuing, and Lino and his pals were only too willing, usually with only seconds to spare.

Commercial Street was empty until Lino got to Howland Street and the beginning of the East End gallery district. People filled the streets here, looking through lighted windows at the artwork, holding hands, kissing. Lino interrupted two men locked in an embrace, busy hands roaming, and asked if they'd seen an elderly woman looking a bit confused, a bit lost.

They hadn't. He kicked himself for not bringing a photograph of her, for not being more prepared, but how do you prepare for this, he wondered. We are all amateurs at the endgame, at the stumbles and falls, the hospital stays, the tubes, the wires, the funerals.

The center of town was like a knot with strands of people filing into restaurants for their seven o'clock reservations. Lino hated it down here at this hour when every breath, every look, every sexy move was directed at one goal: Don't go home alone. Being alone was a painful mix of failure, old age and every inadequacy imaginable injected straight to the heart. No one came to Provincetown to be alone. They came to find love and sex and happiness, even if only for a night.

The sight of Tony Santos broke Lino's thoughts. Tony was undoing a traffic jam at the intersection bordering Lopes Square. Lino waited for the cars to clear, then followed the foot traffic mob across the street.

"Tony." Lino crowded him. "Any chance you've seen my mother?"

"Don't tell me." Tony's arms whirled like rotors as he waved pedestrians one way, cars another. "She wander off again?"

Lino nodded. "She's been gone about an hour. If you see her, don't let her get away."

"You can count on me, Lino. I'll put in a call to the station, put everybody on alert."

"Thanks, and Tony, the tip about the Jackstones worked out. They led me to an old friend of Jerry Dunn's from seminary days. I think you spoke to him. You couldn't forget him. The guy had only one arm."

Tony stepped back as if taking a new measure of Lino. "I may have. So?"

"So why didn't you tell me the truth when I asked if Father Dunn was gay? Could that be the demon Captain Ray was talking about floating around the rafters of St. Peter's? Was somebody blackmailing Father Dunn to keep his past quiet?"

"What happened to stealth, Lino, staying in the background in all of this? I can't talk to you now, I'm busy. Move along now. You're holding up traffic."

Lino did as told and walked through Lopes Square. He descended the stairs down to the beach in front of the Surf Club Restaurant. Maybe his mother sought the solace of the sea.

Low tide was an hour away. In spots the beach already ran out fifty yards before finding water. Lino walked toward the Reggae music that blared from a beachfront condo. He approached the deck and asked the partying crowd if anyone had seen a small, elderly woman come by, looking a bit lost.

A young man wearing red shorts and a yellow tank top waved Lino to the party with a beer in his hand. "Come on up, man. You can do better than an old woman. Come on up and look around, take your pick."

"Some other time."

"There is no other time, man. The ferry back to Boston leaves in a few hours. The time is now."

The music lingered a hundred yards down the beach and mixed with voices from other parties. Lino smelled the burn of a joint. Somewhere an argument flared. Two women angrily yelled at each other. One hurt voice had no fight left. She gave up, crushed and crying. It made Lino feel like he shouldn't be there, like he was looking into someone's soul, and he knew he had no right for even the briefest glimpse.

He hurried along, grateful for the mellow evening light that illuminated the wooden pilings beneath the waterfront houses. A hundred yards from his own dock, a voice shocked him.

"Adilino." It was Katharine, her voice a raspy whisper. "Here."

Lino looked around. Pilings the size of telephone poles blocked her from view.

"Mother? Mom? Where are you?"

She craned her neck around a piling so he could see half of her face. "Shhhh. Hurry. Shhh."

He rushed toward her. "Are you all right?" He slid his hands across her arms. "Did you fall? Are you sure you're all right?" The questions gushed from him. "Why are you hiding?"

"I saw them."

"Saw who?"

She pointed toward the bay. Lino followed the line of her shaking hand.

"There's nothing out there but the usual boats," he said. "Come on, let's go back to the house." He put his arm around her bony shoulders. She was brittle and cold to the bone from standing in the cool shade. "You're freezing," he said, rubbing her arms to warm her. "You're cold as ice."

She stepped out of the shadows and out of Lino's grasp. He hesitated, then followed her over the wet sand to the edge of the tide line, where the *Pico II* floated in shallow water. Katharine waded in ankle deep and stopped. When the boat swung on its mooring line, Lino saw the uneven block letters painted crudely in black paint above the casting deck: *Why didn't you help me, Dad? Why didn't you stop me?*

The air around Lino suddenly felt thick and clammy, his insides confused and frazzled. He closed his eyes, hoping when he opened them he'd see the mistake his vision provided. But there was no mistake. His heart nearly ruptured at the sight of the paint applied in the same harsh strokes Stevie had used when he painted black lines across the living room.

Lino turned to his mother. "You saw who did this?"

Her head bobbed. "Yes. Last night. I couldn't sleep again and was looking out the window at the moon. They came in a little boat."

"Who came?"

"I don't know that, Adilino. At first I thought it was you taking someone fishing, but when your boat didn't go out, I knew it wasn't."

"Why didn't you call me?"

"I meant to." She thought hard, dredging up the memory. "I think I went into your room."

"I'm in the cottage now."

She didn't seem to hear. "I looked into your room this morning, I know I did."

Lino didn't correct her. "I was away."

"Oh."

"Let's get you inside."

Lino held her so she wouldn't fall. After a few steps Katharine stopped to catch her breath. When she did, Lino stole one look back.

For one resounding moment, everything in him seemed to seize up. Then, as if set free by the gatekeeper of his emotions, the accusations scrawled in black paint hurtled through his veins like poison. It didn't matter who had rowed out in the boat in the dead of night or who'd held the brush. Only one person who had seen Steven's handiwork could have hired this done, and only one person would have reason to plunge such a spiteful dagger: his wife. Was she prodded by her new lawyer? Urged on by her father? Or did this nightmare come to her on her own?

"I'm cold." Katharine's voice even shivered.

Lino tore off his shirt and draped it over his mother. "Come on, we'll get you something hot. Be careful of the stairs now." He eased her across the street and into the house, his thoughts jumping ahead to the telephone call he was anxious to make.

Twenty-Two

Lino picked up the phone and punched the numbers as if poking out Linda's brown eyes. When she answered, he let loose.

"What the hell are you doing?"

"Lino?" Shock clung to her voice.

"Answer me. What the hell are you doing?"

He could almost feel her resolve reaching out over the phone lines, getting stronger as it grew into a full-fledged defense.

"You're not supposed to call here. Talk to my attorney if you have something to say."

"Why did you do it?"

"My father thought Solomon would produce a better settlement. Why else change lawyers?"

"I'm not talking about lawyers, Linda, and you damn well know it."

"The only other thing we have in common is the death of our son. Is that why you called? You want to talk about the night you forced him to swallow that poison? He didn't want to take those pills, and I didn't want him to either, but you knew best. You always did."

"That's not fair, Linda, but I'm not talking about Steven."

"Fine," Linda said, her voice sliding from shock to ice. "What are you talking about? Not that it matters."

Lino heard the harsh candor in her voice. "You don't know, do you?"

"I don't know, and I don't care," she said. "I'm too tired to care, Lino, I'm tired down to my bones. Between you and my father, life is a grinding hell. I would have settled our divorce weeks ago so I could pick up the pieces and move on, but my father wouldn't hear of it."

"Why?"

"Because you hadn't suffered enough. He lives for nothing else but to make you squirm."

Lino felt his stomach clinch. "That's bullshit," he spit back. "Have him find his only child hanging from a rope, then get back to me about suffering. Have him ..." Lino heard the phone go dead. "Linda? Goddamn it, Linda, don't hang up on me. Linda? Goddamn you, Linda."

For the longest time after his son's death, Lino did not quite believe it. Even after the funeral, it didn't really sink in. He held on to the thought that any time now, the spell would be broken, and Steven would walk through the door with one of his friends and scurry off to do homework. As reality began to set in, Lino's grief welled inside him like a balloon, shortening his breath until he couldn't speak. On more than one occasion in public, tears flooded down his cheeks without warning. Too wounded to feel ashamed, Lino turned away and kept turning until every emotion was wound tightly inside. Linda said he ticked like a bomb waiting for the right mixture of anger and pain to set off the explosion. The black paint on the *Pico II* produced his anger; the phone call to Linda his pain.

Lino dialed a second number and listened to the ringing, aware of his lungs pumping air like a bellows. When Edwin answered, Lino said, "First you bring on a new lawyer to screw up my settlement, then you hire goons to trash my boat. That's the end of it, Edwin. That's the last fucking straw."

"Are you threatening me?"

"I'm telling you to leave me alone."

"Or else what, Lino? What do you think you could do to me that would be worse than what you've already done? Well? I'm listening."

"Why are you doing this?"

"Because you shifted my priorities, Lino. I used to look forward to my life, to coming to the office every day, to working hard, but mostly to planning for the future. I was a grandfather.

That's what grandfathers do, they plot and plan and offer advice to their grandchildren. You stole that from me, Lino. You crushed those moments I looked forward to and crushed a part of me along with it. Now I live to see to it that you feel worse than I do. That's my life's priority. I don't like it anymore than you, but that's the way it is. Every day we live, I want you to feel worse than me. It looks like someone else has the same idea."

"What do you mean, someone else?"

"I mean that I didn't hire anybody to do anything to your boat. I have Mark Solomon to make you miserable, and it's all perfectly legal. He's all I need."

Lino poured himself another double, trying to drown the dark current of bitterness that pulsed through him. He'd been so certain Linda or Edwin Colas was behind the damage to his boat that learning otherwise shifted the ground beneath his feet. The scotch steadied it, or so it seemed. Lino downed his third drink and grabbed his keys.

He wheeled into the drive in front of the police station just as two officers opened the rear door of their cruiser and dragged a meat-slab of a man in handcuffs to his feet. The man, unshaven and wearing only jeans and the kind of yellow rubber waders fishermen wear while hauling nets, was a billboard for tattoos. From one wrist to the other and across his back, a swirl of blue and rose designs stained his skin. No color was as bright as the purple around his left eye, swollen shut by what Lino guessed was somebody's fist. Lino waited until they had enough time to clear the waiting area, then plowed up the walk and into the station.

"I want to report a crime." Lino leaned close to the glass so he could see the dispatcher more clearly. She caught the smell of alcohol on his breath immediately. "I said I want to ..."

"You've been drinking."

" ...a crime."

She got out of her chair, hands on her hips. "You can't come in here making demands. How'd you get here?"

"Drove."

"Drunk on your ass."

Lino's protest was drowned out by a shout from a door behind the dispatcher. "Who's drunk on his ass?" a heavily built officer asked, stepping out. Lino recognized Chief Bicknell from photographs in the newspaper. "What's going on here?" Bicknell's brown eyes narrowed to slits when he caught the hint of booze. He ran one hand over his crew cut, then down the side of his square jaw. "Who the hell are you?"

Lino told him.

"Ah, yes, Tony's friend."

"I don't have any friends," Lino snapped. "I'm here to report a crime. I want some sonofabitch arrested. Maybe two sonofabitches."

"Want to lock him up for his own good?" the dispatcher asked her chief.

"Me?" Lino's eyes popped wide. "For what?" Lino turned his gaze to the unforgiving Bicknell, looking every inch the former drill sergeant he was. "You're not going to do a damn thing, are you?"

"That depends."

"On what?"

"Giving me your car keys."

"Why should I?"

"Because you don't want to spend the night in jail."

The Lobster Pot is a Provincetown institution known for its chowder and seafood, especially its Friday night all-you-can-eat fish fry. That it had parking nearby and was only a few blocks from Lino's cottage made it an obvious choice for Bicknell, who sat across from Lino in one of the restaurant's many booths. They'd finished their salads and were sipping black coffee when Bicknell said, "I'm going to speak freely, Lino. Because you smell like a distillery, you are going to listen. If you do, you might not get written up."

"I'm all ears," Lino said, as a plate of broiled scrod was placed before him.

Bicknell took a bite of swordfish. "I have friends who have friends in law enforcement all across the state. Sooner or later we all owe each other a favor. I called a few in so I could put together some information about you and your work with Colas, Haggerty and Johnson."

"I saw the files on Tony's desk," Lino said. "Impressive, but they won't tell you much."

"They'll tell us you had motive: Your son's suicide, your assault on Father Donovan and Father Jerry's connection to Sweetbriar. Someone might connect those dots and say you had a very good reason to get rid of the priest and burn down his church."

"If you believed that, we wouldn't be having this conversation. I'd be behind bars, and you'd have a feather in your cap for solving the case before the State Police did. But I'm sorry to disappoint you. I came back to Provincetown for other reasons, nothing more."

"Your mother."

"That's right."

"That checked out," Bicknell said with a slight smile. "I spoke with Dr. Coldwell."

"I wouldn't have expected anything less," Lino admitted.

"I know you wouldn't," Bicknell said, "that's why I wanted to talk with you. You're a trained investigator, you know how these things play out. A bit of evidence here, a bit of evidence there, and pretty soon even a blind man sees the pattern."

"Bring it into focus for me. I don't see anything."

Bicknell dabbed the side of his mouth with his napkin. "The State Police all along have been treating this case as a missing person investigation, not a murder. Why? The plane tickets for one thing. Seems Father Dunn had in mind to take off with someone. The bones found out in the dunes for another. Not human bones. Then a witness saw someone who looked like Jerry Dunn in Miami, followed by a sighting in Tampa, back in Miami, then Dallas and on and on. The last I heard, the Staties were focusing their investigation in and around Detroit."

"The man gets around," Lino said.

"Or somebody just likes calling the tip line. Anything to keep us from finding out what really happened to that priest."

"So you're not buying that Father Dunn is still alive."

"No, I'm not."

"Why?"

Bicknell shrugged. "Like I said, you know how investigations play out. More importantly, you know how the guilty try to stay out of prison by making things appear as they are not. I've solved a crime or two, Lino. It helps to think like a criminal, wouldn't you say?"

"It comes in handy."

"So does knowing your way around the country if you wanted to create a ruse. You investigated insurance fraud cases coast to coast."

"Back to me again?"

"Just thinking. I mean, you took quite a pay cut when you left Colas, Haggerty and Johnson, and then there are your mother's medical bills." Bicknell let the thought hang.

"What do the State Police think of your theory that I'm the guilty one?" Lino asked.

Bicknell slid his plate to one side and folded his hands in front of him on the table. "I haven't told them."

"Why not?"

"I could be wrong."

"You don't want egg on your face."

Bicknell cracked a smile. "No, I don't."

"Why tell me all this?" Lino asked and finished the last bite of his dinner.

"Because I can't shake the feeling that you're the man we're after," Bicknell said evenly. "You're an expert at uncovering fraud, which means to me that you're also an expert in creating it. Maybe one so clever, you'll get away with it, if you invent enough Jerry Dunns and run the State Police ragged."

"That would only leave you trying to prove I'm guilty, is that it?"

"Me and your old friend, Tony Santos."

The hair prickled on the back of Lino's neck. "Tony?"

Bicknell took two twenty-dollar bills from his wallet and set them on the table. "Tony. He's a good cop. Sort of a go-getter like I used to be. I can just see the look on the faces of those State cops when Tony and I solve us a murder case. They'll turn as blue as their uniforms." Bicknell slid out of the booth and stood. "How about a ride back to the station?"

Lino climbed to his feet.

"Once you're there you can fill out a report about the sonofabitch you wanted arrested."

"I've changed my mind."

"What's the matter, you don't trust your local police department?"

Twenty-Three

Morning's first faint light broke as Lino rowed out to the *Pico II* to begin the arduous task of sanding out the stains. The natural oils in the teak kept the black paint from soaking deep into the wood. Still, it would take hours to remove the despicable, accusing letters. Lino started with sixty-grit sandpaper mounted on a wooden block. He worked with the wood's grain, pushing hardest over the paint. The first pass took nearly two hours and only knocked off the shine. The second time around, he focused on individual words, starting with "Dad." He heard his own voice answering: *I did try to help. I did.*

He heard a second voice. "Who could be so mean?" Lino looked up. The tide had fallen low enough for Diane to walk out, carrying two mugs. "They ought to be taken somewhere and shot," she said.

"If I could find them, I'd pull the trigger."

Lino smelled the coffee, took the two mugs and put them down on the deck. He offered Diane a hand as she sat on the gunwale and swung her bare legs inside the cockpit.

"I thought you could use a little pick-me-up," she said and kissed him on the cheek. "I meant my question. Who could be so heartless and rotten to write such a thing?"

"I'll let you know when I find out." Lino sipped his coffee. "Hits the spot," he said. "How did you know I was running low on caffeine?"

"I've been watching you out the window."

"That explains it."

"You work on this boat like you're a doctor, and she is a living, breathing patient. I think it's wonderful."

Lino shrugged.

"Sad, too," Diane added.

"Why sad?"

"Because of how much those words hurt you." Diane ran her hand over the sanded wood, over the faintly discolored area that still shouted out for help. "You can't deny it."

"I'm not denying anything." Lino savored more of his coffee. "Did I ever tell you that you make a damn fine cup?"

"Don't change the subject," Diane chided. "Pain is a sign that something's wrong. You need to deal with it."

"I am," Lino said. "I'm putting my boat back together so I can earn a living. I can't have charters looking at this crap and asking questions about who I didn't help. Definitely not good for business. Thankfully, Hal's covering. I should take you down to Nauset Charters and introduce you. You'd like him. Want to go?"

"You're changing the subject. At least, you're trying." Diane stirred her coffee with her index finger. "You did all you could for your son, Lino. You can't give more than you're capable of. You simply can't give more than what you have. It's impossible, and it's wasted energy to beat yourself with the whip of the impossible."

"Am I listening to the voice of experience?"

"You are."

"Let me guess. You wanted to be a scientist, a biologist studying the comings and goings of the fruit fly."

"Don't tease. I wanted to be a good wife. Every time I stepped to the altar, I told myself that nothing was more important from that moment on than being a good wife."

"What makes a good wife?" Lino asked.

"I don't know. I never was one, and the men in my life walked away because I couldn't figure it out. What drove me crazy was that I was smart enough to figure out what being a good wife was but never proved it to any husband. Maybe I was lying to myself. Maybe it wasn't really important to me after all."

"How so?"

"My parents wanted me to be happy. For them, that meant my being married. I let them convince me that's where I'd find my happiness, too, but I didn't. Still, I beat myself with the whip of the impossible for a long time."

"Why did you stop?"

"Because one day I realized that only I felt the sting. I wasn't punishing anyone else. In fact, no one else gave a damn. I threw the whip down and got on with my life, which has turned out rather wonderfully, if I do say so." Diane's full smile softened the mood. "I like having you in it, Lino. We're good together in our distant sort of way."

"I'd say very good in our distant sort of way. Now you'll have to get more distant, or I'll never get this work done, and pretty soon I'll be destitute." Lino finished his coffee and handed the mug back to Diane.

"Have you told the police what happened to your boat?"

"I went up to the station last night," Lino said without providing details.

"What did they say?"

"They've got more important things to do."

"Which means you really do have to find out on your own who did this, don't you?"

"More or less," Lino admitted. "Mother was up looking out the window. She saw men and a boat, but I'm not holding my breath she'll ever be able to tell me anything more. Too bad you weren't looking out your window."

"I wish I had been," Diane said as Lino gently swung her bare legs over the side. "You're making me walk the plank, and there's no plank."

"You'll manage. You always do."

"Wait a second. I have a message from Colleen. Roger Langsford called this morning. He's starting today." Diane glanced at her watch. "He'll be by the house in about an hour."

"Did he mention gardening tools?" Lino asked.

Diane shrugged. "I didn't speak to him. Should he have?"

"He should have," Lino said. "I'll take care of it."

Colleen heard the ruckus in the shed and hurried out of the house. "Who's in there? Hello?"

Lino backed out, cradling a hoe, a shovel and a spade.

"Getting ready for Roger?"

"He told you?" Lino leaned the garden tools against the shed wall. "What do you think? He's going to work his way into mother's heart as a part-time gardener."

"I suppose it all depends on whether Katharine remembers that gardeners don't sleep over."

"We'll have to ease into that," Lino admitted.

"Anything to avoid the Mrs. Hawkins disaster."

"My thinking exactly," Lino said as Roger Langsford pulled up in front of the red house and parked. When he got out of the car, he looked every bit the gardener from his new baseball cap and khaki coveralls to his boots. Lino's spirit soared. "Maybe there's hope," he said and introduced Colleen to her new associate.

"Pleased," Roger said with the bob of his head. There were handshakes all around.

"Welcome," Lino said. "Sorry we had to move things up a few days."

"Don't give it a second thought."

The three of them walked toward the house. "I understand you spent your career in Boston," Colleen offered.

"That's right, all of it at Mass General."

"Might as well work with the best if you have to work at all," Colleen added. "I was a nurse's aide."

"At the General?"

"No, no. My husband ran a small construction company out here on the Cape. I spent my time at the hospital in Hyannis."

"I'm sure between the two of us, Katharine will get the best of care," Roger said, looking around. "Is she here?"

"In the house," Lino said, taking the hoe that leaned against the shed and giving it to Roger. "The key to her heart is through her flowers."

"I understand. We'll take things very slowly." Roger slipped on a pair of gloves. "Where would you like me to start?"

Lino led the way around back to a shaded area against the fence filled with hostas and competing weeds. He bent down and cradled a plant. "If it has a large leaf like this, keep it. If it doesn't, take it out. We'll give you more instruction when we move to the next bed."

"As you wish," Roger said and began weeding like the amateur he was.

Back on the *Pico II*, a welcoming breeze swirled around the coaming, sending scraps of used sandpaper flying. Lino scurried along the deck, collecting them before they flew over the side. One sheet lodged in front of the console. As Lino reached for it, a printed receipt fluttered by.

At first he thought it was his, since he had an account at Land's End Marine Supply, but he hadn't bought bottom paint for his boat since early spring, and that paint was blue. The receipt, dated three days ago, was for ten gallons of black. Ten gallons would paint Lino's boat from top to bottom fifty times with some left over. Whoever bought that much paint had a boat as big as a trawler, and the only place to haul a trawler for painting in Provincetown was Flyer's Boatyard in the West End. Lino folded the receipt in his pocket and climbed into his dinghy for the row to Flyer's to have a look around.

Twenty-Four

Lino did some of his best thinking rowing. The simple reach forward, the catch of the oars in the water and the pull back with a long, even stroke created a pace for his thoughts; but with each strong stroke across the water toward Flyer's, he felt he was rowing deeper into a sea of confusion. He believed Linda and Edwin Colas were not responsible for the hideous painted words on *Pico II* that went through Lino's heart like rusty nails. But if not them, who? Who else wanted to remind Lino that he'd failed miserably as a parent? Even though he'd tried his best, his best was not nearly enough, and he would live with that shortcoming for the rest of his life. Why would someone other than Linda or Edwin want to remind Lino of his parental failures? Why attack him there? Why attack at all?

The row produced no answers, but the sight of a beaten-up trawler resting out of the water on Flyer's rails gave Lino hope. He shipped oars and pushed a few rental sailboats aside to make room at the crowded dock. He tied his painter around a cleat and hurried up the connecting ramp past the white, cinder block building that housed Flyer's repair shop and offices. A man, his back to Lino, wielded a sander over two new planks on the port side of the dark green trawler.

Lino checked the transom. The *Alice Mae* sailed out of Sakonnet Point, Rhode Island. Rollers, brushes and a ten-gallon bucket of black bottom paint sat on a pallet near the starboard side. Lino checked his receipt. The brand on the bucket was a match.

Lino moved toward the man. "Hey? Say there." The high-pitched whine from the sander's motor blanketed his voice. "Hey?" he shouted.

Lino bent down and unplugged the extension cord. The silence spun the man around, the same tattooed, purple-eyed man Lino had seen last night at the police station.

"I need a little of your time," Lino said.

"Ain't got any," the man snapped and reconnected the sander. He turned back to the boat and froze when the power again went off.

"Won't take much time at all," Lino said, dropping the unplugged extension cord to the ground.

"Who the hell are you?"

"A man with a lot of questions," Lino said.

"I ain't got no answers." The man flipped the remains of his cigarette on the ground and blew out smoke. "Now I got work to do, know what I mean? Get the fuck outta here."

Lino rubbed one hand across the boat's rough hull. "Look, I know how hard it is to keep one of these old tubs afloat. I know how much it costs. That ten gallons of bottom paint you've got runs over five hundred dollars."

"So?"

"So transients pay cash in this business, and you're racking up quite a bill, hauling out for a few days, making repairs, not out on the water making money. Add to that a night in jail. My guess is you couldn't have made bail if someone hadn't paid you well for painting my boat night before last." Lino let the charge hang. "You left a receipt on board."

"I don't know what you're talkin' about."

"Sure you do. What did the cops pick you up for?"

"Kickin' the shit out of a fag," the man sneered. "A crewmate and me seen a bunch of'em swishing around and couldn't resist." He reached toward his swollen eye. "One of the slimy bastards got lucky, but he regrets it this morning. I made sure of that."

"This morning doesn't interest me. I'm interested in what you and your mate were doing two nights ago."

"Same as always. Workin' on the boat and drinkin' a few beers."

"Before or after you had your little boat ride out in the harbor?" Lino asked.

The man's fist slammed into a new plank, a show for Lino's benefit, indicating a night in jail hadn't squelched his willingness to fight. "This boat ain't been nowhere."

"I can see that," Lino said, motioning toward Flyer's rental field. "You borrowed one of those skiffs for a few hours. You already had the bottom paint. All you had to do was find my boat. Who told you what she looks like?"

For the longest time the man didn't move. When he did, he reached down and picked up the orange extension cord. When he tried to plug in the sander, Lino's foot stomped the cord to the ground.

"How much were you paid for the paint job?"

"You're a pain in the ass, you know that?"

"Who paid you to write that trash on my boat?"

"I don't know what you're talking about."

Lino took the receipt from his pocket and handed it to the man. "I'm sure somebody at Land's End will remember all your tattoos."

The man crushed the receipt in his hand and tossed it. "You've got nothing."

"I've got an eyewitness," Lino said coolly. "She saw two men row up in the dead of night."

Silence.

"She saw one of you go on board and do your dirty work. A few words dabbed in black paint. What do a few words matter? They mattered to the person who hired you, and they mattered to me."

Without warning, the man hurled the sander at Lino's head. Lino swatted it to the ground with his open hands as if it were a toy, then lowered his shoulder and charged with startling quickness. The man slammed into the huge rudder but kept his balance and came forward, swinging wide, looping hooks.

Lino bounced on the balls of his feet, ducking and swaying. He targeted the man's swollen eye. Lino connected with a stinging left. He followed with another and another until the swelling split, and blood ran from a faucet down the man's face.

"Had enough?"

"Fuck you."

"Who hired you?"

The man lunged toward Lino, missed and fell awkwardly to his knees. Lino curled back, wrapping one arm around the man's neck while jamming a knee deep into his spine.

"Who hired you?" Lino demanded, jerking the man's head back when he didn't answer. "Who?"

"I don't know. I never saw his face."

"Who?" Lino pulled harder, the man's neck stretched to the breaking point. "Who?"

"I'm tellin' the truth," the man managed through clenched teeth. "You're killin' me. Let the fuck go, will ya?"

"Lino!" The voice moved closer. "Lino! Don't kill the man!" Tony Santos ran breathlessly past a crowd gathered along the docks. "Step back, folks," Tony yelled. "Keep back. Give us some room."

Tony's partner, John Trask, approached from the street, his gun drawn and aimed at Lino. "You want backup?"

"I think we can handle this," Tony said. "Let the man go, Lino. Don't let that temper of yours get the better of you."

Lino gave one last parting tug, then released his grip.

The man wiped blood from his face and worked his neck in circles. "Fucker coulda killed me."

"You want to press charges?" Tony asked.

The man considered it. "No," he spit back. "I wanna get the fuck outta this goddamned town."

"Sounds like a good idea," Tony said, motioning for Trask to put his gun away. "This looks over now."

Disgusted, Lino turned away.

"Where do you think you're going?" Tony asked.

"Away from you before I do something I might regret."

"What's that all about?"

"A conversation I had with Bicknell."

Surprise flashed across Tony's expression. "I thought I told you to stay away from him."

"So I wouldn't find out what you and he were up to?"

"It's not what you think."

"I'll give you five minutes."

"Big of you."

Lino's eyes held fire. "Five minutes."

"Not here where the whole town can listen. I've got a car out on the street."

Twenty-Five

The small plane's engine kicked to life with a puff of white smoke and a throaty roar as it taxied to the head of the runway at Provincetown's airport. Both men watched the plane lift into the air and climb out over the ocean until it became no more than a dot.

"Feel better after beating that man to a pulp?"

"That's not what we need to talk about, Tony, and you know it."

"The business with Bicknell."

"Not a very good move on your part, Tony."

"It's not the way it looks."

"Or the way it sounds? Bicknell all but accused me of killing the priest. You told me you convinced Bicknell that I had nothing to do with any of this." Lino's eyes bore in on his old friend. "Why did you lie to me, Tony?"

"I didn't. Look, at one point or another everybody in town was a suspect. Names were tossed out in an instant and shot down just as fast." Tony held Lino's stare. "I stood up for you, Lino. I did."

"Not the way Bicknell tells it. Somebody's lying, and I don't think it's him."

"Listen …"

"No, you listen," Lino blurted. "You lied about knowing that Jerry Dunn was gay, too. What's going on, Tony? What's your game?"

Tony grabbed the wheel as if strangling some intensely private emotion. "A few things got out of hand, that's all. I never, not for one single second, thought you had anything to do with any of this. That's the truth."

"Then why does Bicknell think otherwise?"

"He's frustrated, that's all. He's like everyone else trying to find a foothold in this case. The State Police think Jerry Dunn is still alive and spin their wheels trying to find him. Bicknell thinks Dunn is dead. He doesn't want to let go of you until he finds something or someone else to sink his teeth into."

"He says you agree with him."

"That's what I want him to think. Besides, if it weren't for me, he wouldn't think Father Jerry died out on those dunes."

"Why?"

"Because I tossed him a bone. Literally, a cross." Tony's gaze settled on Lino. "Do you want me to spell it out?"

"Your five minutes are running low," Lino reminded.

"All right. I was working my own angle in all this when Bicknell got a little close to my theory about what happened to Father Jerry, so I created a diversion to throw him off the track. A bit of genius if I do say so myself." Tony beamed and said, "It was my idea to plant that cross out in the dunes."

Lino's eyes narrowed. "You what?"

"I know it sounds stupid, but ..."

"Stupid? Are you crazy?"

"It gets better," Tony said, inhaling full lungs of air, then blowing them out with a gush. "I had Father Silva help me. I told him where to put the cross."

"There's no question about it, you are crazy."

"He wanted to help any way he could. Besides, I couldn't take the chance of getting caught. Bicknell would skin me alive."

"What about Father Silva?"

"Even if someone had seen him, who would ever suspect a priest of planting evidence?"

"Why did he agree to help?" Lino asked.

"Because I told him it would take me one step closer to bringing in Jerry Dunn's killer."

"You say that like you know who it is."

"I have a pretty good idea. All I need is a few more days."

"Why not bring him in now?"

"Because there's money involved, Lino. Blackmail. I'm setting up the details for the last drop."

"Who's helping you?"

"No one. I'm playing this out on my own."

"You sure you can handle that?"

"I'd expect you to ask something like that, Lino. You were at the top of your game when you worked for Colas, and I was writing traffic tickets and directing tourists across the street here in Provincetown."

"I didn't mean ..."

"I know. Nobody means to question if I'm good enough. Even my own father has his doubts. Tony-the-steady, he calls me. He's right. I'm steady and predictable and capable of more. This is my chance, Lino, and I'm not going to let it slip away. I'm going to solve this case, and I'm going to solve it my way. You'll see."

"If you're right, this person has already killed once. What makes you think ..?"

"What makes me think I'm a match for him?"

"That's one question. Another is how do you keep from getting killed?"

"What if I have you as backup? Would that do?"

"What about Bicknell and members of your own force?"

"Like I said, you were tops when you were with Colas. I'd like to have the best if I'm going to have anyone. What do you say?"

"I'd say I need more information."

"When I have it, you'll have it. That's all I can tell you right now. You'll just have to wait."

"That's my answer, Tony. You'll just have to wait until I see what you've gotten yourself into," Lino said.

Tony reached for the key in the ignition and turned it. The engine fired to life. "I'll see if I can't think of something to sweeten the pot," Tony said, "make you want to jump in."

"You know where to find me," Lino said as the patrol car left the lot.

Twenty-Six

"You look worn out," Diane said as Lino stepped into her studio. She put her brush down on the easel's tray and touched the side of his bruised face. "Worn out and banged up. I take it you found the man."

Lino poured himself a cup of black coffee and took a sip. "I found the man," he said.

"Did you take my advice and shoot him?"

Lino chuckled and shook his head. "Something a little more basic. Something less likely to send me to prison."

"I'd come for the conjugal visits."

"Thanks." Lino sat on a paint-covered bar stool. "You need some comfortable furniture up here."

"The comfortable furniture is downstairs. Do you want to go down?"

"I'm fine," Lino said, looking around at the canvases leaning against three of the walls. The fourth wall was glass, letting in pure, unadulterated light. "I just don't want to go home yet."

Diane heard the weariness in Lino's voice. "Let's go downstairs. I'll make some fresh coffee and get you something to eat, maybe even tuck you up. Come on."

Lino raised his hand and waved her off. "What I'd like is for you to get back to work."

"Don't be silly."

"I'm just catching my breath and interrupting you. Sorry."

"Don't be." She studied Lino's face as if she were about to paint it. "Are you sure?"

"Positive."

Diane hesitated, then picked up her brush. Lino had seen the transformation dozens of times, and each time, her energy replenished him. Diane was now a conductor, her brush a wand, her colors the music. Only the notes were not on a score, they were singing in her soul, desperate to get out. She worked quickly, her speed matched by her confidence, which filled the studio.

While Diane brushed a gray-green foreground for the sky, she glanced at Lino. "You're awfully quiet."

"Thinking."

"About?"

"A kid I grew up with. We were good friends for a while. We planned our lives together. We had it all mapped out, all the great things that we were going to do together right here in Provincetown."

"Like what?" Diane asked, clearly interested.

"It doesn't matter. None of it worked out."

"Why not?"

"Because I went away, and he stayed. Now he's trying to prove something to himself. He's trying to get somebody to pay attention."

"Not a bad thing, is it?"

"In some cases, no. I just have a bad feeling about this. I can't exactly put my finger on why," Lino admitted.

Diane arced a bluish semicircle across the top half of the canvas, then blended it with the green. "Are you still friends with this person?"

"No," Lino said, "not anymore."

"Then why does any of it bother you?"

"Because they were good plans. Deep down, I wish they'd worked out." Lino put his coffee cup down. "I just wonder what went wrong."

"You grew up, maybe," Diane offered.

"That must be it." Lino stood and kissed her on the cheek. "Thanks."

"For what?"

"Energy. I stole some from you. I'll see you later."

Lino found his mother and Roger Langsford in the side yard of the red house, pulling weeds from a massive stand of purple Siberian iris. They looked like old friends, chatting and working at a leisurely pace, throwing uprooted weeds into a plastic bucket brimming full.

In front of the house Colleen adjusted a sprinkler to water the dahlias. She straightened up, and a pleasant smile warmed her face when she saw Lino.

"How's Roger doing?" Lino asked.

"He's doing fine. Katharine really seems to like him." Concern replaced her smile. "What happened to you?"

"Nothing to worry about, just the hazards of a small job I took on. So you think our little ruse is working?"

"Does Katharine think Roger's an RN in disguise? I don't think she has a clue. The big test will be when he stays the night."

"When's that?" Lino asked.

"Sometime this week. We're taking it slowly, letting everybody get comfortable. When the time seems right, he'll stay."

"I like that idea. Don't force anything. We want this to work. It has to work," Lino added.

"I've got my fingers crossed," Colleen admitted, gaining back her smile. "Fingers and toes."

"Me, too," Lino said, walking back around the house to Katharine. He knelt down beside her and gave her a hand with a weed that seemed stronger than she. He pulled it out and said, "You should let Roger tackle the big jobs."

"They're all big jobs," Katharine said, her face red from strain. "Weeds and bugs will take over the world, Adilino. Someday they'll be all that's left."

"Not if I have anything to say about it," Roger chimed, his gloved hands yanking a weed cluster from the soil. He held high his trophy before tossing it in the bucket. "Another one bites the dust, Katharine. We live to fight another day."

Lino hadn't heard his mother laugh in months. He took it as another positive endorsement for Roger and walked back to his cottage. He rummaged through his desk drawer until he found the number he was looking for and placed a call. The phone rang a dozen times before it was answered.

"Father Silva?"

"Lino. How are you on this fine afternoon?"

"Not bad for an old man."

The old priest chuckled. "Everything's relative, young man. What can I do for you?"

"I just had a long talk with Tony Santos."

"A productive one, I hope."

"Maybe. He told me about the cross you buried in the dunes."

"I see." A lengthy pause followed. "Not my finest hour, was it? What are you going to do with that information, Adilino?"

"Am I going to turn you in, do you mean? I should."

"But?"

"But I think we ought to talk instead. I'll be working on my boat tomorrow morning. Low tide is early. Come on out."

"I'll be there. I won't disappoint."

Lino put down the phone.

Twenty-Seven

Joggers and delivery trucks filled the early morning streets in Provincetown. Lino waited for an opening, then crossed Commercial Street and launched his dinghy for the row out to the *Pico II*. It was six in the morning with a falling half-tide. A light southwesterly wind rippled across the harbor, carrying a tease of heat the day would produce. Lino wanted to beat the heat.

He lifted his tools into the cockpit and climbed aboard, tying his dinghy aft. The sight of the stain still took his breath away. Again Lino started with coarse grit sandpaper. He got down on his knees and worked from left to right, pushing evenly along the teak's grain. Progress was hard and slow and reminded Lino of a trip he and his sister had taken with their parents back to Portugal when he and Carol were children.

They had stayed with cousins in a small hillside town that overlooked the Mediterranean. The town had been built on the side of a cliff centuries ago. Its windy streets were so narrow a car couldn't pass, so all deliveries were dropped off at one end of the village and wheel-barrowed in or carried by hand.

During their visit a home in the middle of the village was being remodeled. Workers hand carried truckloads of sand and stone in buckets to the worksite four hundred yards away. One at a time, massive timbers were maneuvered through the tiny streets. The slow, tedious process was repeated over and over for days without complaint. The work was done the way it had always been done. Everyone accepted that fact and refilled the buckets until the sand and stone and timbers were gone and the house made new.

Lino remembered asking his father why the men didn't complain. "Why waste the energy?" Vincent had answered. "They'll need it for the next trip up the hill."

Lino felt the same way about sanding the paint out of his boat's teak. It was hand work, hard and slow, and required all his energy. By the time Lino had completed his first pass over the stain, the tide was almost out, and the *Pico II* tottered in a foot of water. Father Silva rolled his pants to his knees and made his way to the boat. Lino kept sanding, not looking up until he heard the priest's voice.

"Permission to come aboard?" Father Silva asked, holding his shoes and socks in one hand. "I want to do everything right, Adilino, so that I don't offend you. Again."

Lino put down the sandpaper and helped the old man climb in. The priest sat on the combing and caught his breath.

"Long walk," he said. "No doubt good for the soul." He looked around the boat, his attention on Lino's work. "Good Lord, what is that?" He looked closer. "Who put those dreadful words there?"

"I know who did it," Lino said. "I'll find out who hired him before long."

"It's horrible," the priest protested. "Why? Why do such a thing?"

"I'm trying to piece that together myself," Lino admitted, "but we're wasting valuable time. It's low water now. The tide comes back in fast. You've got about half an hour before you'll get wetter going back."

"I understand. You want information from me."

"That's right. Let's start with that tale you told about Father Jerry being taken from the burning church out to the dunes and shot."

"I wanted you to consider possibilities, Adilino. When I first brought up the notion that you help find Father Jerry, you weren't enthusiastic. I wanted to engage your imagination, to pose something that might interest you."

"Even though what you posed was a lie, because you knew how that cross got in the dunes."

"I knew, yes, but it was a small lie. I was given that cross for my many years of service at St. Peter's. When I was reassigned to another parish, I left the cross behind for the next priest. Father Jerry gave it back to me on one of those occasions when I visited Mary Alice. When I mentioned to Tony that I again had the cross in my possession, we hatched our meager plan to bury it in the dunes along with that piece of cloth. I received no pleasure in the act, believe me, and have prayed hours for forgiveness. For Sergeant Santos, too. We should not have done such a thing."

"You and Tony have quite a connection," Lino said, back at his sanding. "You trust each other, confide in each other."

"I suppose that's true. I never really thought of our conversations in those terms, but you must be right."

"Has he proposed any other sleight of hand regarding the disappearance of Father Jerry?"

"I'm not sure what you mean."

"I mean putting the cross in the dunes puts everything we assume to be true about the case in doubt."

Father Silva caught the thread. "If one fact is compromised," he said, "all so-called facts might also be."

"That's right."

"I never thought about that, Adilino. It never occurred to me."

"It must have occurred to Tony. He's a trained investigator running his own show." Lino glanced over at the troubled priest and asked again, "Has he told you of anything else about this investigation that he's manipulated in any way?"

"I'm not sure I can answer that," the priest said honestly. "Not that I'm trying to hide anything, but as I said, Tony only dribbled out a few informational morsels here and there."

"Relating to Leland Ricks?"

"No, he never mentioned him. The first time I heard that name was when you brought it up."

Lino turned back to the black stains. "The first time I spoke with Tony, he was reviewing documents relating to Colas, Haggerty and Johnson."

"I believe he had material about you in that stack of papers, too."

"You saw it?"

The priest nodded. "Yes. That's where I got the phone number for Edwin Colas."

"Did Tony encourage you to call him?"

"He didn't say I shouldn't."

"So he wasn't using you to get information from Edwin?"

Father Silva shook his head. "No need to. Tony had everything he needed in that stack of papers: background about the company, a folder on you, including your run-in with Father Donovan, information about your son's death."

Lino stopped work. "What kind of information?"

Father Silva shrugged. "I'm not positive, Lino. I only saw snippets. What I did see seemed like a police report."

"Police or insurance?" Lino prodded.

"I don't know that I'd know the difference," Father Silva admitted.

"The insurance report," Lino said, pointing to the black letters stained into the teak, "would have words like these on it. The police report wouldn't since it dealt with my run-in with Father Donovan."

Father Silva thought a moment, then said, "I would never forget those vile words, Lino, but I confess I didn't see them in the short time I had. Why does it matter?"

"Steven painted black letters like these across our living room walls. I filled out the insurance claim and took the photos of what he'd written."

"Ah, the photographs. Tony had Xeroxes of them, but they were poor, dark copies. I had no idea what they were. What does it matter?"

"Someone had to see how Steven wrote on our walls in order to paint the letters just like he did. The only place to do that was the insurance report. Apparently, Tony had a copy."

"Tony?" His name came out in a rush. "You can't believe he was behind this."

"I don't know what to believe," Lino admitted.

"Well, I do. No matter what you think of Anthony Santos, he would never stoop to such a thing as this, especially involving you, Lino. You and he were such good friends. There must be another explanation."

"Maybe," Lino said.

"Of course there is. Those files on Tony's desk were open. Anyone could have walked in and seen them. I found it rather embarrassing to see some of the financial records of St. Peter's right there for anyone to look at. After a while I asked Tony to put them away."

"What financial records?" Lino asked. "I thought they'd all burned in the fire."

"Father Jerry's burned. The records I'm speaking of were copies of financial documents held by the Church. Father Jerry was predicting a significant shortfall because of the early snows and extremely cold weather. He requested that the diocese loan St. Peter's some money to cover the anticipated debt. Plus, he'd already asked for money to cover the cost of new wiring."

"How much?"

"About one hundred thousand dollars total. Father Jerry made mention of that in the newsletter distributed at Sunday services. Some parishioners were not happy at the thought that they'd have to drop more into the collection basket."

"Including Tony?"

"Yes. He was certainly not happy. He said he was going to keep an eye on things, whatever that meant."

"Did the diocese give Father Jerry the money he'd asked for?"

"Out of emergency funds, yes. Fifty thousand. The Church has to pay its bills."

"That fifty plus the fifty the Jackstones put in makes for a tidy sum. People kill for a lot less than that," Lino said. "Did Tony ever speculate what happened to the money?"

"Not to me. He moved on to finding out what became of Father Jerry."

"And getting retired priests to bury crosses in the dunes."

"Guilty as charged."

Lino made note of the incoming tide and held Father Silva's shoes and socks while he climbed out of the boat.

"You never explained those bruises on your face, Adilino."

"I ran into a fisherman."

"I see." Father Silva reached for his shoes. "One can only hope it was St. Peter, and he knocked a bit of spiritual sense into you. You could learn a thing or two from Tony in that regard. He walks along the spiritual path as closely as any man can. I admire him for that."

"I'll take it under advisement."

"You should. Just remember, none of us achieves perfection. You, me, Tony. The effort we put forth to live the life God wants is what matters."

"I'll remember."

"What you should remember is that those who ignore God, those who reject His wisdom, have much to answer for on their day of judgment."

Lino motioned toward the water. "You're going to get wet if you don't get a move on."

"You're not listening, are you?"

"I'll talk to you later."

Father Silva turned and walked back to his car through the deepening water.

Twenty-Eight

The sandpaper cut into the teak, leaving miniscule piles of sawdust that Lino swept away after the morning's second pass over the stain. The words were still faintly visible, but the planks above the casting deck were smooth and new looking. Lino worked tirelessly, even though the muscles along his arms and back ached. Still, he kept at it, his mind dragging ideas along as he made measured progress on the wood.

As an insurance investigator Lino would often think through a crime's progression, hoping to understand the mental process that permitted someone to believe they could get away with fraud. There were always paper and electronic trails, informants with grudges to settle, and simple mistakes to help solve the case. With the Father Jerry investigation, most of the evidence went up in smoke with the church, and so far no one with a grudge had been identified. The only mistake seemed to have come from Tony Santos instructing an elderly priest to plant false evidence in the dunes. The mistake might prove harmless if Tony was telling the truth, and Father Jerry's killer was soon to be apprehended. But was Tony telling the truth? Lino wasn't sure and thought of another question to ask Father Silva to help him decide.

Lino looked toward the red house. Father Silva's car was still in the driveway. Lino collected his tools and got in his dinghy for the row ashore. He stopped at the cottage and collected the papers Mary Alice had written on her deathbed. Father Silva, Katharine, Colleen, and Roger were all sitting around his mother's kitchen table, drinking iced tea, by the time Lino arrived.

"I feel like I'm crashing a party," Lino said to no one in particular.

"It is a bit like a party," Father Silva responded as he reached over and placed his hand on Katharine's. "Always a pleasure to reacquaint with your mother." Softly, he patted her hand. "And to see she's doing so well."

Colleen handed Lino a cold glass. "You look parched."

Lino sipped his tea. "I'm fine, really."

"Just like his mother," Katharine chimed. "What was it you said, Father?"

"Strong faith and good genes," Father Silva repeated. "The best combination I know for a long and good life."

Katharine looked at her son. "Did you hear that, Adilino?"

"I did. We're a family with good genes," he said.

"No, no. You're missing the point. Father Silva is worried about you," Katharine said. "The truth be told, I am, too. You need to go to church again. Did you go to the blessing of the fleet with us?"

"I'm afraid I missed it this year."

Katharine turned to Father Silva. "He missed it," she said, disheartened. "Did you go?"

"I sat beside you and Colleen, remember?"

While Katharine searched her memory Lino said to Father Silva, "When you're through here, there's something else I'd like to ask you." Lino put his glass down and opened the screen door.

Roger got quickly to his feet. "I think I should get back to work."

Father Silva followed Roger's lead. "I should be on my way as well. Goodbye, Katharine. I'll be back to see you again soon."

"Soon," she repeated with a smile. "We'll take Lino to the blessing of the fleet."

"Of course."

Lino held the screen, then followed the two men out. He walked down the drive toward the priest's car while Roger, a few feet away, sought out more ever-present weeds.

Lino retrieved the papers Mary Alice had written and said, "I nearly went blind looking over these."

"And?"

Lino shook his head. "Not much to show for it. A word here and there but not enough to make sense of it. But they must be important, or she wouldn't have kept them from her husband. You said she kept many secrets from him."

"According to Father Jerry, yes. Their marriage wasn't one of thoughtful conversation. Robert ran his business and made lots of money, while Mary Alice enjoyed the personal pleasures of giving it away. It must have worked; they were together for years. Why?"

"These papers. She must have kept them from Robert because she was afraid he would make sense of them. I'd like to find out if he can," Lino said.

"How?"

"I want to take them to him."

Father Silva looked stricken. "Impossible."

"Why?"

"I told you Mary Alice let her brother and me see these, not Robert. I promised her that's the way it would be." Father Silva took the pages from Lino's hand. "I keep promises to the dying, Lino."

"Even if it means we hit a brick wall?"

"You'll find a way around it. I have faith. Besides, we understand several words: note, doze, rest, sick. That's something, isn't it?"

"Gibberish."

Father Silva patted Lino on the shoulder before getting into his car. "You will find a way," he repeated, then backed out of the driveway and drove off.

A sheepish Roger looked up from his gardening. "Sorry, I couldn't help overhear. There might be another way to explain those words. Some of them, at least."

"Don't apologize," Lino said and helped Roger to his full height. "What other way?"

"Sounds, just like I heard them."

"Sounds?"

"Sounds. Restic. That's what I heard. Rest, sick, restic. In the hospital around the very ill, nurses were encouraged to listen for possible meanings. Nothing frustrates a sick patient more than not being understood. You have to listen and then put things in context. What were the other words?" Roger asked.

"We think note and doze."

Roger thought a moment. "Not much help there, I'm afraid. What was the patient doing when these words were spoken?"

"According to Father Silva, he repeated the four words and then Mary Alice motioned for a nurse," Lino said.

"I wish I'd seen that," Roger said.

"Why?"

"Well, a patient might motion for a nurse because he needed one, or a patient might motion that Restic is a nurse. Assuming Restic is a person's name."

"Assume that it is," Lino encouraged. "Where might note and doz' take you?"

"Nowhere that I can see."

"How about a first name? Nate? Nancy? Niles?"

"Dan," Roger said, adding, "Doris, Doug, David ... Dave Restic. David Restic?"

"You've got something?"

"I don't know," Roger admitted. 'If you take liberties with the word 'note' and speculate that it's really 'nurse,' you could easily have nurse David Restic."

"Ring a bell?" Lino asked hopefully.

"It certainly does," Roger said. "I didn't know him well, but we worked the same floor at the General for a while. That was years ago, however."

"How long ago?"

"Ten years, fifteen. I'm not certain about that."

"It's the only lead I've got. Let's play it out. What can you remember about David Restic?"

"Not much to tell," Roger said, kicking at the dirt with the toe of his boot. "As I remember Restic left the hospital about the same time Bob Haskell quit. Nurses burn out quickly. All the hours, the intensity of the job. Patients aren't in the hospital because everything is fine. They're sick and moody and, in some cases, dying right in front of you. Some of the finest trained nurses can't take the emotional drain. Bob was a case in point, and too bad."

"Why too bad?" Lino asked.

"Because I had a crush on him," Roger admitted. "It went nowhere because Bob left one afternoon and never came back. David Restic was a different matter. As I recall he was terminated. The reasons were all very hush-hush, but one rumor was that he'd stolen something from a patient."

"Any idea where he went after being fired?"

Roger shook his head. "I don't know, but I might be able to find out. I'm sure I still have friends at the hospital who would know where he is."

"Call them," Lino said, taking the hand spade out of Roger's grip. "I could use any information as soon as I can get it."

"I'll see what I can do," Roger said and reached for his cell phone.

An hour later Roger Langsford gave Lino David Restic's address in Boston's South End and a phone number for the Good Shepherd Hospice in Boston's Kenmore Square. The South End address had an unlisted phone number. Lino called the hospice.

"Good Shepherd, how may I help?" a kind voice answered.

"I'm trying to contact David Restic," Lino said, adding, "I'm not sure if he's a patient of yours or he works there."

"You're in luck," the voice said. "If he were a patient, privacy laws wouldn't let me tell you anything. David is an employee, which means I can't tell you very much. Who wants to know?"

Lino introduced himself. "I want to send him a long overdue gift for his time at Mass General. This is the same nurse Restic, I hope."

"He worked at the hospital, yes, but years ago."

"This was years ago," Lino said, continuing his lie. "David was more than kind when my sister was ill. She made a full recovery in no small measure because of his wonderful care. She passed away recently but never forgot David's generosity and asked that I send him a thank you gift. Is the West Canton Street address in the South End where I should send it?"

A moment passed, then the voice said, "That's the last record we have, yes."

"Thank you very much," Lino said.

"Not a problem," the voice said. "Is this something I should keep a secret, or should I let David know he has a surprise coming?"

"Keeping it a secret is probably best," Lino said, "but thanks for asking."

Twenty-Nine

The brick bow front at 111 West Canton Street had a private entrance below the front stoop leading to a basement apartment. Lino parked in a Resident Only space on a side street, walked around the corner and knocked on the basement door. When it opened, a man of medium height with a shaved head and a butterfly tattoo below his right ear faced Lino. His blue jeans and yellow t-shirt, sleeves rolled up, fit snugly, emphasizing his trim physique. In spite of the youthful dress, Lino guessed him to be over fifty.

"David Restic?"

"Yes."

"Adilino Cardosa. I'm looking into the disappearance of Jeremiah Dunn. His sister …"

"Don't mention her vile name in this house," Restic said, a sharp sting riding each word. "I've been expecting someone ever since Jerry disappeared. I don't know anything about it, if that's why you're here. I read in the newspaper that Jerry went missing. That's all I know."

"I'm here to talk."

"Are you a cop?"

"No, I'm looking into this for a private party."

"Then I don't have to say a word, do I?"

"You don't, but if you have nothing to hide, why keep quiet?"

Restic flipped a cigarette ash near Lino's feet, then opened the door wide enough for Lino to step into the small, colorful apartment. The two men faced each other awkwardly. Finally Restic pointed to the yellow and white striped sofa. Lino sat. Restic sank down in the matching chair opposite him and lit another cigarette from the one in his hand.

"I know people like you," Restic said smugly. "You say you want information, but you're really here to pass judgment."

"Not me."

"Yes, you. You may not even know it, but you are. Gays get used to it, some more used to it than others, but we all get used to it. You're passing judgment right now. I can see it in your eyes. They're hard and cold and full of disdain." Restic took a long, defiant drag from his smoke. "Is it because I slept with a priest?"

"Father Jerry?"

"Maybe."

"You don't deny it?"

"I deny everything, but that's why you're here, isn't it? You're picking up the club Mary Alice used to beat Father Jerry. She was a nasty woman. How did she get so nasty, I ask you?"

"I don't know," Lino admitted. "I never met her."

"You're lucky."

"Maybe she didn't approve of your interest in her brother?"

"Or his interest in me?" Restic shot back.

"Which was it?" Lino asked.

"That answer is more complex than you might imagine. Let me just say that my relationship with Jerry was very special. If it suffered from anything, it was that our time together was so brief."

"How long?" Lino asked.

Restic laughed enough to make Lino uncomfortable. "Most men who ask me that are thinking of something anatomical." He laughed again. "Am I embarrassing you?"

"Possibly."

"I can see that I am. Good," Restic said, savoring the moment. "Half the world's problems would go away if we weren't so timid about sex. What's to be ashamed of, huh?" Restic batted his eyes flirtatiously. "Tell me, darling, where's the shame?"

Lino looked away to the windows above the kitchen table. All he could see of the people strolling by were feet. He turned back to Restic, now in full jeer.

"I'm glad you're enjoying yourself," Lino quipped.

"Always." The smile held.

"You were telling me about the time you and Father Jerry had together."

"Was I?"

"Yes."

"I thought we were talking about sex." Restic puffed on his cigarette and watched the smoke drift across the ceiling. "That was Mary Alice's problem, you know. She didn't know how to deal with it. Worse, she didn't know how to enjoy it. Too bad, don't you think?"

"How do you know about Mary Alice's sex life?" Lino asked.

"I know everything."

"Did Father Jerry tell you?" Lino pressed.

"No," Restic said, his eyes declaring a stalemate. "Ask something else."

"Tell me about the time you spent with Father Jerry."

"It was wonderful. Like most things wonderful, here, then gone. Too bad."

"Why did it stop?" Lino asked.

"Mary Alice died, and the world changed. Simple as that." Restic snapped his fingers. "Poof. Disappeared like dear old Jerry."

"I'm not sure I follow."

"Because you don't see the crumbs at your feet. That's how everybody gets home, following the crumbs, Mr. Portuguese man. You are Portuguese, am I correct? You don't have to answer. I've seen the dark skin, shiny black hair and hard look several times in Provincetown. You folks work the boats, don't you? I think I'd like that for a weekend, working a boat, I mean." Restic aimed a line of smoke toward Lino.

"Did you visit Father Jerry in Provincetown?" Lino asked.

"Lots of people did. Saturday afternoon mass at four-thirty, Sunday morning at seven, nine and eleven."

"Did you meet Father Jerry other than at mass? Did you meet on social occasions?" Lino asked, liking Restic's game less and less.

"Yes."

"In Provincetown?"

"There and here in Boston. One afternoon, I even stopped by the Connellys' house to see if I could be of any help with the deathwatch. Big of me, don't you think? Very generous."

"So you were with Mary Alice."

"Not for long."

"Just popped in and out, did you?"

"You do have a way with words. 'Just popped in and out' like a quickie in a bathroom stall." Restic tapped the ash into the tray. "I was invited one time because of my highly refined nursing skills but couldn't stay long because I had a job interview or something equally boring. Besides, Mary Alice was hostile."

"Then why did she invite you?" Lino asked.

"I didn't say who invited me."

"Father Jerry?"

"Do tell."

"I take it this visit to the Connellys was after you were fired from Mass General?"

"On to bigger and better, is the way I put it." Restic lit another cigarette from the one he held in his slightly trembling hand, then rubbed the old one out. "Ask something else."

"What did you steal from the hospital?"

"I forgot."

"Narcotics?"

"Never touch the stuff."

"Let's go back to your time with Father Jerry."

"I don't kiss and tell, unless I've had too much champagne."

"How would you say he handled his sister's illness?"

"The problem was he couldn't handle it. He felt responsible. He came to believe Mary Alice's cancer was punishment for his being queer. It was God's revenge. I told Jerry his problem wasn't with God. I told him it was with Mary Alice. He needed to clear the air with her while there was still time. If he didn't, the missed opportunity would consume him, and I was right, wasn't I? Jerry went up in a puff of smoke."

"Did he have that conversation with Mary Alice?" Lino asked.

"Robert made it happen, yes," Restic said with a devilish laugh. "He's very clever in how he manipulates his world. Very clever."

"How did he make the conversation happen?"

"By taking advantage of that old bothersome priest, what is his name?"

"Father Silva?"

"That's the one. Father Silva was supposed to hear a confession Mary Alice requested, only it wasn't clear to Silva whose confession."

"I'm not sure I follow," Lino admitted.

"Because you don't understand how Mary Alice operates," Restic said. "She didn't trust anyone to tell her the truth. That's why she hired private investigators by the dozen."

"To look into what?"

"Sweetbriar, her brother, or to follow her husband once he'd left their house. Robert didn't want to lie to his dying wife, so to avoid that little rub, he convinced Father Silva that the confession Mary Alice wanted him to hear was Father Jerry's."

"It was supposed to be Robert's?"

"That's right. Mary Alice wanted to know the truth about something and couldn't imagine that her husband, a devout Catholic, would lie to a priest. He'd lie to her, yes, but to Father Silva during confession? No."

"What did she want to know?" Lino asked.

"She wrote it in one of her notes that no one can read," Restic said. "Who really knows?"

"You seem to know a lot. How is that?"

"I pay attention."

"Who's doing the talking? Father Jerry?"

"I told you, I don't kiss and tell."

"Was he the one who invited you to the house when Mary Alice was dying?"

"Maybe I couldn't stay away. I have a weakness for everyone who's been pushed into a space they don't fit."

"And who might that be?"

"You said it, Father Jerry. Mary Alice created a priest out of a simple boy whose only sin was attraction to men. When she learned that horrible little secret, she led the charge up the hill of moral decency and placed her brother on the very top. All well and good, except that Jerry was afraid of heights. Every day he lived in fear that he would prove unworthy to God or his sister. He didn't want to disappoint either."

"But he did disappoint when you came along," Lino said. "What did you do? Photograph him in a compromising position and then blackmail Jerry to keep his affair with you quiet?"

Restic leaned forward, amused. "Blackmail?" He gushed a throaty laugh. "Would I be living in a basement apartment if I'd been blackmailing anybody? I don't think so."

"I do," Lino answered. "Your past history with Father Jerry makes you a prime suspect in his disappearance."

"Didn't know I had a past history," Restic said, unfazed. "Sordid little history, is it?"

"I'd say stealing from a patient qualifies."

Smoke fell from Restic's mouth as he spoke. "That incident never got out of internal review. You are guessing."

"Something got you fired from Mass General."

"I wasn't fired. I quit."

"What happened, did Father Jerry find out why you lost your job and end your relationship? He wanted nothing to do with a common thief?"

"You can't end what never began," Restic said, delighted with the confusion sweeping across Lino's darkening expression. "I'm delighted to see you mystified. It does me a world of good."

"How do I know you're not lying?" Lino asked.

"You don't know anything, Mr. Portuguese man," Restic taunted through a bluish cloud. "Is there anything else I can help you with?"

"I think you've done quite enough."

"Good, because I don't do manicures, and I don't do hair. Too bad, your nails need some attention."

Lino stood. "I know the way out."

"Ta, ta."

Thirty

Jack Moore arranged lunch with Lino at the Capital Grill on Newbury Street. The steak house was a few blocks from Jack's Boylston Street office and a short drive from David Restic's apartment. Jack had just arrived when Lino walked through the front door.

"Perfect timing," Jack said, shaking Lino's hand. "How was the drive up?"

"Not bad, but I wouldn't do it every day."

"Some poor bastards do." They followed the bowtied waiter to their table. "Not from Provincetown, but I represented the wife in a divorce case from Hyannis. Her husband drove up and back every day."

"Maybe that's why she got rid of him," Lino offered. "Too much time on the road, not enough time at home."

"More like the guy was cheating on her," Jack said and beat the waiter to the punch. "Dry martini, straight up, two olives. Lino?"

"Scotch on the rocks."

The waiter disappeared.

Jack put his elbows on the table and pressed his fingers into a steeple. "You know what I miss most about restaurants? Not being able to light up after a sticky dessert and double espresso. Sugar, caffeine and nicotine are the holy trinity of culinary experiences. I miss the combination, I really do," Jack said, collapsing his steeple and his wistful mood. "I have news that requires a response."

"If it's bad news, I don't want to hear it. I had a little dose already this morning."

"How so?"

"You remember the P-town fire at St. Peter's church?"

Jack nodded.

"I've been doing a little moonlighting on the side, trying to find out what happened to the priest who disappeared the night of the fire."

"A friend of yours?"

Lino shook his head. "Doing a favor. Anyway, when I was investigating suspicious fires for the insurance company, the key to the truth was like peeling away the layers of an onion. After enough layers, the truth was right there in front of you. Nobody could miss it."

"And this time you missed it?" Jack asked.

"I missed something," Lino admitted. "I was so sure that an affair and blackmail were major parts of the mix. The more I chased that idea, the more it led me to a priest and a nurse."

"Priests fall in love, I guess."

"I'm now not so sure this one did."

"What'd the nurse tell you, or didn't she didn't cooperate?"

"This nurse is a he."

"Oh." Jack felt stupid. "I keep forgetting that this is a Provincetown story and little out there resembles the rest of the world."

"That can be a plus," Lino offered.

"It can also be confusing," Jack countered. "In the normal world nurses are women, priests are men, and affairs between men and women are a part of everyday life that keeps my business running full tilt. Do you want my advice?"

"I pay you for advice, Jack. Go ahead."

"My advice is not to give up on your peeled onion. Stay with your male nurse a little longer and see what shakes out. If it were my case, and a female nurse was breaking up a marriage, that's what I'd do. What have you got to lose?" Jack rubbed his palms together in anticipation as the drinks arrived. He savored a sip. "Nothing like a well-made martini to ease the day's pain," Jack said.

"What's the cause of this pain?" Lino asked warily.

"Your wife. She's the reason for our meeting, Lino."

"Figures."

"You don't mind if we get to that, do you?"

"Fire away."

"Wonderful. Remember a few weeks back when we almost settled, and then her father dragged Mark Solomon into the picture to play some hardball?"

"How could I forget? She wanted part of everything, even my boat."

"Not anymore," Jack said, glancing at the menu.

A knot cinched in Lino's stomach. "She wants more?" he asked.

Jack shook his head. "She wants to settle. Not at bargain basement prices, but she wants to put an official end to you and her. I think she's being pushed along by her new boyfriend."

Lino's eyes arched over the rim of his scotch glass.

"That might be the painful part for you," Jack said. "She's playing house with some guy on the weekends."

"How do you know?"

"Your wife's never been off the radar screen, Lino. We've been keeping track on the chance she'd do something to help our cause. She knows moving in full-time would be a bad move until the divorce is settled, but I think that's what she plans on doing. Right now it's just weekend hanky-panky. Does that bother you?" Jack asked.

"I'm not sure," Lino said honestly.

"Fair enough," Jack said. "Some guys can't deal with it. Their moods swing from furious to depressed. They take their wife's new romance as one more attack on their masculinity. They fight back to the point of ruining any reasonable deal. That's why I always like to pass this information along in person. Get a good reading on my client, you know? See where we really stand before we make our next move."

"What do you suggest?" Lino asked.

"Be grateful her attention is on the future, not on you and what happened to your son. With any luck we can wrap this up before we all die of old age."

"What happened to Edwin's role in all this?"

Jack shrugged. "I don't know for certain, but my read is that Linda stood up to him for once. She's calling the shots and wants closure."

Lino drove out of the O'Neill Tunnel an hour ahead of rush hour traffic. All through lunch and during his drive back to Provincetown, the idea of Linda with another man festered until his mind could think of nothing else.

He wasn't angry as much as he was curious. How had they met? Did she know him while Lino and Linda were still happily married? Did the man have his eyes on her even then? Or was it Linda who set her eyes on him during one of the dinner parties their circle of friends held throughout the long New England winters? Cocktails at six-thirty, dinner at eight, lingering over dessert, then home by eleven.

Chatter around the dinner table rarely focused on children. Talk of home improvements, horrid contractors, job changes, job failures, job hunting, neighbors' divorces, neighbors' drinking problems, neighbors' drug problems and other assessments of failure filled the time.

Lino thought the absence of kid talk, given that every couple had at least one, purposeful. You regain your youth when not reminding yourself and others that Johnny starts college next year or that Sheryl's thinking of law school. Youth regained means play, and who better to play with than someone else's spouse?

Lino pled guilty to scanning the dinner lovelies and imagining flirtation leading to lies to Linda about working late to be with his new love. But it all stopped in his mind, even though he felt sure other party goers spent the night in unfamiliar beds.

Even when traveling, Lino returned alone to his hotel room. He didn't want the hassles of an affair or the worry over someone else not keeping his secret. Besides, he loved his wife.

He wasn't sure what Linda did when he was away. Not that he searched through the phone records or credit card receipts looking for a paper trail that led to a weekend at some hotel. She was attractive enough to be sought after and adventuresome enough to be caught. It would be a game to her, Lino thought, something like skydiving where the risks and thrills were equal. Still, he couldn't see her making the jump.

And now? How did Lino feel about Linda playing house? She should seek happiness, he thought. As much as it is possible to experience happiness, she should grab her share, but Lino knew it would not be easy for her. The death of a child blots out part of your heart. It darkens the sun and dulls the bloom in the garden. Nothing ever again is the same.

Nothing.

Happiness? What is that?

Lino stopped in Orleans to check on how Hal had been getting long with Lino's charters. The parking lot held a few cars and Hal's red truck and boat that he trailered to and from the launch ramps. A cluster of men were trying out a new fly rod in the practice area on the back lawn. Lino had his head in a tray of peanut bunker flies when Hal came out of the back room.

"Well, if it isn't my savior," Hal boomed. "Don't tell me you're going back out on the water anytime soon."

"I'm not, if you can still cover," Lino said. "I need one more day working on the boat, then I'll be ready."

"Boat? I didn't know there was a problem," Hal said.

"Nothing big, just a little this, a little that."

"Consider it done. Those charters for tomorrow confirm?"

"They did. Five-thirty and three."

"I'm there, pal," Hal said ringing the cash register and removing a money envelope. "I figured you'd be by sooner or later. Got to pay mama's doctor bills, right?"

"Right." Lino put the money in his pocket. "You got your cut?"

"Always pay the boss first. How is your mother?"

"She's pretty good, Hal. Good days and bad, like the rest of us. How's the fishing? You keeping my clients happy?"

"Happy and tired from reeling in the big ones."

"I'll bet."

"You'll be betting on a winner, Lino. Don't worry about a thing on the water. Everything out there is fine."

"Thanks, Hal. Wish I could say the same for conditions on land." Lino picked up a handful of flies he didn't need and paid for them. On his way out Lino turned back. "On second thought, I might need two days, Hal. I might have to run up to Boston to sort something out."

"Another doctor appointment for mom?"

"Sort of. Another appointment with a nurse."

Thirty-One

Lights were on in the red house even though the sun had not set. Lino pulled in front of the cottage, turned off the engine and got out. When he opened the cottage door and stepped inside, a showered, dressed and agitated Roger Langsford waited for him.

"What are you doing here?" Lino asked, not pleased with the sight.

"Your mother won't let me in her house."

"Oh, great. Why not?"

"I'm the gardener." Roger crossed his arms over his chest and pouted. "Gardeners stay outside."

Lino was exhausted from the drive up and back from Boston and didn't want to deal with this. "Can Colleen handle it?" Lino asked.

"No, Colleen cannot handle it," Roger bristled. "Colleen has gone home. This is my first overnight watching your mother, and she won't let me in. I've been keeping an eye on her from here so she won't walk away, but I can't stay here. I need to be inside."

Lino inhaled a chest full of air and sent it out in a sigh. "I'll talk to her," Lino said, not moving. "Are you sure you can't handle this on your own?"

"Once I get inside I can handle it. It's the first part that's holding up matters." Roger shifted nervously on his feet. "I'm sorry, Mr. Cardosa. I can see you're tired, but I didn't want to force the issue with your mother. I thought it best to wait until you got back, and then the two of us could ease into things. By the way, if you don't mind my asking, how did your chat with David Restic go?"

"I'm not really sure," Lino admitted. "We need to talk again to clear up a few things."

"Wonderful," Roger said, catching movement out of the corner of his eyes. "Oh, dear."

Lino followed the direction of Roger's gaze. Katharine was stepping outside and closing the side door of the red house behind her. The two men hurried out.

Lino put his arm around Katharine's shoulder. "Nice evening, isn't it, Mother?" he asked. "Thinking about taking a walk?"

She looked at Lino blankly, then at Roger. In time an idea formed that she could understand. "Now I remember," she said. "A strange man came knocking at the door and wanted in the house." She pointed at Roger. "You've caught him, Adilino. I knew you would."

"This isn't a strange man," Lino corrected. "You and Roger have been working in the garden together. Remember? You liked working together."

"We did." Roger was upbeat. He pointed to immaculate beds heavy with yellow roses. "Every weed, Katharine. We rousted every one and will tackle more in the morning, but first we need a nice dinner and a good night's sleep."

Katharine hesitated, looking at her garden. Something sat on the edge of her memory.

"You must be hungry after all that work," Lino said, gently nudging his mother back to the house. "I'm starving myself."

Roger pulled the door open, smiling. "I'm pretty handy with pot and pan. What would you like?"

"Mother's a pushover for macaroni and cheese."

"My favorite," Roger chimed. He offered his hand, and Katharine took it. He helped her inside. "You'll join us?" he asked Lino beseechingly.

"Sure, I'll join you," Lino answered, his mind on David Restic and Jack Moore's advice not to give up on his peeled onion. Lino asked his mother if she'd like a sip of wine while Roger cooked.

"Who's cooking?"

"Roger." Lino removed two wine glasses from the cupboard. "White or red?"

"I don't know a Roger, do I?"

Lino filled one glass halfway with white and filled another with red for himself while Roger busied himself at the stove.

"To your wonderful garden, Mother." Lino lifted his wine in toast. Katharine joined in and clicked glasses. "It's the best on the block."

"Do you think so? Really?"

"Yes, I do. We have to do each other a favor."

"We do?"

"Yes, we do, if we want to keep the garden nice."

Katharine sipped her wine and thought about it. "I'd like to keep the flowers nice, Adilino. You know I like my flowers."

"I know you do. Roger likes them, too. To help you keep the flowers looking nice, Roger has to be up very early."

"Like me."

"Like you, yes." Lino swirled the wine in his glass and drank a soothing swallow. "He lives far away."

"Like me."

"Not like you. You live here in your own house."

Katharine nodded.

"The favor we need is a place for Roger to sleep. Would it be all right with you if he stayed here in the house, so he could get up early and work with you in the garden?"

"Here?" Katharine couldn't quite picture it. "In this house?"

"Yes, in the guest room. As a favor and just for a while." Lino looked into his mother's eyes. "And I'll return the favor."

"How?"

"The woman who stays with you now and again? Colleen?"

"I don't know why that woman ever comes here," Katharine mused.

"I know you don't. I'll send her away for a few days," Lino said. "That's my favor to you. Roger stays to help with the garden, and Colleen goes for a while."

"She doesn't need to come back."

"I know, but she might."

"There's no reason."

"I know."

"She's only in the way."

"She might seem like she's in the way, Mother, but she's really a great help. But I'll talk to her about staying out of your way."

Roger put a bowl of salad on the table and went back to the stove. Katharine picked out a green leaf and held it in front of her lips. Slowly, it made the trip to her mouth.

"The gardener can stay," she said.

"Thank you."

"You're welcome."

Thirty-Two

A religious man might have said that God gave him a sign by brewing up a small low pressure system and spinning it south of the Cape, producing so much early morning rain that no work could be done on the *Pico II*. You can't sand wet wood.

Lino chalked it up as confirmation of his own good judgment. He'd decided last night as he finished dinner with Roger and his mother that, like the Portuguese carrying their pails of sand in the village Lino had visited as a kid, he would put in his time and effort and drive to Boston again. The receptionist at the Good Shepherd Hospice had told Lino that Restic only worked half a day on Fridays, so Lino needed to get to the city before noon. Before leaving Provincetown he popped into the red house to make sure no battles had raged overnight.

"All is well?" Lino asked Roger, who was reading the morning paper and lingering over coffee at the kitchen table.

"Quite," he said. "She slept like a baby. You're off?"

Lino nodded. "For a few hours. Call Colleen and tell her to take today off, will you? If mother remembered anything about last night, I don't want her to think I was lying to her about Colleen being gone for a while. You can manage alone, can't you?" Lino asked.

"Don't you worry. I can, and I will," Roger said, and Lino left.

Cape roads in the early morning before work are a zigzag of contractors, construction workers and fishermen headed for the rising sun on an empty beach. Lino missed being on the water, missed the simplicity of the life he'd cobbled together for himself. He let himself think about the future: a settled divorce, a boat ready for charters, his mother taken care of, and Father

Jerry's case resolved. Lino was certain that David Restic could help with the last if Lino could get him to talk freely.

The Good Shepherd Hospice was located a few blocks outside of Kenmore Square on Beacon Street in a six-story brick building. Lino double-parked and checked inside to make sure he was at the right address. The office directory in the foyer identified the building's occupants as doctors, lawyers, accountants and the Good Shepherd. It was here that caregivers received their home assignments and returned with a written summary of their activities.

Lino checked his watch. It was ten forty-five. He got back in his SUV and drove around to the alley where the receptionist said Restic and others parked in reserved spaces behind the building. Lino drove past and backed into a space on the alley's other side. Fishing had made Lino an expert at waiting. You never knew when or if a fish would strike. All you can do is hope you're in the right spot and wait. This time the strike came early.

After fifteen minutes the back door opened, and a cautious David Restic stepped out. He looked around as if anticipating being watched, then quickly got into his car.

Lino followed him back onto Beacon Street, through a congested Kenmore Square and onto Storrow Drive inbound. Past Mass General, Restic avoided the entrance to the I-93 tunnel and veered right onto the surface road toward TD Garden, where the Celtics and Bruins play. A block before the Garden Restic turned right and pulled into a parking lot where the attendant opened the gate, gave Restic his ticket and waved him through. Lino slowed a half block away and stopped at the curb just as Restic walked across the lot and stopped at the street. Lino slid down in the seat to avoid being spotted. When he raised his head, Restic was gone.

Dread clutched Lino's heart as he scanned the area. Left. Right. Back left, settling on a light gray Mercedes flashing its hazard lights twenty feet from the parking lot. In seconds, the trunk lid opened. Restic jumped out of the passenger side door, ran to the back and removed two knapsacks, which he passed through the open back window. When Restic retook his seat and closed the car door, the Mercedes slipped into traffic with Lino trailing a few cars behind.

Past South Station in a light rain, the Mercedes ran with the traffic into the tunnel and onto the expressway. Lino kept pace and followed the gray Benz as it headed toward Cape Cod when the highway split at Braintree.

The rain let up at the Canal and gave way to hazy sunshine by Hyannis. One exit before the rotary in Orleans, Restic slowed and got off the highway onto a narrow, blacktopped road that curved around ancient cemeteries, ponds, horse farms and small vegetable truck farms. It took Lino a while to understand where these back roads were leading, but when he saw the turn for Paw Wah Pond, he knew they were headed to the house that Robert Connelly had rented. Could he still be there? Lino wondered. What really did David Restic have to do with Robert Connelly, and who was driving the car? Father Jerry?

The Mercedes turned into the driveway just before the end of the road. Lino drove to the end where a boat ramp shared room with a few parking spaces. Lino pulled into one, shut off the engine and got out. Connelly's house was a hundred yards back up the road. An anxious Lino ran the distance crouched low, hidden partially by a stone wall that paralleled the blacktop. When he heard children's voices, he stopped, his heart pounding, and peered over the wall. David Restic, Robert Connelly and the third man Lino did not recognize ushered two small boys no older than twelve or thirteen out of the car's backseat and quickly toward Connelly's house.

A knot formed in Lino's stomach as one of the boys, a terrified shriek in his voice, swerved out of Connelly's open arms and ran hastily back toward the safety of the car. Connelly gave chase only to stop in his tracks when he saw Lino leap over the stone wall into the yard.

"Doesn't look like your little friends want to stay and play," Lino said.

"What the hell are you doing here?" Connelly demanded. "This is private property, get off."

"Or you'll what? Call the police?" The frightened child raced toward Lino, who scooped him up. "It's all right," he said to the whimpering boy. "I'm here to help you, do you understand?" The words painted crudely on the *Pico II* surged through Lino like acid. "I'm here to help."

When the second child broke toward Lino, a panicked Connelly backed into his house and slammed the door.

A rattled David Restic turned to the man beside him. "Do something," he cried out. "Don't simply stand there."

The man raised his hands in submission. "I drive, nothing else." He turned to Lino. "You got that? I ain't no chickenfucker. I drive. Period."

Lino heard the screen door slam out back, then saw Connelly race down the path at the side of the house toward the dock.

Restic heard it too and ran after him. "Wait," Restic yelled. "Robert, wait!"

Lino set the child down. "Everything's going to be okay. Do you hear? No one's going to hurt you." Lino's loathing was etched across his face as he turned to the driver. "You stay here, and watch these kids until I get back. Understand? Don't run, or every cop in the state will be tracking you down. If they don't find you, I will."

The driver nodded.

Lino tore off, passing Restic, who had fallen. Connelly scrambled along the dock.

"He's afraid, can't you see that?" Restic scurried on all fours, trying to get up. "Robert's afraid. Let him go. Please. Let him go. He's not going to hurt anyone."

Lino sped past Restic and reached the dock as Connelly threw off the bow line tied to the Boston Whaler. The engine fired with a throaty roar. Connelly looked up and tossed off the spring and stern lines. He jammed the Whaler into reverse, smashing into the catboat tied behind him. Connelly seemed momentarily at a loss, giving Lino enough time to hit the end of the dock in full stride.

Connelly cranked the wheel hard for the turn into deeper water as Lino launched himself like a long jumper. Lino flew right at Connelly who thrust the boat's transmission into forward. The instant acceleration sent Lino crashing onto the cockpit floor. Quickly he was on his feet, grabbing the handrail on the back of Connelly's seat as the boat picked up speed.

"Give it up," Lino demanded. "The charade's over."

"Leave me alone," Connelly shouted over the engine's roar. "All I ever wanted was to be left alone."

"With kids?"

"Fuck off."

"At Sweetbriar?"

"You don't know what you're talking about," Connelly sneered.

"I'm talking about my son!" Lino shouted and reached over the seat for Connelly's throat with both hands.

Connelly leaned forward and clawed free, then cranked the wheel left and right, trying to shake Lino off the boat. When that failed, Connelly shoved the throttle all the way forward. The boat leapt ahead full speed, slamming into the small harbor waves at over forty knots.

The longest dock in Paw Wah stretched out in front of them. A move to the left and Connelly would clear the dock into the channel and charge out into Little Pleasant Bay; a move to the right and the Whaler would crash into the dock at nearly fifty miles an hour.

Lino leaned into Connelly's right ear and shouted. "Listen to me, you crazy bastard. Do you really want to die? Do you?"

The boat plowed ahead, Connelly seemingly unable to move. Lino reached forward and yanked the steering wheel hard to the right.

"You may not want to," Lino shouted, "but you deserve what you get."

Nothing could stop impact with the dock fifty feet ahead.

Lino used the handrail and all the power in his legs to send his energy backward high enough to clear the engine cowling as he flung himself over the boat's transom. He hit the water tucked into a tight ball, his arms clinched around his knees, his head buried into his chest. Like a rock, he skipped across the water in the Whaler's wake, spinning like a top until he was aware of nothing but the water around him quivering as the dock's pilings ripped out of the seabed, and the boat exploded like a bomb.

Debris rained down around him. Splinters of wood and floating chunks of burning fiberglass fell nearby. Dazed, Lino reached out and grabbed a piece of wood large enough to keep him afloat. He treaded water trying to discover if anything had broken. His legs worked. His arms worked. He could breathe and see and hear the distant sirens. He tried to swim a full stroke to shore, but a pain sliced through him like a knife. He must have torn something, a muscle maybe or a ligament. He decided to float until the man wading out to help got closer. The man tossed a line. Lino reached for it and was towed to shore.

"You okay, buddy? You all right? What the hell happened to Dick's boat?"

Lino had a hard time finding his voice. "Dick?" he finally said. "Who's Dick?"

"The guy you were with. Richard Gregory." The man helped Lino sit upright on the sandy shore. "No one onboard could survive that crash. You're lucky you got off."

Lino sat in silence.

"Can you stand?" the man asked.

Lino decided to find out. He went slowly. With the man's help, Lino stood. Keeping his balance took all his energy, but he managed an uneven step toward David Restic, who looked past Lino with red eyes.

Lino saw two EMTs racing toward him. "I'm going to be a while," he said to Restic. "Go back to the house and wait for me."

"You killed him," Restic said, dabbing a tissue at his eyes. "How does it feel knowing what you did?"

"Everything hurts but that," Lino said, catching the feeble slap Restic sent in his direction. "Go back to the house."

Thirty-Three

David Restic sat in a large room in front of a baby grand. Beyond the piano a wall of glass overlooked a small, sculpted pond full of red and gold koi. On the opposite wall hung several framed watercolors, all Cape Cod landscapes. Lino had been probed by EMTs and questioned by the local police long enough for Restic to cry himself dry and fill half of an ashtray. Tired and wet, Lino stood in front of Restic, who seemed small and frail. His stare was fixed on something not in the room.

"I know it's not possible," Restic said, his voice as distant as his gaze. "I saw the crash, the boat and dock in flames and splinters, but I still believe Robert survived. Funny how the mind plays tricks, isn't it? But Robert has a knack for tumbling off the edge and reaching back just before the fall like a cat with nine lives. He always managed to walk away. Always."

"Not this time," Lino said.

"No, not this time." Restic looked up at Lino. "I always knew he would meet a tragic end. It was part of his personality, part of who he was. He couldn't help it."

"Why was that?"

Restic lit a cigarette. "Demons."

Lino pulled up the piano bench and sat. "The same sort of demons that tormented Father Jerry?" Lino asked.

"The same sort, yes. Demons always win," Restic said, all his wisecracking of yesterday gone. "You can delay them for a while but not forever. They come back again and again and worm their way into your head until you can't stand it anymore. Robert said the feeling was like a thousand bees buzzing inside his skull."

"How do you know all this?"

Restic watched his cigarette smoke drift, then said, "I was a nurse on his floor when he was first admitted to Mass General.

Robert overdosed with sleeping medication. That's where we first met and where I first learned that he was a tortured soul who needed my help."

"You said first admitted. I'm guessing there were other times?"

"Yes, many. Each time kept hush hush. That was one aspect of Robert's life that he managed well, he and Mary Alice. His secrets never got out. She made sure of that. Robert's secrets would have ruined Mary Alice."

"And they were?"

"That he was suicidal and couldn't keep his hands off young boys. One was a manifestation of the other, of course."

"Yet he married Mary Alice," Lino said.

"Because he learned growing up that you don't win fights with a family like the Connellys, and not to marry would have caused an enormous fight. You fit their mold, or you're shown the door, and their mold was the traditional Catholic family headed by a self-made father who knew what was best. It wouldn't do in Robert's family to be gay, even though there were suspicions that Robert was not quite straight. Suspicions, of course, that were not pursued. They didn't really want to know. Besides, Robert's father would never allow an openly homosexual son to wave the Connelly banner, and Robert could never stand up to his father, although he promised himself that once his father passed away, he would confront his mother and tell her the truth. By then the truth had gotten lost, and Robert had married Mary Alice to complete his disguise."

"Not quiet complete," Lino corrected. "There's the matter of Richard Gregory."

Restic managed a half-smile. "A nice little twist, don't you think? A separate life down here on the Cape. It worked very well, except for the fact that stealing Gregory's identity and handing it over to Robert got me dismissed from the General."

"So that's what you stole," Lino said, "a man's identity."

"A dead man's identity," Restic admitted. "He died in the hospital. I waited months until I found a patient who had no relatives, and when Gregory died, I swooped in. It was perfect until one of Mary Alice's detectives found out what Robert and I were up to. That bitch pointed the finger at me, and the hospital did the rest."

"But she let Robert get away with his deception."

"She didn't let him get away with anything," Restic corrected. "Not unless she approved, and she approved of the creation of Richard Gregory and this house on the Cape."

"Why?" Lino asked. "Why not divorce him? Or more to the point, why did she and Connelly marry in the first place?"

"Because the Connellys did not have male lovers. They had wives and lovely children and traditions to uphold. The foremost was not embarrassing the family. Robert embarrassed them enough when he announced he wanted to be an architect instead of following in the financial footprints of Connellys before him. Robert hadn't the strength to challenge anything else, so he married, and by doing so went along with expectations while conducting business in Boston. He carved out another life, a more secretive life, down here on the Cape."

"What about Mary Alice? Why did she put up with it all?"

"Robert was a catch," Restic said. "He was handsome and charming and successful. What woman wouldn't want to spend her life with him?"

"Even when she found out about you?"

Restic laughed quietly. "Not just me."

"You and others. Why not get rid of him then?"

"Mary Alice thought she could change him, turn off the gay switch, make Robert a one-woman man lusting only after her. It was a challenge for her, a game she intended to win, just like she had with her brother. Besides, Mary Alice loved her image, the power her foundation gave her in Boston. She wasn't about to give it up without a fight. So man and wife had a meeting of minds. Robert would be the dutiful, hetero husband in the city, and Mary Alice would turn a blind eye to his life on the Cape as long as he remained discreet and away from Sweetbriar. Unfortunately, he didn't do either, but it took a while for Mary Alice to find that out. When she did, she threatened to expose Robert to his family."

"Why not turn him in to the police?" Lino asked.

"You wouldn't ask that if you'd spent any time with Robert," Restic said and lit a second cigarette while extinguishing the first. "He was very clever in the way he used people. He had the knack of hurting someone, being forgiven by them, only to hurt them again. That's the one thing Mary Alice and I had in common. We were both fools when it came to Robert, and he took advantage by cheating on both of us. The worst part is he didn't really love either one of us, and we both knew it."

"Yet you both stayed with him. Worse, you delivered children to a monster," Lino said bitterly.

"You would never understand."

"Try me."

"You don't know what it's like when a gay man loses his looks. It's all over. You can lift all the weights, have all the hair tints and facelifts you want, but when that freshness, that spark is gone, you're left on the rack like an old suit, especially when the man you love has his eyes on the boys. To be near him, I ran errands."

"You trafficked in kids," Lino seethed.

"I did what Robert wanted. I did what I had to."

"You ..."

"Don't judge me!" Restic shouted. "I know what I am, so don't you judge me." When he'd regained his composure, he said, "Besides, it's all over now. Robert, Mary Alice, Father Jerry—all gone."

"Tell me about you and Father Jerry," Lino said, "the truth this time."

"The truth is there was nothing between Jerry Dunn and me. When I met him, he was a priest living the straight and narrow."

"You had no affair?"

"No affair."

"How did you meet?"

"Mary Alice brought him on staff at Sweetbriar to watch after her husband."

"Jerry didn't run the camp?" Lino asked.

Restic shook his head. "Hardly. Jerry had trouble balancing his own checkbook. He was at Sweetbriar for one purpose, and that was to make sure Robert behaved himself. Jerry continued in that role long after Mary Alice died."

"Why?"

"Out of respect for his sister, I suppose. He knew she was looking down on him, watching him from above. Even when she was dead, Father Jerry didn't want to disappoint her."

"But eventually he did when he quit Sweetbriar," Lino reminded. "Why did he leave?"

"There was another incident."

"Involving Robert?"

"Yes."

"When?"

"About two years ago."

Lino felt as if a hot coal had been dropped in the pit of his stomach. "Two years ago my son was at Sweetbriar."

"Was he the boy that ran?" Restic asked. "One of the boys got away. Was he the one?"

"You tell me," Lino said.

"He must have been. All I know is that Father Jerry called the police. He could no longer do his sister's bidding. He wanted as far away from Sweetbriar as he could get, and he wanted Robert arrested."

"Why didn't that happen?"

"I don't know. All I know is that Father Jerry was friendly with a policeman in his parish. That's who he called."

"Tony Santos?"

Restic shook his head wearily. "I don't know."

"I think I do," Lino said, looking through a side window. An Orleans police officer walked toward the house with a child on either side, hurrying to keep up. Behind the officer the Mercedes driver was still being interrogated.

"The cops will be here any minute," Lino said. "They're going to want answers about you, Connelly and those kids."

"There's nothing to hide now," Restic admitted. "I'll just tell them the truth. The bees finally killed my baby. Look no further than the bees."

"Bees, hell," Lino said and took out his cell phone. He dialed the Provincetown police and asked to speak to Tony.

"He's out on his shift," the voice came back. "It ends at three."

Lino checked his watch. He had an hour.

Thirty-Four

The traffic up Route 6 toward Provincetown crawled along for miles until coming to a complete stop in Wellfleet when four lanes narrowed into two near the Wellfleet Drive-in. A frustrated Lino looked for room to pass. Finding none, he flipped open his cell phone and dialed. He got an answer on the fifth ring. Light, romantic music and a man's low, yet happy, voice in the background filled Lino with unexpected sadness.

"Linda?"

"What do you want?" she asked coolly.

"I don't want you to hang up, okay? Sounds like I crashed a party."

The music dimmed, and the man's voice faded to nothing.

"It's none of your concern, Lino. It really isn't, not anymore." Her voice sounded pained, less angry.

"I understand," Lino said, "I'm not butting in, I'm ..." He felt out of place and feared that the purpose of his call was even more so. He regrouped and said, "I talked to my lawyer. I just want you to know that we're going to work something out. You there?"

"I'm here." He heard her suspicion.

"We were doing all right before your father stuck his nose in. How'd you get him out?"

"He took himself out, Lino. All that hatred, all that energy trying to turn back the clock, took its toll. His doctor said he'd be dead in a year if he didn't stop. I told him I couldn't stand to lose another man in my life. That would kill me, too."

"Yeah, well," Lino stumbled. "You've got to take care of yourself. All of us do." Lino heard the man's voice in the background again. "Sounds like you're getting along."

"I'm trying."

"Yeah, well," Lino said again. "I'm trying, too. I don't know if you heard on the news, but there was a boating accident down here on the Cape. A man died."

"I hadn't heard."

"He was connected to Sweetbriar."

"I thought you were done with all that. When Father Donovan dropped the charges ..."

"That I made an ass of myself accusing a priest doesn't change the fact that our son is dead, Linda. I need to know the truth. I've been looking around, putting the pieces together. I think I've got something."

"Let it go, Lino." He could hear the plea in her voice. "Let it go."

"I was in Cincinnati, finishing up a case for Colas, when you called. You'd picked Steven up a few days early from camp. You brought him home, and he wouldn't leave his bed. You phoned to say you were taking him to the hospital. What happened at Sweetbriar that you've never told me?"

Linda hesitated, then said, "You know the answer, you just don't know the details."

"The details are what I need. You wouldn't hide the boy's rape. That would be impossible. What else could be so horrible?"

"It will crush you, Lino," Linda finally said. "Let it go, please."

Lino felt his insides flutter as if he'd stepped over a cliff. "Crush me?"

"Yes."

"I guess there's only one way to find out."

Linda paused and gave in. "Stevie and a friend were walking back to their cabin after a late afternoon swim. They were afraid of being late for dinner so decided to cut through the woods. You know how thick those woods can be, how dark they can get even in bright sunshine."

"I know," Lino said, picturing the long, threatening shadows of the forest.

"They got disoriented. Stevie's friend got frightened and started to run in the wrong direction. Stevie hollered after him to come back. He waited and waited, and when his friend didn't return, Stevie went after him. That's when he saw the man in the woods bent down over his friend. Stevie froze at the sound of the screams, the pleas for help. He couldn't bring himself to move, he couldn't bring himself to help his friend. Terrified, he ran back to camp."

Lino imagined the horror. "Dear God," he murmured. "What happened to his friend?"

"He found his way back. He wanted to know why Stevie didn't help him. Why Stevie left him the woods. Why he ran. Stevie didn't have answers and called me to come get him."

"Why didn't you tell me?"

"Your son made me promise."

"Why?"

"Isn't it obvious? Your job is to rush at problems, to solve them, to get the bad guys. Stevie did what you would never do: he ran like a coward. He looked up to you, Lino. He loved you more than anything and wanted to be just like you. How could he ever overcome the shame he felt if you knew the truth? He was humiliated. He wanted to die."

"My God," Lino said, his voice hushed. "I would have understood."

"Like you understood Father Donovan's explanation when he denied his involvement? Stevie thought you were going to tear the priest's head off."

"I would have understood about my own son," Lino tried again. "I would have talked to him, explained."

"You were his hero. He wanted to be just like you."

"I don't know what you're saying, Linda. Should I apologize for that? A son wants to be like his father."

"So much that it kills him?"

A flash of anger welled within Lino. He banged the top of the steering wheel with the flat of his hand. "Okay, I get it," he stumbled. "It will always be my fault."

"You wanted the truth, Lino."

"Yeah, well, the truth is that we don't have to worry anymore about this happening to someone else's child. The man responsible is dead."

"Did you kill him?"

"I was there, yes. It's over, Linda. Now we can move on. That's what you want, isn't it?"

"I'm seeing someone, if that's what you mean."

"That's what I mean," Lino admitted, adding, "I'm seeing someone, too."

"Really?" She sounded suddenly hopeful.

"Yeah. Nothing serious."

"Me either. Maybe someday."

"Maybe someday," Lino repeated, the words caught. "We did our best, Linda. We shouldn't ever forget that. With Steven, we …"

"I know." Linda cleared her throat as if shutting off tears before they got a good start. "Good luck, Lino."

"It's got to be good, we've already had the bad."

"I hope so," she said and switched off.

Lino drove down Snail Road to the Shore Road intersection. He turned right and then made the left at the fork onto Commercial Street, his regrets about his son rippling like the harbor waves.

Lino's thoughts froze when he saw a rake and spade dropped across the driveway of the red house. Beside it, a trickle of water puddled into a small lake. Katharine treated garden tools like coveted prizes and never left the water running, even on her worst days.

Something was wrong.

"Mother?" Lino called from the empty kitchen. "Mom? Katharine? Is anyone here?" he shouted from the doorway to the living room. What he saw nailed him to the floor. "What the hell?"

Roger Langsford, bent forward on the sofa, head in hands to stop the bleeding, looked up, mystified.

"What happened?"

Roger's eyes strained to focus. "He hit me."

"Who?"

Roger shook his head and swooned. "I'm going to be sick," he said and bolted into the bathroom.

Lino climbed the stairs two at a time and searched the upstairs rooms. When he came back down, Roger held a wet cloth to his forehead.

"Where's my mother?"

"He took her."

"Who took her?"

"The policeman who came to the door. I said there must be some mistake and tried to stop him. That's when he took out his gun and hit me."

"Where did he take her?" Lino pressed.

"He said you'd know where, and you'd know who had sweetened the pot."

Thirty-Five

The large, dark green umbrella cast a shadow over Diane, who was stretched out reading on a chaise lounge. She was so engrossed in her book, Lino stepped quickly onto the deck, unnoticed.

"I need a favor," Lino announced, "a fast one. I'm in a hurry."

Startled, Diane nearly dropped her book. "Not a good thing to do to somebody who has a bad heart."

"You don't have a bad heart," he said, reaching out his hand. She took it, and he pulled her up to her feet. "You know those things I took out of the red house and brought over so my mother wouldn't find them and get herself into trouble?"

"I do."

"I need to take one back."

Lino followed her inside to the downstairs utility closet. She opened the door and said, "Everything's in the back, just like you left it."

Lino crawled inside and came out carrying what looked like a tool box and a crooked pole wrapped in blankets and tied with thin line. He cut the line with his pocketknife and unrolled the blankets to reveal a bolt-action Winchester rifle, the metal barrel shimmering in a protective coating of oil, the wooden stock darkened from years of use.

"My father sometimes carried this on his dragger," Lino said, opening the tool box and removing a box of shells. "Often big sharks would attack the nets when he hauled the catch onboard." He held up a three-inch shell. "They didn't last long when he hit them with one of these."

"And you've seen a shark?" Diane asked.

"A Great White." He slipped one shell into the chamber, pushed the bolt forward and snapped it closed.

"I hate it when you lie to me."

Lino stuffed his pockets with shells. "Who says I'm lying?"

"Me. You haven't been out on your boat in days." Her dark eyes bore straight into his heart. "Tell me what you're really doing with that gun."

"I'm going to bring my mother home."

Diane's eyes popped. "What's happened to Katharine?"

"Tony Santos knocked Roger unconscious and took her."

"What! Why?"

"That's what I'm going to find out." Lino returned her gaze as long as he could. "There's a certain symmetry in all this. I was nagged into looking for a missing priest because Father Silva, with all the Catholic guilt he could muster, said rightly that my father would have wanted me involved. Now, at the end, it's my father's rifle that I'll carry into the dunes."

"To what, kill a man?" Diane said tersely. "Or worse, get yourself killed. You don't have to take that chance, Lino. Let the police handle it."

"Tony is the police," Lino said. "I've got to go." He kissed Diane on one cheek. "I'll be back."

"I'm counting on it." She followed Lino to the door.

"Where are you going?"

"To see if Roger needs any assistance."

Lino turned off Route 6 and parked his SUV two hundred yards into the woods on a sandy road that stopped at the base of the dunes one quarter of a mile from the red house. As children, he and his friends used to ride their bikes through here until their wheels bogged down in the soft sand. Then they'd race up the hill, the sand falling away under their feet, until they reached the top. They'd race down the other side and up a second, larger hill where the prize of their efforts waited: An abandoned dune shack overlooking the sparkling, blue Atlantic. It was little more than a rickety tree house built years and years ago on sand. The one-story structure had neither electricity nor running water. The sparse interior was shared with mosquitoes and sand flies and spiders, which made it a boy's dream.

Inside, on warm summer days, Lino and Tony Santos talked about their dreams for the future. They would go to the same college and play in the same backfield, breaking tackles and records along the way. They would marry sisters, have two boys each and own a fleet of fishing boats together from Maine to the Carolinas. They would build dune shacks for their children but live in waterfront homes overlooking their growing fleet of fishing boats. There was no reason their wives and children wouldn't get along splendidly, so they plotted their lives as well, creating empires of imagination, a fairyland of possibilities and goodness. They promised each other that when circumstances were at their bleakest, they would rendezvous at the shack where they revealed their dreams. They would meet to figure out what went wrong, and they would fix it.

Lino carried his rifle like a hunter, the barrel pointed skyward, his thumb on safety, his finger off the trigger, just like his father had taught him. He climbed halfway up the second dune, using a line of scrub pine for cover. Impressions in the sand indicated someone had come this way before him. Fifty yards from the shack, Lino stopped and knelt down.

"Tony?" Lino hollered. "You up there?" He listened for an answer and moved ahead cautiously when none came. "Mother?"

Lino stood twenty yards from the shack when a tattered curtain moved to one side. Tony's face filled one broken pane. "See anyone on your way up?"

"Who I want to see is my mother."

Tony stepped aside, leaving room for Katharine to stare blankly out the window. Lino's heart sank.

"What the hell is this all about, Tony?"

Tony moved to the door and yanked it open, his rifle pointed at Lino chest. "Put that cannon above your head and step inside."

Lino did as told, plowing the remaining distance through the sand. When he stepped inside, Tony grabbed the Winchester, removed the shell and leaned the rifle against the far wall.

Lino put his arms around his mother. "Are you all right?" he asked her.

She couldn't find an answer.

"I knew you'd remember this place," Tony said, loosening the top button of his uniform. "We had some bold talks up here, didn't we? Mapped out the world for each of us right here. Funny none of it worked out."

"You weren't a rotten cop in the lives we planned," Lino said, helping Katharine to a chair along one wall. "You killed Father Jerry, didn't you?"

Tony didn't flinch. "I killed him. I took the money. I set the church on fire," he said as if ordering fast-food. "Sit down, Lino." Tony motioned to the straight-back wooden chair beside the small table. On it sat a pen and pad of paper.

Lino sat, his eyes locked on the Winchester a few feet away.

"Don't try for it, Lino. I don't want to kill you before you've served your purpose." Tony stepped back from the table.

"What purpose is that?"

"To help Tony-the-steady-and-predictable get away with the perfect crime. I told you this was my chance, and I'm not going to let it slip away."

"Why bring my mother into this?"

"To make sure you'd come to the shack. Without you, I've got nothing. You're the key to all this, Lino. You make everything work."

"Why did you do it?" Lino wanted to know.

"Kill Father Jerry?"

"Yes."

"You won't believe this, Lino, but I prayed for guidance about that. Far be it for a mere mortal to shoot his own priest without answers from on high."

"I take it you got those answers?"

"I got those answers, yes." Tony laid his rifle on the table, its barrel pointed at Lino's chest, Tony's finger still on the trigger. "A priest is the voice of God, God in the flesh. As a consequence a priest must be judged by the highest godly standards, and when he fails, he should be sentenced to the most severe punishments. Besides, I didn't want any witnesses."

"What was Father Jerry's failure?" Lino asked, his mind cranking options for getting himself and his mother out of this without getting killed.

"He mingled with the scum of the earth," Tony spit out. "Leland Ricks is one case in point. I wore my State Police hat when I chatted him up. Smart of me, don't you think?"

"Very," Lino said absently. "How did you find out about Ricks?"

"I found out about everything, Lino. That's what expert investigators do, isn't it?" he chided. "I found out about Robert Connelly and the filth at Sweetbriar. I found out about all of it when Father Jerry asked how best to proceed with the arrest of Connelly."

"Which you never got around to."

"No." Tony worked a satisfied smile. "I told Father Jerry that to act too quickly might ruin all the good work his sister's foundation had done for the children. Father Jerry didn't want to be a party to that. He was a man in deep, deep conflict."

"Which you took advantage of."

"Of course. How often in a man's life does such an opportunity present itself?" Tony asked excitedly. "First, the opportunity to blackmail Connelly, and second, to lay the entire neat package at your feet. I hadn't clearly seen the ending until you came back to town, Lino. I thank you for that. Your confession will allow me to walk out of here, not only a free man but a hero for capturing the man who killed Father Jerry, stole the church's money and burned St. Peter's to the ground."

"Why would I do any of that?" Lino asked, buying time.

"Because you're one angry man who's already attacked a Gloucester priest and proved once again, for all to see, what an animal you can be when you beat up that fisherman at Flyer's."

"Then it was you who hired him."

Tony nodded. "And told him what to paint on that boat of yours. I knew it would set you off. I planted the receipt so you'd know where to find the stupid bastard. All I did was wait for the explosion."

Another blast was slowly welling inside Lino. "Why did you burn the church?"

"I wasn't sure if Father Jerry had left any records that might point to me and my business with Connelly. He was more than willing to pay handsomely to stay out of jail. I added his money to the hundred thousand I took from the church."

"What did you do with Father Jerry?"

Tony stomped on the floor with one foot. "He's under here."

The noise startled Katharine. "Adilino?"

"It's okay, Mom."

"I think I'd like some tea. Can I make some tea, Adilino? Would your friend like some?"

"In a bit." Lino glanced in Katharine's direction. Her gaze was back out the window. She didn't see her son's concern. "What about my mother?" Lino asked. "You can't afford to let her go free."

"Why not? A woman with Alzheimer's? A court would have a hard time believing anything she said."

"What about Roger Langsford?"

"What about him? Your mother needed to come with a police officer, and Mr. Langsford got in the way. I knew you'd come after your mother. Besides, at the time Langsford was the least of my worries. Connelly had just called in a panic. He said you followed two kids to his house. He was going to tell Bicknell about the blackmail unless I did something right then to get you off his back. I'm delighted you took care of Connelly before I had to kill him myself. You did me a great favor, Lino. Thank you."

"What do you want from me?"

"Your confession."

"I gave up confessing a long time ago," Lino said. "I don't plan on starting again now."

"I'm afraid you have no choice." Tony pointed to the pad and pen on the table. "Say you're sorry for all you did but that you couldn't live with the grief caused by your son's death. Write it and sign it."

"No one will believe that, Tony."

"Sure they will. You're a godless man, Lino, a man full of rage. A good trial lawyer could make the case that you really came back to Provincetown to kill Father Jerry because of his association with Sweetbriar and the suicide of your son. Vengeance is mine, sayeth Adilino Cardosa." Tony pointed to the pen. "Pick it up and start writing. Your signed confession will be the icing on the cake."

"It is a nice little package," Lino admitted..

"Isn't it?"

"There's only one problem."

"And that is?"

"I'm not going to sign it." Lino jumped up from the table and attacked with stunning swiftness. Tony's rifle skittered across the floor as Lino flung his adversary against the wall with such force a sharp tremor shook the cabin.

Tony fought back, grunting with pain as Lino's blows landed. Tony fumbled for the Glock automatic in his service belt, only to have it drop when he raised his arms to block the chair Lino kicked at him. Tony gasped for breath and backed away. He had one chance at victory, and he took it, lunging across the shack for the closest weapon, his handgun. Face down, his body stretched to its fullest length across the floor, Tony clutched the weapon's grip.

"You don't want to move another inch," Lino said, jerking a shell from his pocket and reloading. "I've got my father's rifle aimed at the back of your head."

Tony cranked his eyes around but couldn't see Lino clearly. He guessed he hadn't had time to grab his rifle and reload. "You're lying," Tony said, his chest heaving.

"I don't imagine killing a priest will earn you a friendly greeting at the pearly gates, Tony. Do you want to find out?"

Tony's eyes darted left and right as he slipped one finger inside the trigger guard. Before he moved that warned inch, Lino fired the gun that killed the sharks.

Thirty-Six

Pain surged through Tony's body with each slogging step through the sand. At the bottom of the hill, Chief Bicknell waited, surrounded by patrol cars, their blue lights flashing. Lino pushed his prisoner, one hand wrapped and bleeding, toward the line of officers. A female officer hurried after Katharine, who moved close to Lino's side.

"You can put those guns away," Lino told them. "Tony's done fighting for the day."

Bicknell nodded. The Glocks slipped back in their holsters. A young officer put Sergeant Santos in the back seat of his patrol car.

"Read him his rights and get him to a doctor," Bicknell ordered. The car sped off. "We'd have been here sooner, but ..."

"I don't want to hear it, Bicknell."

"Look, about your involvement ..."

"Talk to Sergeant Santos, not me."

Lino put his rifle in the back of his SUV, then helped his mother into the passenger seat. "There's a dune shack about a half mile up," he said to anyone who would listen. "Father Jerry's buried under the floorboards. Tony can tell you where he hid the church's money."

"Damn," Bicknell said.

"That about covers it."

Lino started the engine and drove off.

Lino slept like he hadn't in years and woke only when the smell of bacon wafted into his bedroom. He pulled on his clothes and descended the stairs. Diane's smile brightened the already sparkling morning. She poured a cup of black coffee and handed it to him.

"How do you feel?"

"Alive."

"Rumors are all over town," Diane said. "Just like when Father Jerry went missing, stories are all over the place about what happened up there in that shack."

Lino tipped his cup. "Did I ever tell you make a fine cup of java?"

"You're not interested?"

Lino looked out the window. Katharine and Roger warred with the weeds while Colleen carried groceries into the red house. "Looks like everything is going well over there," Lino said. "What time is it?"

"Almost nine. You were dead to the world." Diane turned the bacon strips and lowered the heat on the burner. "One of the rumors is that Tony begged you to kill him right then and there. He was loaded with guilt over what he'd done and wanted to end it in that shack. Somebody said they found a pen and paper up there, and Tony was going to write his confession."

Lino picked up a piece of bacon draining on paper towels and bit off half. "Is there anything better than bacon? It makes everything taste wonderful, even the air you breathe."

Diane checked her irritation. "Another rumor is that he shot at you with two guns and missed. Emptied every bullet, and you were still standing without a scratch. Some say it was a miracle."

"You can never be sure about rumors."

"I guess not."

Lino savored the second half of his bacon. He reached for another, and Diane lightly slapped his hand. "Don't eat all that. It's not just for you."

"Who else?"

"Father Silva. He's on the *Pico II* and has been since early this morning. He's sanding the last of the stain for you, Lino. He said he wanted to do it. He said he owes you that much, probably more."

"He doesn't owe me. I may owe him."

"Why?"

"I found the answers I was looking for. I got my life back."

Diane added more bacon to the pan. "Do you want to explain that?"

"It's tied up with my son. I haven't sorted it all out yet, but I learned why he died."

"Why did he?"

"Because of me. Because he was embarrassed and afraid." Lino sipped his coffee. "He should have seen me up in that cabin if he wanted to know fear. We could have had a long conversation about it. A conversation like that might have kept him alive."

"How did you stay alive up in that cabin?" Diane asked. "Did Tony really fire every bullet he had at you?"

"No," Lino said. "It was a rifle aimed at me. Would have caused a big hole."

"You want to hear the last rumor?"

"If you're sure it's the last."

"The last and the most interesting." Diane looked at Lino, holding his gaze for the longest time. "This rumor says there was a fight up in that dune shack, and you finally got the best of the man who was trying to kill you. He laid face down on the floor, crawling inches to get his hand on his own gun. You already held your father's rifle and aimed it at the back of Tony's head. You warned Tony one more inch, and he would die. He moved that inch, and you shot without changing your aim."

Lino lowered his eyes.

"You wouldn't miss that close," Diane said. "The people spreading that rumor say you're a dead shot just like your dad. You couldn't have missed."

"Then what happened?" Lino asked as if he didn't really know.

"Part of the miracle," Diane said. "You not only found out what happened to Father Jerry, but you proved he was a good, caring priest. He wasn't a thief. He wasn't taking lovers. He was doing his best and got killed for it."

"That was the miracle?"

"Part of it," Diane said. "The hand of God moving that bullet was the miracle."

"That's the rumor?" Lino asked.

"That's the rumor." She moved more cooked bacon onto paper towels to drain. "Any truth in it?"

"That's a good question," Lino admitted. "I'd like the answer myself. I'm sure Father Silva will provide his own version when I take him his breakfast. He's a man who loves miracles."

"I thought you gave up listening to priests."

"Maybe I changed my mind."

"Then that last rumor was right, wasn't it?" she asked. "You did shoot to kill, only ..."

"Put Father Silva's plate together, will you, Diane?" Lino poured the priest's coffee. "I want to walk out on the low tide and have a chat."

Meet Author Larry Maness

Larry Maness is the author of three previous novels, *Nantucket Revenge*, *A Once Perfect Place*, and *Strangler*, a Detective Book Club selection.

Pulitzer prize-winner William Inge introduced Larry's first collection of plays, which have been produced in New York, Boston and other venues in the United States and Europe.

He lives with his wife Marianne in Hull, Massachusetts. For more information about Larry and his work, visit www.larrymaness.com, or contact him at ljm@larrymaness.com.

CPSIA information can be obtained at www.ICGtesting.com
Printed in the USA
BVOW07s1811201013

334127BV00001B/10/P